When Dreams Come True

BETTY LOWREY

To order additional copies of this book, contact:
Bookwhip
1-855-339-3589
www.bookwhip.com

When you're in a desperate situation and

You are relying on hope to see you through

"That's on a wing and a prayer"

And then one day things begin to happen

"That's When Dreams Come True"

CHAPTER 1

IF DREAMS COME true no one would be happier than Samantha. It had been her life plan to have a shop of her own, even before Blake she had asked for Kentucky but the boss's daughter had more rank. Her plans had been put on hold when she thought she and Blake would marry, but when her love life went south and all her plans seemed to go down the drain, she began to rethink the shop deal. Recriminations not only left a person in despair but turned one's personality around. Through it all, she had returned to her upbringing, the teachings of her youth, at the hand of her grandmother. "Above all, Samantha, believe on the Lord. There will be troubles and trials but if you stay strong with him you can get through anything and He will open new paths for you."

She had a lot of time to think on the trip from Michigan to Missouri. She was leaving behind her home for the last five years, the church she attended and where she planned to marry Blake. It had been with great embarrassment she had faced the people, returned the shower gifts and tried to dismiss the whispers behind her back. The engagement ring was no longer on her hand, nor her dearly intended by her side. If ever it hit home they were different it was when he told her he wanted out of the engagement, she was too straight laced for him and he had found someone who wasn't.

Her class, the Inner Circle had finished the pre-marriage seminar a week earlier in which the leader had posted on the board at the front of the room, 2 Corinthians 6:14. "Be ye not unequally yoked together with unbelieves for what fellowship hath righteousness with unrighteousness and what communion hath light with darkness." Blake declared afterwards he didn't agree with the instructor or the scripture. "We are doomed before we begin," Blake said. That was when she realized it was foolish to think he would change after they were married.

She shook her head, remembering the many subjects the class had discussed, sometimes the leader laughing and saying they were chasing rabbits again. One couple had openly questioned the meaning behind the scripture, if one was Christian and the other not, what difference did it make? The instructor's reply was that marriage was difficult enough without adding problems and whether to attend worship became the stage for Sunday morning battles if they were of opposing mind set and that was only the tip of the iceberg when they had children there would be decisions that would cause great friction in the marriage.

One subject seemed to intrigue everyone, the idea in the workbook that took the subject material farther, in today's world that couples remain chaste until the wedding nuptials were said, when many of the couples were already living together. The fact she and Blake had never lived together left her feeling relieved now that circumstance had proven there was no future for them. The same couple had been more liberal in their view, "On what are you basing it is wrong to live together biblically before marriage?" And the teacher had replied that sex was all about marriage and commitment and in biblical teachings the privilege of having sex required the consummation of marriage and he had given them scripture to read.

The pre-marriage workshop had covered about any question those attending could ask and one person questioned what if one experienced the magnetism of being drawn to another, so profound the effect left one inept to behave as one should. Teasing, the class had said, let us find that person, and everyone laughed, but the teacher's advice was to hurry to the nearest minister and get married. Samantha remembered thinking she had never experienced such and wondered if the one asking the question had.

After a week of weeping, hoping no one knew her heart ache and staying out of public view she had wandered to the office where she ask Carlos to allow her to set up shop away from those she normally worked with; she didn't feel up to seeing sympathy written on their faces. Together they searched the internet and what was hoped became reality. She would be on her own, proving her shop would make it; that was the plan, but first she must find the right place. With that thought she began her journey.

She entered the area they had marked on the map; it was half way between two major cities. The merchandise should sell and if she picked up local vendors, that would make it all the better. It was truly a rural area, well-kept and that was a plus, already she could imagine it in spring when everything was green. Then she saw the barn and her heart started pounding, it was what she imagined, her mind could describe it in detail. She let the car roll to a slow stop. After driving hours it was a wonder she had not driven past, but there it was.

She stared at the old wooden barn. It would be perfect. She sighed. Was it possible a person really could find their dream? Sliding her purse under the seat, she pulled the keys from the ignition and climbed out of the car. Already, she could visualize the whole thing.

A line of trees crowded each side of an overgrown path. The branches definitely would have to be trimmed. Oh, yes, her heart caught as she neared the barn. It was as magnificent as she thought. The view from the road would be great once the trees were trimmed. She could have a sign painted and hung at the path's entrance. Samantha's Barn. Country Barn. Country Interiors by Sam. If Carlos would let her pick up the line of fabric as well...she laughed. She had only found it and already before the preliminaries was naming her business.

She had wanted this for as long as she could remember even when she went to work for Carlos to learn the trade; a business with her name on it, an opportunity to design beautiful items for whoever darkened the door; that was her dream and heart's desire. Once she made the decision to break loose from Carlos and Interior Design, in her mind things were falling into place. The long meeting in Carlos office with considerable hashing brought them to his agreement to be her partner and to let her go with his blessing.

Surely this place was empty. No one let a path grow up like that or abandoned their building if they were still using it. Did they? Chewing her under lip she had a fleeting thought; this project would need a lot of muscle grease and hard work. Was she biting off more than she could chew? She had physical stamina but this place was a wasteland. There we go again, she thought, doubts trying to stall her before she began. First there had been the heartache, since she and Blake broke up; with hours of loneliness she tried to fill his absence by working on areas she thought would be necessary if she swung the deal.

Recrimination brought her to the point she tagged herself the world's biggest fool and decided she must put space between her and Blake. It was obvious Blake was not coming back. He didn't have to. Any man would be a fool to turn down his big deal. He had fallen for the boss's daughter, lock stock and barrel. The bosses little darling needed him while Samantha had nothing to offer, except a business degree with a second in design not to mention she had given him undying love and devotion, but that was not all he wanted. Evidently he had never loved her because with a bat of her false eyelashes, Carmody had brought him to her side and before their wedding rumor was they were already living together.

Shrugging off the memories that made her sad first and then angry, she stared hard at the landscape before her. It was a jolt to the system to remember once they planned a business together but now he was nothing and she would be going it alone. There might never be a man that loved her. It was true she had never had an interest in any man compared to finding a spot to build the business she had in her head. Cautious she was moving down the overgrown path, slowly, one foot in front of the other, wondering all the while if the roadside revealed well-kept holdings what was wrong with this picture. The weeds were taller and denser than any she remembered. She had to guess each foot forward would land on solid ground. Sweat was running down the side of her face into her ears as the weeds brushed against her legs and now and then she heard a sound that momentarily brought a catch to her breath, but she trod on to find more weeds and saplings grown around an object that blocked the path.

Just ahead was the structure, she surmised it was built from cypress, which explained why it had aged well. But it appeared too sound she thought as she tried to find a door, glancing around dejectedly to see the reason the path was blocked. An old trailer, its hitch broken, was visible from this side. Unable to reach the front she chose to investigate what she thought was a side entrance. This door was completely enshrouded in half grown trees. She felt through the branches until she found a large hinge and worked herself to the other side and pushed hard. When it balked she tried a full body slam and the door creaked open. "Inner Sanctum," she whispered pushing through the saplings while some item hanging down from overhead brushed against her hair making her stay on her knees. Mice and rats scurried, as she came to steps and raised herself to walk up them. "So that was the entrance," she spoke aloud. She could only guess at what had been touching her head and keeping her to the floor.

"Well, this is a surprise." Carlos words came to her now, as she stepped onto wood floors. "Even if you find a barn, it will be old and dark and smelly with nothing but a dirt floor, to say nothing of the cribs with left over dredge of rotten corn." Samantha chuckled. Wouldn't he be surprised? Squinting she bent to study the floor wondering who years earlier had the foresight to meet her need? It was as though Carlos was in her head, talking trying to extinguish the excitement fueled by hope she was now experiencing. A bit exasperated he asked, "How can you expect to find what you have described to me and if you do it will require an exorbitant amount of funding to bring it up to par. Twenty thousand is all I have invested in my other partners. It's up to you but after that you are on your own."

She had been saving the gifts of money from her grandmother for years. Now she was ready to pitch it all into this venture as Carlos termed it. That and a bit more she had managed to save. Saving had not been easy. Renting apartments, buying a car, plus the insurance she must keep and her own daily expenses had pushed her to the limit of human survival. Now and then Carlos parting words popped up to question her unwavering search for the right place. "You always struck me as a very practical level headed young woman, Samantha. Dreams can be very expensive and sometimes they are very elusive."

"But this is exactly what I hoped for." She hugged herself thinking of Carlos in Michigan. This was like a great room. True it was boarded on the sides in typical stalls and a loft overhead she hadn't seen yet that she supposed covered the whole area. It was the outside worried her. Sure there was mucking out on the inside, but out there? Taking a deep breath, she wondered if that would be taking on more than she bargained for, physical stamina was something she had, but this was a wasteland. How badly do you want it, she'd questioned herself on the drive down, "as much as you wanted marriage and a family?"

Yes, she wanted Blake but he had other ideas. First there had been the heartache to deal with and hours of loneliness to fill, then recrimination that turned into cursing herself for being the biggest fool of all. Of course Blake would fall for the Boss's daughter, any man would be a fool not to, a business came with the deal and what did she have to offer in comparison? Nothing.

Love, her mind insisted. You loved him; he was your heart's desire. You thought the two of you would build a life together and a business but it wasn't to be and you need to put it behind you. Months had evolved, seeing the two of them together, Blake looking the other way, the boss's daughter smiling.

She needed to see the loft and then find the owner of the barn. Surely he would want to make a dollar off of a piece of land setting idle. "Excuse me?" A voice interrupted her from the doorway.

Heart thumping, Samantha whirled around. "Yes," she said, breathless. "I didn't hear you come in."

It was obvious he startled her. A beam of light from a crack in the roof caught the woman's hair, making a halo and diffusing her face. He knew she was trying to see him through the darkness. One hand was splayed across her chest and he'd bet her eyes were scared big as saucers. Still she was trespassing.

"Do you have car trouble? I saw your car in the lane."

"It wouldn't take the drive, all those saplings," she began. "I just wanted to see this barn."

"You're trespassing." The light was dim but she made out a tall man, late twenties or thirties, she guessed. She edged towards the door, knowing he was in direct line with it. "There's no phone here, if that's what you're wanting." He was quiet a moment but when she didn't answer he drove his point home. "I'm sure you noticed there are no poles for electricity, the barn had wiring years ago when an old coot lived here, but that's long since been torn out."

"Why?"

"Why did he live here or why were the electrical wires torn out?"

"Both, I guess."

"Are you with the realtors?" His voice was abrupt as if to say I'm through with this let's go. "Since Old man Jessup died this place has been overrun with curious people. They want to see the inside of our only landmark, Old man Jessup's barn. I've had about all the oohs and ahs a man can stand out of strangers."

"Was he the old coot that lived here?"

He ignored the question, stepping up onto the wooden floor, the boards creaking under his weight. He was a fairly large man, wide shouldered; she could see the form of him as the door behind was open and the meager amount of light outlined his body as he came toward her.

Bemusedly he wiped sweat from his face knowing his shirt was damp from a day's work. He was near enough to her now he caught a whiff of some fragrance, wondering that it was always so even in a musty stall. She was backing away. Good, he'd teach her a lesson. He could be dangerous; Lord knew he was big enough. How in the world did she expect to make it around him? He pretty well filled up the space between her and the door. Was she planning to make a run for it?

Samantha was calculating the space to his side, could she slip through and what would be in the floor that she couldn't see in the dark that might cause her to fall and break a leg. He eluded an earthy smell.

"Are you with the realtors?" His voice was softer, with just the slightest lisp of a southern accent.

"No, no, I'm not." She extended one hand. "I'm Samantha McKinsey, formerly of Flint, Michigan. I'm hoping to ummm," she swallowed hard, her throat dry as cotton, "I'm hoping to establish a business in this area and this looks like a perfect setting."

His hand met hers. "It's not for sale or rent."

She heard the sharpness in his voice. "Then it's not for sale or rent? And you do own the land, right?"

He shrugged. "No, I farm around it."

She scrutinized the man, standing there one hand on his hip, the silence growing between them as his attention span was gone from the two of them and on something in the distance. "Don't mean to be rude," he said, "But I got work to do and least I can do is see you to your car."

She started to protest, instead tried to walk past him, when he grabbed her arm and lifted her up, all the while stomping three times on the floor. Not thinking to set her down, he was striding to the door, pushing it out to allow full daylight into the room. Now she screamed a blood curdling scream. A huge snake longer than the length of a broom handle lay wriggling helplessly; the head crushed and bleeding. Without a word, her benefactor lift her up and carried her down the steps to the outside. He held her for a minute looking down into her face, a mocking smile lifting his lips. "It's harmless. I was afraid you'd scream if you knew it was there and it would strike. Couldn't you smell it?"

"I thought it was you." Her body rebelled against her bravado. Her eyes closed and for a moment she thanked heaven she was up away from that floor, those stalls and God forbid an attic full of snakes as her body went into a shudder that promised a full shake down. Almost, he started to pat her arm, but she saw the coldness enter his eyes and his demeanor shaped into a wide shouldered stance as he stood her on her feet. She realized he was a man who did not like women and she wondered why.

"It is not safe for a woman to be lurking around odd places like this. There are men who would hurt you." He was buttoning a shirt that had been hanging loose. "I was trying to let my shirt dry. Anyway, as I said it isn't safe for a woman to be out here, alone."

"I'll be all right," she bluffed and started walking.

"Not if you're going that direction."

For the first time she thought perhaps he did have a sense of humor. "Why?"

"Because you are three feet from where an old house was pushed into a hole and buried and since it was a few years back the rains have ravaged a hole of sorts in the center and I'd imagine it would smart to fall in there." They walked, rather he walked, and it was all she could do to stay up. "Don't you have any kind of home to go too?"

"No, I don't and I don't like your tone of voice."

"Too bad. Too bad." His long stride lengthened as he strode away. "Suit yourself. But remember, no more trespassing. I can't keep you from falling into sink holes. You are on your own."

Where he had been walking her to the end of the lane that led up to the barn, he now turned toward a white pickup truck in the back field. "Stay away from this place at night. Don't have any ideas."

"What are you some kind of male chauvinist?" She called back. "Women have been let out of their cages, you know."

"Too bad. Too bad." Then he threw his head back and laughed. "Lady, you will get what you ask for."

Samantha's blood boiled. Oh, men, she thought, they make you so mad. It's all to get out of helping.

Almost as if sensing her thoughts, he turned. It surprised him, she had the face of an angel but what he was seeing was the fire of anything but...fire angel he thought and it made him laugh all the harder.

"Go away," she screamed, stomping her foot like a three year old. "I don't know why you are laughing. I just want a place to set up shop and earn a living." Bending to the waist, hands on hip, she glowered at him, standing there studying her. "You couldn't possibly understand another person's hardship, could you?" Tears threatened to overflow her eyes. For a minute she thought of all the past hardships.

He would wonder why he bothered, as he stalked toward her, bending at the waist like some kid whose feelings were hurt and wanting to cry, he picked her up off the ground, brought her eye to eye, his own squinting dangerously. "You are acting like a school girl. What you need is a good spanking."

"You wouldn't dare." She was kicking her feet, "Let me down." He did, dropping her the two feet onto the ground, catching her hand as she stumbled and almost fell backwards and then pulling her roughly to his body, as he bent to kiss her.

"I would dare," he said, his eyes half closed, daring her to retaliate and she did. He caught her arm as it came up. "You slap me and I'll kiss you til dark comes in just to show you I can...and not even enjoy it."

"Oh, yeah. Who says you wouldn't enjoy it? You...you... oversized bully."

"Enough. This has gone far enough." He turned and this time he didn't look back.

It finally occurred to her if she was to rent this barn she probably needed him on her side. "Wait....." she followed his footsteps, but if he heard her he wasn't stopping. "Wait," she was out of breath. "Please." He stopped so sudden she barreled right into his back side. "I'm sorry." She stuck out her hand. "Could we start all over? I'm Samantha McKinsey from Flint Michigan. I was passing through your community when I saw this barn and I didn't think I'd harm anyone if I just went in to look at it."

He was eyeing her extended hand, his eyes in that hooded way she'd already recognized as a man used to having his own way if he had to make it. "Landon King," he said, giving her hand milquetoast shake. "Nothing's changed. Stay away from the barn and off the property."

"It's not yours." She stared him down. "You said you rent the land but you didn't say you rent the barn."

"The barn goes with the land." His mouth did a strange side to side swish as one chewing tobacco might do. "I've this terrible tooth ache," he explained. "Are we through now?" For a second he saw a glimpse of accusation followed by frustration in her glance. The humidity was causing her hair to curl; tendrils framed her face and he couldn't help but notice she was attractive, black hair up off her neck, ivory skin and that rose bud mouth he'd found enticing. But there was a hollowness of cheek made him wonder if she'd just come out from under some trial or burdensome time.

"So you're not going to give me the owner's name?" He looked dumbfounded. "Owner of the barn. I'm not interested in the precious land you rent. Just the barn. I assume one can use this path to get to it?" She tried to focus on him, not so much as a blink of the eyelash, but he was close and looking dangerously male at the moment. Something fluttered inside her and she tore her gaze away. "I guess you're afraid I just might make you eat your words that the barn is not for rent. I just might talk the owner into letting me rent it, mightn't I?"

Landon King eyed this misfortunate young woman who dared challenge him. He'd have to get to the Jessups first but if he asked they'd not rent the barn out if the president came asking. Something in his heart softened for a moment, she'd probably cry. His soul groaned within him. He'd not thought of a woman's feelings in five years and now this stubborn piece of fluff was challenging his patience. Why on earth was she stirring sensation in his body and mind? He resented it. "Jessup," he said. "Alice Jessup."

She watched him turn and walk away, the damp shirt clinging to his body in all the right places, wide shoulders, narrow waist, and muscled arms. She shook her head. Forget it cup cake. Mr. Macho is off limits. Well defined muscles, her mind recalled, tight skin stretched taunt against a wall of bones and that brisk mat of chest hair she'd seen before he buttoned his shirt. She shook her head in aggravation at herself. A sudden blush of color spread up into her face. She was ashamed. What was wrong with her?

He was well across the field when he dared look back. A furtive glance at first then a hesitant halting of his stride, he stood there his arms hanging loose. What had just happened? The woman irritated him. She was one of those that wouldn't take no for an answer and he'd had enough of that in his marriage. A marriage marred from day one, had he known his sweet little bride had a sugar daddy on the side; older, richer and more patient who knew his money would draw her back, what was brawn in a young buck compared to money unlimited to a young woman?

Jason Powers, landowner, paper mill king pen, entrepreneur for all the locals who had dreams and patents they could neither afford to launch or the knowledge to pursue, so who came to their rescue? Jason Powers, his ex-wife's Daddy. Sometimes Powers won and a few times he lost but even in losing he won because he tied grateful followers to his side. No one was surprised when he entered politics. And all those followers voted him in. Rosalind Vandervoot made a great politicians wife, she could shop and wear beautiful clothes, rub shoulders with the rich and famous and if she was lucky never have to do a day's work in her husband's mansion. She trained her daughter well and he wondered from the beginning why Lila looked at him, when the world was at her feet, so to speak.

Samantha was almost to the car when she heard a slithering sound; it could only mean one thing. She broke into a run, jerked the door open and slid behind the wheel. Her mind quickly turned to the landscape around her; she was a mile into town, farmland in between the barn and Riverdale, population eight thousand and one. Who in the world could claim that spot? One?

Carlos had mentioned he had studied the map; Riverdale was located equal distance between St. Louis and Memphis by way of Interstate Fifty Five. Checking the records, he found no distributors to compete with his or Samantha's interest. Samantha had a different ace up the sleeve; Tessia lived in the next town. Riverdale was a town of old homes, aged trees and an agricultural background; Rich fertile loam, soil in some areas referred to as ice-cream, what every farmer longed to own a piece of before they died.

And Tessia owned a piece of that pie, six hundred and twenty acres to be exact but Samantha had vowed early in life she would never infringe on her grandmother's wealth, like all the women who had come before her she would make it on her own. Tessia, born Contessa Mae Winters McKinsey, a young widow with a small son named Sam McKinsey, was a scholar, educated and refined who taught third and fourth grade students the love of art and music when she was called to Granview in the sixties, while the school board was set on a male to override the absence of the communities boys that had rather be out on the farm than attend a musty old schoolroom for six hours a day, unable to find a male, they settled on young widow McKinsey and ask her to prove her ability, if she could cajole the young boys to stay in school, teach them reading and writing and the need for arithmetic she had the job and if not she must leave. If she stayed she could also teach the two classes she loved most, art and music.

Teach them she did and married one of the boy's widowed fathers. Andre Petit was nine years older than Tessia, from a long line of family used to making their living from the soil, it was a match of wits, brawn and passion; His passion for the soil and hers for making life beautiful. Born in nineteen thirty eight, Tessia was now showing the strains of life, her body beginning to fail but her spirit indomitable. She had raised Andre Petit's son as though she had borne him herself and wept bitterly when he and his father were killed in a train accident in the seventeenth year of his life. She often reminded Samantha, having Joseph helped bridge the gap between her and Andre and Sam being young was loved and treated fairly. Unlucky in love, Tessia survived alone until in her sixties she married Samuel Cleveland.

Noticing the fuel hand was on the down side of half full, Samantha began to watch for a gas stop. It was while she was filling the gas tank she noticed the man working on the other side of the street. Driving across, she found a parking spot and approached him. "Sir, I wonder if you could tell me anything about the owner of the barn just outside of town, Jessup's the name I believe. I'm looking for the owner," she repeated.

He straightened, chewed a wad of tobacco, his jaws working it to a softness he could handle, then he spat a stream of juice, clearing miraculously Samantha's feet as it hit the sidewalks water alley. "Ain't here, that she lives," he said. "But down the road a piece in the house her husband built for them." The emphasis was on *them.* "Her lands on West end of town, that what Landon King farms. You wantin' her or him?"

"Just Mrs. Jessup."

"I did hear she was changing her name. She was Mrs. Collins. But you won't find her home. Why do you need her?" His black eyes scanned the car. "City license," he said. "I know where she works."

Waiting impatiently for him to form his words, which seemed to come slow from the top of his head, she explained, "I want to rent that barn from her if it is at all possible."

"Her barn?" He gave a quick push of the broom, emptying debris into the down shoot that let him down to check on the necessary pipes if someone reported a stopped up line causing overflow. "For that, I suspect you'd have to see Landon. He's in charge of her place. Now a twinkle came into his eyes. "Why would anyone give a lick to see that old barn of Jessups?" He threw back his head and gave a cackling laugh. "That old place ain't been cleaned in years and I hear tell there are snakes galore. Sides, Old man Jessup was crazy as a coot."

Studying the man's unkept appearance, she doubted they should be discussing the citizens of Riverdale on the town's sidewalk. "Thanks," she said, turning to walk away. "Which way is the highway you referred to Mrs. Jessup living near?" He pointed an Easterly direction. "Fairly nice lookin'."

CHAPTER 2

$\mathscr{I}$T WAS EIGHT o'clock when Samantha rang the doorbell. A woman appeared and stood there examining Samantha through the screen. "Yes, may I help you?"

"Mrs. Jessup?"

"Actually, Alice Jessup Collier, but everyone around here has a way of remembering their own by the maiden name." Green eyes sparkled, with a mischievous grin spreading across her face. She flipped the hook free and held the screened door open. "Come on in. We'll have a cup of coffee in the kitchen, if you'd like and discuss whatever it is you're interested in." She yawned. "Decaffeinated? I can't hack the other after five."

"Will it disturb your family, my coming in at this late hour?"

"Nah." Alice studied her, the green eyes friendly over a nose that bore a sprinkle of freckles. Her brown hair was pulled back to the nape of her neck and clasp in a tortoise barrette. "It's only me, now. I'm in the process of a divorce." She buttoned the top button on a short summer housecoat. "I have to take a bath as soon as I come home from work. You wouldn't believe how grimy I get."

Smelling the fragrance of talc and aware of the yawning, Samantha realized the woman was ready for bed. "I'll get right to the point," producing a small white card from her handbag, Samantha began, "I'm employed by a company in Michigan, and we are seeking a place to distribute our line in this area."

"Carlos Ware, Interiors of Distinction," Alice read, glancing up, "And you are Samantha McKinsey?" Now she studied Samantha. "This will be your business or his?"

"Being friends with the president of the company has its advantages," Samantha confessed, "But having just been through one of the stormiest years of my life, when Carlos considered expanding in this area, I jumped at the chance."

"A man?" Alice guessed, "Caused you a stormy year." It was more a statement than a question.

"How did you know?"

"Put it there." Alice extended a hand. "So have I. After twenty years there should be some justification, somewhere, right?" She shook her head. "So what does Interiors of Distinction stand for?"

"It is the parent line for Country Makings, which is a line of paraphernalia that supplies home makers and craft enthusiasts with everything they need. Candles, ribbon, wires, pegs…you name it. We have it. But what I have in mind is to bring in a sideline that will last as the fads come and go. Fabrics and furniture, even carpets or area rugs, that is if I can handle the expense. But that's a long way down the road. Basically, we want to start out with accessories. We have been successful in other areas of the country, bringing in the native residents art."

"You're an Interior Designer by trade?"

"Something like that." Samantha grinned. "There's more to it than meets the eye."

"Honey, I wouldn't touch another woman's wants with a ten foot pole."

"Hey, its fun."

Dubious, Alice examined her. "You look like a pretty high toned dame for this area, I don't know."

"Gee." Samantha met her gaze. "You're seeing me in my dress clothes. Wait until I let my hair down and start to work. That's why I'm here; I wanted to talk to you about a place to start this business."

"This man, Carlos, does he have, well does he do well with his endeavors in other parts of the country, and it's worked?"

Samantha nodded. "Indiana, Illinois and Kentucky, and now's the time for Missouri. In fact, six months or a year ago would have been a good time for me to come down here." She grimaced.

"But I didn't realize…" She grinned, "But that's another story." She peered around the kitchen, except for a pair of small oil paintings there was no decorative touch.

"Pretty drab, huh?" Alice grinned, "When you're working your butt off to keep your head above water, you neither have the time nor energy, let alone enough money to display pretty things. Rather than knick knacks, I have a daughter in college."

"What I need is a place large enough to display the products. It really is a wonderful line."

"Lots of work involved in introducing something new around here." Alice brought her shoulders up into a body yawn, thinking. "Crafts are popular and we have some talented people here in Riverdale."

"Where would be the nearest town to exhibit one's work?"

"About fifty miles, some travel all the way to the Ozarks, but they could try closer to home."

"Just a trip to the Ozarks would be considered a happy and healthy atmosphere, but what I was thinking," Samantha was visualizing the whole thing, "if there was a place, on a local level, one that distinguished really good work that could be distributed to the larger cities, then everyone would benefit."

Alice was pouring coffee into two mugs. "Cream or sugar?"

"Black."

"Why here in Riverdale? There are larger populated towns within a hundred mile radius. There's Newhaven and farther North, the Cape, not to mention Grandview. Why here?"

"The cross roads. Everything that goes to the city passes on the Interstate and isn't this the route touted to tie the states together, the corridor from the South all the way to the North?"

"That's going to take some doing. There's never a big hurry there."

"I haven't read up on everything concerning this area, but I did read several large industrial plants are already here and the Chamber of Commerce rolls out a new add about this location and the need for new business to break in." Samantha took a sip of coffee. "Oh, yeah, that hits the spot." Alice smiled and winked. "And, when Carlos received the brochure and I was familiar with the area, say from Riverdale to Titusville, he said he felt better about the whole deal, considerably since I knew Grandview."

"Why were you familiar with Titusville and Riverdale?"

"I have a grandmother nearby. As a child I've probably visited these towns at least once but I'll admit things have certainly changed. My Grandmother is now at Grandview, but I don't know for how long."

Alice was considering the information. "Grandview means money", she said, "not for the less fortunate."

"I know what you're thinking."

"You do?" Alice grinned. "So tell me."

"I'm not rich and while my grandmother doesn't suffer, most everything she stands for is tied up in land." Samantha found it pleasing to remember her grandmother. "She has this grand old home but she's considered moving into an assisted living apartment. She would be near people and that counts with Tessia, she enjoys meeting people. Until about the last two years, she was teaching people who resided in nursing homes to paint or to play piano if they were of that mind. She's a grand old girl."

"You aren't thinking of driving all the way to Grandview, are you?"

"No, I just wanted to speak to you about the barn and then I'll be on my way. I think I'll stay over in Titusville, while you consider renting or selling the barn, I'll kind of observe the money spenders from a safe distance and if you say yes, then…I'm just dying to see the loft of your barn and understand the barn's potential. I already know it's perfect. It even has a floor."

"Don't remind me," Alice winced. "My grandfather built that barn and lived in it. Folks back then called him a crazy old coot.

Now does that seem fair when people all over the earth now live in barns?"

"What did you think of your grandfather?"

"That he was great. I loved the loft, his kitchen room, but mostly I loved him. I thought he hung the moon. He took those stalls, boxed in the back and made regular rooms out of them." Alice yawned, trying to hide it behind her hand. "My grandparents' house burned. It was located just a distance from the barn and sadly grandmother didn't get out." Alice shook her head, remembering. "He was such a lonely old man after she died and almost grieved himself to death. I guess my being a kid I didn't realize the full extent of his loneliness, but now I do with Jade gone."

"Jade?"

"Crazy name, isn't it? My husband. Anyway, Grandfather had always loved that old barn and taken such pride in it. When Grandmother died he added the floor and moved in. Have you been there?" She waited for Samantha's nod. "Did you see the walls?"

"No, it was too dark and a snake scared me off."

"It's because it's so damned grown up. Jade never cared a fig about the place. Then when he left I was lucky Lan took over. He's clearing it up, but the fence rows and field ditches come first."

"Lan?"

"Yeah, a local farmer. Tall, good looking, the silent type, Lan's all work and no play." Alice grinned, "But don't get any ideas, he's too young for me; he's the type can get a woman's body actin up." Alice laughed. "Sometimes I think he flirts just to see if he can get a rise out of a woman. For me, Land's more like a brother and frankly one man's enough in this life. I've done good to last through Jade."

"You're not that old."

"I'm thirty nine, forty come October. I plan to celebrate with a bang. Maybe the second half of my life will count for something." She yawned tiredly.

Samantha stood. "You need to get some rest. Could we talk about this another time?"

Stifling another yawn, Alice gave a slight shrug. "I honestly don't know. Land's in charge of the place. He's a strange one, too."

A serious tone entered her voice. "You understand, I have to have a good farmer an honest man in charge and Lan's that on both accounts."

Nodding, Samantha was gathering her things. "I'll call tomorrow night. Right now, I need to be on the road."

"Where are you going from here?"

"Back to Titusville, or Grandview if necessary to find a room."

"But that's fifty miles don't you have other relatives around here, besides your grandmother?"

"No, that's one reason I want to move back."

"You mean you are all alon, except for your grandmother Cleveland, when she dies, what then?"

"Almost alone," Samantha corrected. "I have a mother I haven't seen in eight years."

"We all have a story, don't we?" Alice yawned. "Come with me, I have an extra room. Bed, bath, clean sheets. You're welcome to stay if you want." She shook her head, hand over her mouth trying to control the yawning. "Sorry, I'm that tired; the job I'm on is mind boggling. Saps my energy." She was leading the way. "It's my daughter, Kimberly's room but she's away at college."

"You're sure?" Samantha was pleasantly surprised not to have to drive back at this late hour and grateful Alice would offer the hospitality. "I'll pay, just as I would if I went to the motel. Please?"

"No. You'll have to fend for yourself because I leave early. If there's anything you need just look for it."

One trip to the car for her overnight case, and clothes for the next day, she locked the car and within the hour was laying in Kimberly's bed smelling the fresh sheets, scrubbed clean and thanking her lucky star Alice had invited her to stay. Her eyes were fixed on a wall of dolls, no doubt from Kimberly's childhood. She wondered if the years Kimberly played with the dolls were happy years because according to her mother the last had been fraught fighting with her father and filing divorce.

Twelve, at the time her own parents decided to part ways, Samantha remembered Clarissa's words.

"Some people should never marry, darling. What your father and I had was a physical attraction and after that, nothing. There's more to life than that, there's companionship and mutual interest."

The bitterness in her heart had dissipated but that period of time when her father invited her along to ballgames, fishing and activities away from home, she remembered. He never asked her mother and before she knew it they had their divorce. "Why?" She questioned her mother and the reply was, "Your father wants to spend his life working in the plant weekdays and fishing on the weekend. I want to travel and do things together. Obviously, I want someone to care about me."

Clarissa had her own problems to deal with. She'd found Walter next door, a willing listener. They shared a hobby of growing roses; he encouraged her in the jewelry making that would become Clarissa's funding when she left Sam. She wore the jewelry; women saw it and visualized their self as attractive as Clarissa. Soon there were parties where Clarissa displayed the pieces, women ordered and Clarissa delivered. Occasionally Walter accompanied her on those deliveries.

Now, Samantha sighed, wondering how long it had taken Tessia to make her see both sides of the picture. There was something they weren't telling her, she felt it. She found she was truly her father's daughter, he took care of her. Her loyalty belonged to him. Obviously Sam was on to something. When he suffered the first heart attack he asks for Clarissa. She heard him on the phone talking to her mother. "You shouldn't have left us, Babe. I couldn't stand losing you."

There had been a moment of silence and then Sam had asked, "What ever happened to Walt's kids? Did you help raise them?"

"No, Elise remarried, after she moved back to Shreveport. That's where her family lived. Remember? We traveled a lot, Sam. Elise wouldn't let the kids come those first years, and now Walt has filled his time with teaching."

Everyone left the same year. Elise, Jim and Bubba, and then Walt disappeared mysteriously about the time Clarissa got the divorce.

The only ones remaining in the houses whose yards bordered next door were Sam and Samantha.

"She's your daughter, Sam, all the way through. I doubt she'll ever forgive me," Clarissa gave a nervous laugh. "You were right to demand she be named after you, she'll never forgive me."

"I forgive you, Clarissa," Sam had replied, and then as naturally as if he'd been asking about the weather, Sam asked. "Walt takes good care of you?"

"Yes." There was delayed silence, again. "You were the best, Sam. Now, I know, after all these years."

Her dad gave a bitter laugh. "That's a hell of a thing to say to a dying man, Clarissa." He gave a groan of sorts, "Small comfort…but I guess it's better than nothing"

Samantha decided if her father made it through, the next time she wouldn't call her mother. She hadn't forgotten their conversation and still wondered what Clarissa meant; Two years later she buried Sam McKinsey the way he'd intended with his friends from the plant in attendance and his mother and daughter. Tessia had visited often after Clarissa left.

There was a history of heart disease in the McKinsey men; Tessia's own husband had died young. She'd remarried, an older man and outlived him, too. Content to do what she could, Tessia had tried to bring a woman's world into that of her granddaughter's and she loved her son, understanding his pain.

It was Tessia's blue eyes Samantha saw in her own, but later awakened disturbed from a dream where she had seen Landon Kings dark look observing her as though she were a nuisance. Why had he lingered holding her before he stood her on the ground, or had she imagined it? He had held her staring into her eyes with that mocking smile on his face. A flush warmed Samantha's body. Why?

An early riser, Samantha padded quietly into the kitchen, noticed the time and found the coffee. Surprised, Alice entered a few minutes later. Coffee and toast were waiting. "How'd you know?"

"You looked like a toast and jelly girl to me," Samantha grinned. "Me, too. Maybe it does take one to know one." She eyed the denim jeans and cotton t-shirt Alice wore. "So where do you work?"

"For now," Alice eyebrows arched a dubious expression on her face, "I work at an aluminum factory." She sighed. "Someone claimed discrimination and they hired a few women. Do you know how hot it is in the pot room?"

"I imagine that's what saps your energy."

"Honey, I sweat like a politician at an election. The first few days I was scared to death around that boiling liquid. Then, you get so tired you forget to be scared, just careful. If I didn't need the money, I'd quit."

"What about your husband, Jade?"

Alice gave a bitter laugh. "Listen, why don't you stay over? Go examine the barn. Find Lan King and make an appointment for the three of us to get together. Why drive all that distance to Grandview when you can stay here and we can get acquainted. That is, if you are sincere about the barn."

"You mean it?" Surprise sounded in her voice as a smile spread across her face. "I'd love to."

"I'll expect coffee in the mornings," Alice grinned. "But now I've got to be going. Anyway, you need to meet with Landon. First things first, and see what he think." She noticed the look on Samantha's face. "What's wrong?"

"I think I already met...I mean I know I met him when I stopped at your barn. Tall, dark, moody, all musk and muscle? Unfriendly?"

"Landon, unfriendly?" Alice laughed. "Quiet and reserved is more like it, until he knows you, but unfriendly?" A frown wrinkled her brow. "That's another story. Listen, I gotta run. See you tonight."

"What about a key, do I lock up when I leave?"

"There's an extra key in the sugar bowl on top shelf by the frig. It really doesn't matter, if they want in, they'll get in."

"Who?"

Alice laughed seeing Samantha's alarm. "How do I know, some of these country yahoos that don't work." She was on her way out the door, when she called back, "don't worry. It's safe here."

Using her cell, Samantha called Grandview, her grandmother didn't answer but the answering machine picked up the call.

"Grandmother, I'll try to see you tomorrow, if all goes well, if not, I'll call."

Next she searched for Landon King of Riverdale. There was no listing. She dressed ready to find Mr. King. Denim jeans, a loose sleeved white shirt tucked in by a silver belt with turquoise studs, and her leather boots she'd pulled from the trunk of her car and she was ready to tromp through the weeds again, with Alice Jessup's permission to explore the barn. Finding the key, she secured the bolt and hurried to her car. If everything went the way she hoped, she would return to Flint for her things, or better still ask Carlos to bring them, when he came to make his inspection. For now, her wardrobe consisted of what two suitcases and her overnighter would hold. She carried a small pouch of cosmetics in her purse complete with eu de cologne.

Alice had left for work wearing little make up. In the pot room with the heat it would be a wasted effort. Sympathetic to Alice's day at the plant, Samantha turned on the Air conditioning, backed out of the drive and headed to Riverdale. By end of day she already knew she would rue her choice of wardrobe for the day.

Driving the streets she watched for Landon King's truck. Outside one of the town cafés she saw a half dozen parked trucks, stopped and went in. A number of men were seated around a table drinking coffee. The buzz of conversation dropped a pitch when she entered the door.

"Can I help you, honey?" An auburn haired waitress asked from behind the counter.

"I'm looking for Landon King."

The waitress shrugged, turning toward the table. "You fellows got any idea Lan's whereabouts?"

"Yesterday," A burly man drawled, "he was over at Jessup's place readying his combine. Course that don't mean he's there now."

"He doesn't come in here, honey," the waitress explained. Her eyes rest on the group of men. "Landon, now he's a hard working guy. This bunch, they gotta have the latest gossip, whether the crops in or out."

A groan went around the room. "It' the coffee and the good service, we're addicted to it."

"He's out by his house," A young man came from the back, studying Samantha with interest. "I passed by there on my way in to town. Take one fifty three, four miles north, then there's silver grain bins," he grinned. "Heck, you can follow me; I'm going right by there."

"Thanks." He was holding the door for her and Samantha noticed the noise around the table picked up. Fifteen minutes later, she was standing by a green combine. Three men who had directed her toward the path where the combine sat were now watching curiously from the wide open shed where she'd found them. "Mr. King?" There was no reply. She called again, tapping her foot impatiently while she surveyed the holdings. A modern shed, grain bins and beyond that a thick growth of trees concealed the house with only the roof visible. She wondered if that would be Mr. Landon King's home.

Land had seen the car drive in. He recognized it as the one parked in the lane to the Jessup place the day before. She didn't give up, did she? With his back flat on the roller, he shook his head wondering at her persistence. So snakes didn't scare her off? He'd watched her approach, saw the long legs clad in denim, the tan leather boots; at least they'd seen a day's work, good leather though. Remembering her face, he stared up; his thoughts were that the bosom was more than he'd thought her slim body would have. Yeah, he felt a tightening in his loins and cursed himself, what the dickens was going on in his own mind and body that he had no control over earthly lust and for that matter why her, he'd kept himself in check for five years. She was calling his name. Damn. He finally rolled out.

The worn work boots with the Double H imprint came into view, followed by faded denims and a more faded denim short sleeved shirt. With slight effort, Landon King stood, wiped his hand on an orange grease rag and stared moodily down on her.

"Can I help you?"

"I came about the barn."

25

"Haven't we already discussed this?" His eyes pinned to something in the distance. "It's not available."

"I met Alice Jessup. Collier. She said the three of us should sit down together to discuss the barn." Turning she stared the direction he seemed interested in. A field of beans, lush in green growth lay in the line of view. She wondered if he even heard her. "With her divorce, I think maybe the rent of the barn would be an added income she could use. You and Alice are friends?"

"You might say that. I knew Jade, too."

Evidently he had an opinion. "Alice said we could discuss…"

"No need of discussion," He said abruptly. "If Alice decides there's nothing I can do, it's her property."

"But, I wouldn't want to interfere with previous agreements. You understand I intend to put in a business there, would you mind that?"

Landon folded his arms to his chest and continued to stare out across the field. "What's my opinion got to do with anything, seeing as how you and Alice have decided?"

"But you rent the land. There's even a compromise which regulates who can come and go on your property."

"I rent the land," He was brisk as he corrected. "I had hoped to dress for dinner when we had our sit down, maybe be a gentleman. As I was saying, I haven't taken my machinery inside that barn, I'm careful. Only a fool would take good machinery in there to clean up that mess."

"I guess I'm that fool, then," she replied.

His eyes held hers. "You got your work cut out for you." He tipped his finger to his brow and left her standing there.

"I believe there's a matter of my reimbursing you for the rent, and whatever it takes for Alice to receive her share." She grit her teeth when he kept on walking, paying her no heed as he headed for the shed where the men stood gawking. "Oh," she uttered the word in disgust and hurried to her car.

She heard one of the men call to him, "Hey, Boss, great set of legs."

"If you say so."

His reply made her smart. How dare he? She turned the key in the ignition and spun her tires as she backed out of the drive.

"What gives, Boss?"

Landon eyed the youngest member of his working team. "You're nineteen, Jimmy, and a ladies man, I hear. You tell me, what gives."

"Well, she's a real filly, like I said, great legs, sturdy stuff and I'll wager she didn't back down even when you scowled. Did she?"

"That's all you have to say?" Landon gave Jimmy a searing look.

"Oh, come on, Boss. It's obvious." Jimmy shrugged. "So I'll say it. Great legs and nice chest."

The rest of the men laughed as Landon stomped off toward the combine again. "Get back to work," he barked and they all scattered. "Show's over."

CHAPTER 3

$\mathscr{S}$AMANTHA BROUGHT THE tea pitcher to the table. Settled into her chair, she paused from pouring tea into Alice's glass. "He didn't say no to my renting your barn." She was hesitant, but then continued, "He did say only a fool would clean up that mess."

Alice winced. "I did try calling him from work, but he wouldn't answer his phone. It doesn't matter. I know Landon King. He will be direct, but fair."

"His actual words were, "Only a fool would take good machinery in to clean up that mess. Since I have no machinery, I figure it will be personal toil and hard body labor. Mine."

"You're kidding, aren't you?" Alice's fork paused midair. "You're out of your mind."

"No." Samantha grinned. "What else is new? Look, it took me months to realize Blake Donovan was not to be a part of my future. Now that I think about it, Carlos daughter taking my ex to the altar, instead of me, was the biggest hurdle I'd ever faced." Her eyes twinkled as she said, "Maybe that grown up lot won't even faze me, one bit."

"I'm sure you gave Land something to think about and this other fellow, his name was Blake?"

"Not as daring as Jade, huh?"

"Forget Jade. If you want a real man, concentrate on Landon King."

"He seems a cold fish, but tell me about him, anyway. You said there's a story there."

The phone rang and Alice went to answer. Her voice lift in despair. "Why me?" She was shaking her head, Samantha saw the arched eyebrows. "Because I'm the last one hired? Lucky me." She slammed the phone on to the cradle, returning to the table. "Well, kiddo, we'll have to postpone our little discussion, I've got to go back to work."

"You'll be dead on your feet."

"That's what they want." Alice eyes narrowed, dangerously. "They're trying to push me out, along with the other women. We made a pact we'd show those balled bastards we could handle it. Excuse the bad language. I only do that when I'm pushed to the wall. If you'd known my grand dad, cursing is almost natural." She was pacing the room. "Here we are, most either widowed or divorced and we need a paycheck as badly as they do but to them, it's a man's world. They're not looking at the whole picture of survival."

"Oh, so," Samantha eyed Alice judiciously. "All things considered, no discrimination charges if the women prove unable to stand the test. They'll just load you down with double shifts and break you physically, and then they'll say, "We knew they couldn't take the heat.""

"I know," Alice was removing a pair of denims from the dryer, an unironed T-shirt from a folded pile and ready to step into them. "We all agreed we had to try and if we get our toe in the door there are ladies in the office."

"You mean you're looking either for friendship or sympathy from the office ladies and you're in."

"Exactly."

"Let me fix a sandwich for you to take."

"Great, I'll need it about three in the morning." Hunching her shoulders forward Alice grimaced. "There's muscle in there I didn't even know I had." Dressed, she went over to the stove, lifted a small thermos she'd sit there earlier and poured coffee into the thermos. "Thanks for the supper. I haven't had time to cook lately. You won't be afraid here will you?"

"I've been alone most of my life."

Later, having stored the left overs and clearing the table she was standing at the sink washing dishes when she had time to reflect how many times she'd been left alone to do the finishing up of one job or another. She decided to take a bath in Alice's old fashioned tub. Thirty minutes in the tub soaking and she was ready to slip into bed for a leisurely hour of reading. Thinking Alice's soap bore a lovely fragrance, she applied her usual talc, let her hair down onto her shoulders and heaved a delicious sigh that for the first time in ages she'd been given an hour to herself. It was then she heard a knock at the front door.

Wrapping her terry robe firmly around her body she hurried the short distance down the hall to the living room foyer. Maybe the plant manager changed his mind and Alice didn't have to work after all. "Who is it?" She called out. "Alice?"

"Lan King."

Her breath caught. "Alice isn't here. She had to go back to the plant. This is Samantha McKinsey. I was by your farm today."

"I know who you are. Must we talk through the door?"

"But Alice isn't here."

"Miss Mc Kinsey, "A tired note sounded in his voice. "There was a message on my answering machine to come by. What did Alice want? I only have so much time, Miss McKinsey."

Considering the dim-lit room, Samantha secured the robe's belt, straightened the front and opened the door. "Come in," Mr. King. "IF you'll be seated, I'll go slip into my clothes. I just got out of the bath…"

"Is that necessary? I'll only be here a minute. I've not been home nor had supper. What the heck?" He rubbed the back of his neck.

"It's been a long day and I'm tired. Alice said we had business to discuss."

"I think she meant about the barn, what I mentioned to you."

He turned to leave. "I assumed it was more."

"Take a seat. I'll be right back." She left before he could say more. Conscious of his eyes on her back, Samantha hurried into the bedroom, closing the door firmly behind. Thumbing through the suitcase she pulled a blue jumpsuit from the contents, shook it out and wondered if he would know the wrinkles were part of the material. Pulling on underclothes first, then the jumpsuit and last looked for her shoes and found only one. "What's wrong with bare feet," she muttered, heading back to the living room.

Landon glanced at his watch; seven minutes, he'd expected twenty. All the while his stomach rumbled and reminded him it was time for food.

"Shall we go into the kitchen? I can find a cup of coffee or a glass of tea."

"Tea will be fine." He followed behind.

She thought she heard the rumbling of his stomach. "Did you say you haven't eaten?"

"I had a cookie for breakfast."

"That's all?" She eyed him disapproving. "I stopped by the market and bought a roast that cooked very nicely with potatoes and carrots. Could I fix you a plate?"

"I'll be all right," he replied, but his arms were wrapped rather tightly around his stomach. "Just tell me what Alice wanted, now that you've got me over here." This time his stomach practically roared.

Samantha was busy taking a plate from the cabinet and removing containers from the refrigerator.

"Two minutes in the microwave and you can eat." She filled two glasses with ice cubes and poured tea.

"I'm impressed," he said, and for a minute the scowl almost lessened on his brow. He was washing his hands at the sink waiting for her to hand him a towel. "I didn't know city girls could cook."

The micro wave beeped. She brought out a steaming plate and set it on the table. "Who says I'm a city girl?"

"It shows."

"You mean the snake?" She shrugged. "Do your country girls like snakes? I doubt it." She reached for salt and pepper. "Now." She sat opposite him and suddenly laughed. "I guess you need a knife and fork, too."

A slight smile lifted his lips. "I could eat with my fingers."

"Hey, you smiled." She clapped her hands. "Maybe I could do tricks and you'd break into a whole hearted chuckle."

"Thanks," he said dryly. "I chuckled already, today."

"When?"

"When you left."

Irritation flashed in Samantha's eyes. "So the men were making dirty remarks about me. I thought there was a certain leer in their eyes."

"Actually," Land held one hand in the air. "They complimented you."

"Do I want to hear this?" A serious tone crept into her voice.

"I don't know, do you?" His gaze met hers.

Intrigued, Samantha stared back. At least he was talking. "Yeah, why not," she said, "After all, we're strangers. What can you say about a stranger?"

"Well," Land leaned on one elbow, chewing the roast. "This's not bad food." He indicated the plate. "Thanks."

"You're welcome." She waited, her eyes narrowing to a slit.

A mocking grin crossed Land's's face. "Jimmy, now he's a natural woman watcher. His observations come from daily practice."

A shiver of anticipation tingled up Samantha's spine. "This has to be interesting. Which one was Jimmy, and how old is he?"

"Nineteen." Land's eyes held hers. "He said…you…"

Samantha's mouth became a thin line.

"Are sturdy," Land chuckled, his eyes slipping almost roguishly to gauge her reacation. He was wondering what she'd said if he had relayed Jimmy's truthful remark.

Samantha blushed. "Well, I'm grateful to your Jimmy, but somehow I feel there's more, and no," she held up one hand warding off further comment, "I don't want to hear it."

"The way to a man's heart is through his stomach, they say." A slight edge came into his words. "Do you try this often, to get your way?"

Rebuked, Samantha fingered the blue place mat on Alice's table. "Actually, no, I don't have to."

"Plenty of male suitors, huh?"

"Yes."

"Why are you moving here?"

"I have a grandmother in Grandview." Noting his body stiffen, she asked, "You know where I mean?"

"Yeah, the town of the hallowed Nursing home named for it. Grandview."

"You have something against homes for the aged who need help?" She felt the coolness. The curtain had closed again to his inner thoughts. "Actually," she explained, "Grandmother has retained most of her faculties. its age that has played a hand against her, memory and strength of body; she has chosen Grandview, herself."

"No need to explain," he replied curtly. "Usually they are for the elderly who have no one willing to take care of them and they palm them off to some care unit. Grandview has its purpose. Everything does."

"About the barn, Mr. King, do I speak to you or Alice concerning rent of the property?"

"So she's decided to make the deal?" He questioned, rising he pushed his chair back to the table. "She'll be fair. Alice always is."

"Funny, she said the same thing about you."

"I appreciate the meal," he said, "Best I've had all week."

"Alice said that, too."

"She's a worker. If she had the knowledge, of chemicals and fertilizer and such she'd farm her granddaddy's land. I don't know how long she'll last at this present job, because those old boys are going to give her a hard time. They don't take to women getting their jobs."

"Men do that, don't they?" She hadn't meant for the critical tone to kick in, but there it was out in the open between them. "Give a woman a hard time and maybe she'll quit. It's always their job, isn't it?" She stared in stony silence as the distance widened between them. But he stepped forward.

"And women play their games," he replied softly.

"I'm afraid I don't know what you mean."

"This." He touched the front of the blue jumpsuit.

Puzzled, Samantha glanced down, a tinge of color washing into her face. She'd buttoned that top button, but in her haste, perhaps not good enough. It had come open. She hadn't intended to show cleavage. "An honest mistake," she said, anger thickening her words.

"And this?" His hands touched the curls of hair that lay on her shoulders, then cupped the shoulders pulling her to him. With deliberate care and much forethought, Landon King lowered his head, covering her lips with his own, parting and teasing he demanded a response. He had planned this moment.

Something stirred within Samantha. Caught off-guard, she tried to pull back but his hold was unrelenting. With subtle persistence his eyes burned into hers. It was as if he probed the inner core of her being. Slowly the ember that had lain barren flamed. She knew when her hands crept up to the back of his neck even as his own caressed her. Bending, pressing, Lan wielded her body to his, purposeful and intent and then suddenly he loosened his hold. She almost fell.

Heart pounding, Samantha met his eyes watching as he turned toward the door, tipped his fingers to his forehead and was gone. As quickly as he left, she rushed forward and threw the bolt, her body sagging against the door. She knew when he paused on the porch, returning to try the knob ever so gently but it held. Then came the chuckle as he moved on down the steps and out into the night.

The night air felt good on his skin. He needed the coolness to put out the fire she had created. Maybe she hadn't intended to entice him playing Susie homemaker, her hair curling on her shoulders, those pouty lips; he thought it was part of her plan. She was a fire angel.

Breathing deeply, whether from disappointment or relief, Samantha wondered what had possessed the man. First the challenge, then the tortured look, she'd seen both in his eyes. Had he taken her in his arms to prove a point? What point was that and for that matter what possessed her to respond?

Disgusted, she scrubbed at her lips. He had smelled of sweat and earth. Turning, she leaned her back against the door. Again. Pressing back she stared up at the ceiling. Suddenly she grinned. He was strong. He smelled earthy. Blood rushed through her veins as laughter came in a clear tinkling sound. She had him going as much as he did her and it wasn't planned at all. From now on, she must be careful.

CHAPTER 4

*G*RANDVIEW WAS AS she remembered nicely manicured lawns, and the elderly wearing windbreakers still enjoying being outside. Tessia, overjoyed with her granddaughter's visit, suggested they take a walk, away from the prying eyes of the other residents. They stopped when Tessia needed a short rest and resumed when she said, "Let us continue." Late blooming flowers were her interest today. "It's amazing, flowers just like people are different even when they come from the same family. Not one's alike. People get them all confused, calling Periwinkles an Impatient and vice versa but one takes to the sun while the other dies if not in the shade. One takes hard knocks, the other succumbs. Which are you, my girl?"

Samantha stalled. "You tell me."

"Well, let's see. I'll have to garner your merits." She tilt her head, the sun catching her hair done up in a bun top of her head, the sun making a haze around it, a halo of sorts Samantha thought. "You've left a very lucrative employment in the city, driven for hours to begin your search for an appropriate barn in which to start your new business. I'd say your adventure will lead you to what you want." She paused for a moment, placing one hand lightly over her chest, breathing deeply. "I'd say you are probably a mixture of the two, you'll take to the work, stand tall in the sun as the Periwinkle but there'll be times when you'll bow to the onslaught of it, too. That's when you'll remember the Impatient because you'll want to take to the shade."

"Run for cover, huh?" She heard her grandmother's breathing and it concerned her. Taking Tessia's hand she paused for a moment in the middle of the path. "I'm curious; did you do that, too? Daddy always said that I have a lot of you in me. Perseverance and a genuine feeling of winning. Did you ever run?"

"We're discussing you, not me, young lady. Now, what about furnishings? I want you to take all my old things out of storage. Lord knows I've kept them long enough and have no further need for them."

"You mean it, Grandmother?" Samantha's pleasure was obvious by the smile in her eyes and on her face.

"Why not?" The blue eyes twinkled mischievously. "Besides, you know they're saved for you. You're the one who appreciates old furniture and who else would want them, anyway?"

"They're antiques," Samantha corrected, "A hot item on the market and you always have good taste."

"Your grandfather used to ask what I'd be bringing home next." Tessia's eyebrows arched. "But I liked fine wood and I liked to move it about in the house. So it was only his misfortune if his bed was in a different place, some nights. When he complained, I told him what mattered was that the same woman was in his bed each night."

They laughed together, as Tessia sat on the nearest bench and Samantha tried to ignore the fine mist of perspiration on Tessia's face. "You're sure you don't want to come live with me?"

"In a barn." Tessia's voice was droll. "I think I'll pass on that. I couldn't climb those stairs, sometimes my mind just wanders and that means I'd embarrass you in front of your customers. Then there would be the day you mention fabric and I would drone on and on about the strength and beauty of damask." She started to chuckle, "and heaven forbid they mention music. You know my passion for music."

"You don't even like damask."

"I know, but it does have strength and beauty. But a woman wants something that will wear out before she does, otherwise she will never have opportunity for change and change keeps life interesting, just as a woman who changes with the times keeps her man interested." Tessia paused. "I notice you aren't jumping on that subject. There is a man, in the picture I assume."

"Not unless you count Carlos."

"Who's he?"

"Carlos is the distributor who is backing me. His money, my talent, this being a new area we hope it works. Partners."

"Partners?" Tessia studied Samantha's face. "I thought you wanted to be free of all men's trappings. Haven't I heard this Carlos name before?"

"Yes, he's Blake's father in law, but more than that he is my friend and willing business associate."

"I thought you wanted a business of your own." Tessia snapped. "But this Carlos, I don't know and Blake, the same Blake you brought to meet me?" Samantha nodded. "I'm glad you didn't marry him. He's not worth the effort to wipe your shoes on. So he married the boss's daughter? Good for him. Now you just wait 'til he comes running back to you and says, she doesn't understand me. I made a mistake. Forget him."

"How long does it take to forget a man?"

"Well, I haven't forgotten your grandfather. Every morning I wake to remember him." Tessia's eyes flashed, "If they're worth anything you won't forget them." Memory rushed her brain, her eyes narrowed, "They're like fire in the blood, the one you love."

"Your grandfather," her voice softened. "There was a man. Some said a bit standoffish. But others set great store by him. Erect in the way he carried himself, he was a gentleman. Most of all he loved me. Your grandfather did. I was always glad I bore no children by another husband."

"Maybe I shouldn't say this but any man worth his salt that's had a woman between the sheets won't be easy to forget. You'll see. I'm talking about a woman who holds her own and waits until the wedding day and a man that honors her, not saying he won't try you, men are men. So if you're hung up on a man's good looks forget it." She searched Samantha's face. "Now, what about this Blake fellow?"

Samantha felt a warm flush. "Thankfully, on this trip I realized I can forget him. He was just a pretty face but the things that count like loyalty and me being the only one, were not there."

"So I was right, he wasn't worth his salt." She laid a hand on Samantha. "You'll be just fine without him. I'm glad you found that out." Suddenly, Tessia's hand was on her chest. "Leaving you for the boss's daughter, didn't speak well for him. That kind of man would never stand by you when life gets rough."

Samantha leaned close to peer into her grandmother's eyes. The old woman was trembling. "I already realized Blake wasn't worth my hurt pride." She reached for Tessia's hand. "My gracious, you're like a summer storm. Is this about me or is there something else going on?"

"Well, you're all I have." Tessia snapped. "I didn't like Blake Donovan at all."

Hugging her grandmother, Samantha apologized, all the while smiling. "I'm sorry I brought him here to meet you."

"He was too perfect."

"That's easy for you to say. You had three husbands to compare him with. I simply grew up my father's daughter."

Tessia ignored reference to her son. "You'll do all right if you look for one of these country types. Find a man with a firm hand grip that will look you in the eye when he talks with you."

"I'll try to remember that."

"Your daddy always said as long as he had you there'd be a piece of me around."

"You think I'm like you, Grandmother?"

"Too much, child." Tessia's eyes blurred with tears, her voice softened. "We're independently stubborn, willful and persistent, and when we love, we love with all our heart."

"I'd settle for growing old gracefully as you have, and maybe in time there will be someone to love me."

"I've gone as far as I can go," Tessia admitted. "Let's go back now."

"Don't worry over me, Tessia. I can tell you do."

"I'm just reminding myself how good it would be to have you near. But I forgot I shouldn't get emotional as it wears me out." She sighed. "It makes my heart beat too fast."

"It's remembering all that passion made you tired," Samantha teased.

Leaving Grandview, she reflected on their visit. Tessia's shortness of breath bothered her. In the months since their last visit her grandmother had grown thin and the lines in her face had deepened. Now she trembled. Bringing herself up short, Samantha wondered, had she thought she'd have Tessia forever?

Tessia had been there to pick up the pieces when her parents divorced. "You don't know what went on between your parents?" She questioned, but Samantha had no answers. "Much as I loved my son, he may have neglected his wife. Your mother was a good woman." Yeah, Samantha thought, tell that to the woman I've not seen in years. "She left daddy," she said out loud. "I guess she left me too."

"There may have been problems you weren't aware of." The years between disappeared as she remembered the conversation. Tessia had a fondness for Clarissa; she had mourned Clarissa's leaving.

"Of course," Samantha had snapped. "Clarissa wanted out. Walt Smith tired of his wife and children and conveniently for him my mother was next door."

"As I recall," Tessia replied, "You had a choice of staying or going. Furthermore, Elise Smith thought nothing of her husband and all for the children." Tessia's mouth set in a firm line. "The boy and girl were spoiled brats. Didn't you tire of giving in all the time to them?"

"What had it mattered?" Samantha shrugged. "They were there to play with, I suppose I loved them. Walt and Elise's children were the brother and sister I never had."

"Bubba and Barbara." Tessia shook her head. "Forget them. It's your father and Clarissa you have to understand and I must admit I'm having a bit of problem doing so, myself." Sighing deeply, Tessia stared off into space. "Clarissa loved her rose garden and nothing pleased her more than to stay home in the sunshine tending those plants. You have no right to judge her harshly."

"Whose side are you on? Clarissa never wanted to go with my Daddy."

"I don't have to take sides, Young lady," Tessia replied. The blue eyes settled firm and disapproving on her granddaughter. "Clarissa did very well establishing her jewelry business."

"What if she was the cause of my daddy dying too soon?"

"Get that out of your head. God decides. We're all on a time table. His."

Samantha saw the troubled look on her grandmother's face. "What? What are you not saying?"

"All McKinsey men die young. His dad, too. "

"How do you think Elise felt; it was her husband ran off with my mother. Bubba and Barbara's daddy."

"Elise married within two years," her grandmother replied, smoothly. "Don't you think that accounts for something? Perhaps the new man in her life was allowed to correct the children and make better persons of them. Heaven knows Walt wasn't allowed to and they were spoiled. I felt sorry for them."

Samantha was twelve when the divorce was final. Sam was thirty when she was born and Clarissa six years younger than her husband. She remembered the hurt on Clarissa's face when she declared she would not go with her to her new husband's house to live. There last conversation was, "Don't come to the funeral, there's no need our upsetting each other."

Staring at the line down the center of the road, she wondered why she was rehashing her relationship with her one remaining parent. Forty seven wasn't old when you compared Clarissa's age to her grandmother's. The blare of a horn brought her back to reality. She wasn't familiar with the roads, yet. She needed to call Carlos. Pulling off the highway, she found a spot and found Carlos number.

"Couldn't you find a more suitable building?" He had given her a long list of questions probing the wisdom of establishing a business in a barn.

"I did," she laughed. "It's perfect. You'll see. Just ready the supplies and send me enough advance for six months' rent, and don't worry." She paused for a moment. "Carlos?"

"Yes," weariness crept into his voice. "I know there's more. I can tell when you grow suddenly quiet."

"Well, my things are stored at Meanie's. Could you send the boxes marked clothes?"

Carlos groaned. "Are they packed for shipping?"

"Yes, I was thorough."

Silence indicated Carlos was thinking. "What about the others?" He was hesitant. "Surely you don't expect me …"

He would be thinking of the wedding gifts intended for her and Blake. "I returned everything," she replied, her voice so low he would have to think what she was saying. "As I said, I was thorough."

"Sure, Kid." Almost apologetic, Carlos softened. "I'm sure you were. Only the purge of fire could do any better."

"Yeah." Samantha swallowed. "I'll expect a package soon. Huh, Boss?" She gave him Alice's address.

"Your box?"

"No, a friend's. Send them by UPS, Carlos."

"O.K., Kid. See you in the funny papers."

Closing her eyes tightly against the thought, she shook her head to clear the cobwebs and swallowed a bitter laugh. What did he think that she'd let the gifts set corroding in Meanie's Storage? Blake hadn't the heart to tell her until after the bridal shower that he'd changed his mind, or Carlos daughter changed it for him. In her heart, she felt his delay had created a common thread among her friends; they felt sorry for her and she couldn't stand their pity.

The best thing Carlos could do was transfer her to Kentucky. "I'm sorry, Kid," he'd said. "I can't."

"Sure, Boss," Samantha's mind went into a tail spin. Blood's always thicker than water. Right? I'm the water, she thought. Presumably, Blake and his precious were building a flourishing business in Kentucky. "I've got to get away," she told Carlos and still feeling guilty, he agreed. "Go check out Missouri. Someone needs to build a thriving business in Missouri." She was pumped and ready.

She had five days to make a dent in the barn lot wilderness before the first order arrived. There had to be a spot clean enough for storage. Grateful for Alice's offer of room and board, she made a mental note to stop at the supermarket on her way out of town. If Alice could provide the room, she would provide the food. But for now, she drove into the lot with the sign on the front that read equipment for rent.

CHAPTER 5

"You're kidding?" Alice's brows knit together in consternation. "You have rented a tractor?"

"It's not much larger than a riding lawn mower," Samantha admitted. "But he called it a tractor and said it was best suited to a person who knew nothing about one." A nagging worry surfaced again, although she tried to push it to the back of her mind. "I told him I used to mow my Dad's lawn."

"That's all the credentials you need to rent a tractor?"

"He's delivering it, tomorrow. Eight o'clock sharp." She gave a stirring imitation of the Rental owner. "Yes, Sir, I knew old man Jessup, the one that lived in the barn? Alice, now, she's the granddaughter. Nice girl Rents the land to Lan King. He'd clean that lot up for you, if you'd ask."

"But you won't, will you?" Alice eyes twinkled. "You're almost as stubborn and of pride as him."

Remembering Landon Kings words, Samantha hesitated. "I can't help but wonder why he hasn't already."

"Oh, Honey, you can't imagine the shape Jade let things get in. Now you see straight rows of crop. Before Lan took over, it was a grown up mess. Jade tried something new every year, and actually never completed a crop. He would plant but never follow through."

"Why'd you let him? I mean," Samantha shrugged, embarrassed. "It was your land."

"I appreciate your thinking, Honey, but that man was a cross between a man and a bull. You didn't tell him anything." Alice sighed. "If my daddy had known, he would roll over in his grave and my granddad; he would have boarded up the barn."

"Enough said." Samantha pat her shoulder. "Sit. Eat. For tomorrow, If I'm as tired as you think I'll be, we will either have left overs or starve."

"Tell me about your family." Alice lifted a fork full of rice to her mouth. "Ummm. What's the secret?"

"A can of crème of chicken soup, a can of celery soup poured over the rice and the chicken breasts."

"Dinner in a dish," Alice agreed, nodding. "What's your family like? You don't mention them. Secrets?"

"No secrets." Samantha slid into her chair. "A mother named Clarissa, my father, Sam and a grandmother we call Tessia. When my parents divorced I was twelve and Tessia filled in as surrogate mom. My mother left with the man next door. Appropriately his name was Walter Smith. Mr. Smith honored me with having a step brother and step sister, who my grandmother dubbed as very spoiled."

"You were an only child?"

Samantha's fork paused, "Yes, I suppose I was, until Bubba and Barbara came along. Elise moved back to Louisiana and remarried after two years, and I did miss them, for a while we were good friends, but we aren't in contact often."

"Where's your mother now?"

"Ironically, we're in the same state. Walter transferred here. Worked his way up the ladder, so to speak and now they travel while he trains others in his field."

"Prosperous?"

"Yes." Samantha pushed her plate away. "I suppose that's the answer to Clarissa's dream. Dad hadn't gotten as far, but then he died young."

"You sound bitter."

"Why not, I was still a kid when she left."

"Your grandmother seems to have done all right. Except for the bitterness I'm hearing, you appear level headed."

"No thanks to Clarissa's influence. Sam was like that though."

"How old is your mother?"

"Forty seven I haven't seen her in a number of years. I don't know how she's aged, but I'd guess very well."

"Samantha," Dismay rang in Alice's voice. "She's only a few years older than me. For Heaven's sakes, you could be great friends."

"I doubt it." Samantha's voice was dry. "Now, eat your apricot salad or I'll have to give it to the dog."

"We don't have a dog?"

"Right." Samantha grinned. "Then you'll have it tomorrow night. So, that's enough about me. Childhood spent, Mother lost. It's your turn."

"Well," Alice rest both elbows on the table. "I thought Jade Collier was the end of the world." An amused gleam came into her eyes. "He almost was. When the implement dealers started retrieving pieces of machinery I became suspicious. If Dad hadn't held on to the deed, we'd probably have lost this place, too."

"But, how did you make a living if he was such a lousy farmer?"

"I worked as well. Factory, piece work, then the factory closed. There's a greenhouse near here and I helped out." She sighed. "It was difficult. Agricultural areas don't have a lot of available jobs. Unless you prefer seasonal work you are without employment." She glanced at her hands. "When I was a teenager I used to have blisters, and then callouses on my hands every year, we went through that, from holding a hoe handle chopping cotton."

"What about the farm aren't there guidelines, as in every business?"

"Sure. But if someone owns the farm, it has to produce and Jade didn't know how to make that happen. Taxes still came at the end of the year and those bills he forgot to pay…" For a moment sadness clouded her expression. "It hurts when your possessions are taken."

"I'm sorry."

"I know. Most people don't understand. In farming there are good years and bad, you have to know enough about it to make it through. How are you going to make a crop if there's no bank account?"

"But aren't there lending facilities?"

"Yes, but what will you use for collateral if they have already collected everything? Who funds a loser?"

"You have suffered."

"Dad wouldn't take the farm because I was Jade's wife, his own daughter." She grimaced. "You have to understand, when a farmer retires and rents his land to someone else, he still depends on that land to make a living for him, too. That's why the situation became critical." Alice remembered the moment as if it were yesterday. "By the time I decided Jade Collier's lies were not worth a good night in bed, once in a while," her eyes lifted to Samantha for understanding, "That's when our life together came to an end. He had already killed our love by taking another woman to bed, more than one, actually. I filed for divorce."

"Dad died shortly after. He wanted to hang on for me, forever, but it wasn't to be." Tears filled her eyes.

"Maybe we could have turned things around. As it is, Lan King is doing a pretty good job of it. At least the farm is making money again."

Samantha wiped the tears from her cheeks. "We are pretty emotional, aren't we? Father's love their girls pretty much don't they?"

"Yeah, they do. Daddy loved me. Grandpa loved the land. That crazy old coot. That's probably why I agreed to rent you the barn. It's great. Isn't it?" Now she laughed. "He went to extremes, using cypress wherever he could and those oak beams. They are to die for. It's a landmark, but what he went through constructing it." She sighed. "How can they call him crazy when he built something like that?"

"But they smile when they say it," Samantha recalled. "I think there's an understanding of his determination and they feel a real fondness for your grandfather, and I'm sure it is a landmark.

"That's why it's still standing and I'm not selling the land. The truth is if I sold the land, how long would the money last?" Alice stood and stretched. "I've always worked," she laughed, "That's why I have this great body."

"And a wonderful sense of humor." Samantha quipped. "So what's next?"

"Maybe I'll find myself a lover, have an illicit affair, spawn a child in my old age and name him…"

"Grandpa Jessup." Samantha bowed to Alice, reached out a hand and they did a do-si-do.

"Oh, Lord, what's in this soup? I bet you laced it with rum."

"Wrong. Vodka," Samantha teased. "Odorless intoxication."

"How would you know? I can almost guarantee you don't drink and neither do I."

"No, my grandmother taught me the woes of drinking. She didn't drink but a few of her stories about those who did and I just didn't want to and where I've lived the last five years, believe me, they drink."

Looking thoughtful, Alice sobered and said, "I might take it up, if those guys at work don't stop the harassment."

"It's that bad, huh?"

Alice nodded. "A thin skinned gal would have folded by now."

❋ ❋ ❋ ❋ ❋

Amused, Lan King watched the proceedings at the old Jessup farm. Little escaped his attention. The rental truck arrived with a tractor, a small mower attached. There was a trailer parked in the lane when he arrived at work, holding what, he could only guess. On one trip past the lane he had seen the McKinsey woman's car with an assortment of tools protruding from the rear, even handles sticking out the back seat windows. The letters on the license plate said SAM 1-2. He wondered what that meant.

He kept track of the days by her progress. First she worked clearing the lane; several trips over the tall grass with the mower brought the path visible. Next she started cutting the clumps of bracken that had grown around the trees. That would take a while. Curious, he made it a point during the day to drive by, although his men were working on the home place. Loathe admitting it, her progress piqued his interest. Her manner of dress brought a certain diversion to the order and similarity of his days. The first day she wore designer jeans, he could tell, a green scarf around her forehead and it was ninety degree heat. She must have been dripping in sweat.

Concerned and wondering why he cared, he noted she wore boots. Heaving a sigh of relief he hoped there were no poisonous snakes, but one never knew. Eyes narrowing, mentally he reviewed the lot. He'd warned her about the old storm cellar and the place where the old house had been pushed in. There was an old metal pile where Jade junked everything, but there was no reason to think she would work that far back.

The heat index rose and the drought bore down around them. Lan's men moved along the turn rows, one on the tractor, the other two laying plastic tubing that would swell and carry water to starving plants. Another was assigned to starting the motors. Trying to water Alice place was a struggle and they were headed that way. Whereas his own ground was put to grade and irrigate able, the Jessup farm was completely out of kilter to running water by way of tubing. The best they could do was to try flooding it. Put to grade meant the rows received the water with minimum loss, but Jessup's was a wilderness when he followed Jade's farming.

There were low spots where the water welled up and would drown out the plants. Around the barn, his men stretched flat plastic tubing. "Don't break on me now," he said out loud, staring at tubing coming to life. The tubing was economical, laid once and discarded at the end of the season, but there were also disadvantages. An occasional tear when animals decided to find out what was keeping them out. Stripping bare to the waist, Lan waded in wondering if he dared flood this field from the upper turn row to the lower ground on the South end.

Using his shirt he wiped the sweat and grime from his arms and climbed into his truck. He needed things from home. He was backing down the lane, a cloud of dust obscuring his vision when he saw her. Damn! He'd nearly run over her. Slamming on the brakes he was out of the truck and by her side in a flash.

"Are you crazy? I nearly run over you."

Visibly shaken, Samantha lay over the steering wheel of the small tractor, her hands were clenched around it and both feet were jammed against the brakes. "Get off," he demanded. She couldn't move. Lan reached across and threw the tractor out of gear. The tractor was lodged against a small tree with one wheel in the ditch. He bent over her and pried her hands loose from the steering wheel. Seeing the fright on her face, his anger dissipated. "Look, I'm sorry. I couldn't see you. I nearly run you down." She must have suntan oil on her face, because it was covered over with dust, all he could see was her eyes. "My word, woman, you must have been barreling through those trees like a mad woman."

She was coming around, but the shaking of her body hadn't stopped. Tears stung her eyes. She had hit the tree hard, he'd bet she would be bruised. "What are you doing?" He was ignoring the giddy feeling he was experiencing pulling her from the tractor. There was more bare skin than that covered. The twist of halter was an interesting concoction but the dust settled on her face gave her a clownish look that made him chuckle.

Thinking to be alone, she had left off the confining garments and gone for comfort. Working behind the barn, no one would see her. But she felt his hands on her ribcage trying to dislodge her from the tractor. Truthfully she had hit the tree hard enough to knock her out, or maybe it had, she felt all disoriented. Mesmerized by the strength she felt in him, she reacted almost hypnotically, wondering what would be his next move. Evidently Mr. King was not a man to miss an opportunity. Somewhere in the mix of emotions she heard his breath catch, or was it hers. Her halter was caught on the lever beneath the steering wheel, and she was too groggy to take matters into her own hands, trembling, thinking it was all a dream, she tried to rise but she was weighted down. "I need help," she groaned, her arms going around his neck. "Lady. Lady." He couldn't remember her name. "Help me here. Your clothing's caught on the ..." How could he resist. He kissed her. For an immeasurable time he kissed her and she kissed him back, his lips on hers. It was as if an electric current passed between them and a flame began to stir they neither could afford. She was bracing her hands against his chest but too weak to push him away. His hands were caught between the mechanism of the steering wheel lever and her halter. "How in the world did you do this?" Finally seeing her troubled eyes, he backed away. "Let me find a knife and I'll cut the fabric and you can cover yourself and I promise I won't look."

He returned to find she had wiped away the grime with her free hand and the storm brewing in her eyes sent up warning signals. She would blame him for only the Lord knew what. Anger flooded his mind.

"Please." His hands lingered, he heard her but the memory of times past with someone else beat out her moment's need. He managed to pull the piece of tattered material over the end of the lever. The storm in his own body was abating. Later he would wonder why he spoke. "I thought you found it enjoyable, too."

"I did." She was too addled and confused to lie. "This is the second time you've kissed me. It's quite unnerving. I seem unable to resist your unorthodox manner. I don't know you. You don't know me."

Surprised by her truthfulness, Landon reluctantly released his hold, watching as she straightened the halter, pulling it down over the band of the loose fitting shorts she wore. "You think we should become better acquainted?" A mocking expression replaced the sincerity he'd briefly felt.

"Undoubtedly." Summing what strength she could, Samantha resolved to squelch the fire that raged within; she felt sapped of energy as she stared at the tractor. "Will you drive the tractor out of the ditch, if it will start?"

"Yeah, that was my intention until you went giddy legged on me. Nice trick."

Fresh irritation rankled through her veins. "You thought I was playing a game, nearly killing myself?" Her eyes flashed. "How dare you."

He saw the agony and hurt cross her face, followed by the anger that flared. Still, his mind went back to another woman that teased. He watched as she stumbled away from the tractor, disdaining his outstretched hand. He climbed onto the tractor, slammed his foot on the brake and turned the key to the ignition. The mower rumbled, stopped, caught again and fired up. She watched her jaw set in a disa-proving way. When he dismounted she took the seat, vaguely aware of the return of his mocking smile, the touch of finger to his forehead and the blur of the white pickup truck leaving her there, alone, to find her way back to the path that led to the barn.

She wanted to hate him. Instead she could only wonder that there was magnetism between them that they neither wanted. He was a maddening man. The best they could do would be to avoid each other.

CHAPTER 6

As SHE WORKED the meadow became shaven clean, enough grass laying in swathes to make a hay man envious, and the musings come. Landon King resurfacing as clearly in her mind's eye as if he stood before her. He was a stranger. How could she possibly savor his kiss? She groaned. Tessia had warned her of this. If she closed her eyes she could see his face, the dark eyes questioning; the rake of sun tinted hair darker near the nape of is neck, his skin superbly tanned. She glanced at her own body, covered in a film of sweat and dust, her hair pulled tight that morning in a ponytail had escaped to tendrils around her face. With her eyes open she could feel his body, lean and hard against her own, the wide shoulders tapering to narrow hips and the ripple of muscle, the way they had felt beneath her hands.

She could not delude herself, all the while a demon of righteousness kept reminding her that she did not like his rude behavior, but like a fire in the blood he uprooted every conscious thought.

It was dark when she parked the tractor behind the barn and dark when she pulled into the drive at Alice's house. A light was on in the kitchen and she made her way to the kitchen door. Dressed in shorts with a loose fitting blouse, Alice turned to stare as she entered the door. "Honey Chile, what have you been doing?"

Sinking into the first chair without a cushioned seat, she heaved a sigh and stared at her scratched arms and the layers of dirt on her skin. "Would you believe, I was nearly killed being run over by a truck today?"

"What?"

"A truck going backwards faster than a speeding bullet," she replied. "For the first time I'm wondering is it worth starting a new business if it's going to be all this trouble?"

Immediately interested, Alice sat across from her. "Do you know who's truck it was?"

"Landon Kings."

Alice mouth fell open. "Not intentionally?"

"I don't think so." For some reason Samantha's eyes filled with tears.

"Honey, was it that bad?"

"Nooo." Samantha wailed. "Yessss." She cried, the sobs gaining momentum and volume. Until finally she hiccuped and said, "Don't be kind to me. I'm so tired." Trying to understand her own outburst beneath Alice's curious stare, her shoulders drooped. "It's the physical labor, I guess, making decisions. The things I have to do just to clean up an overgrown barn lot. Maybe I took on more than I can handle." Her body continued to tremble. "I'm sorry. I don't mean that hateful. I'm grateful but just tired."

"You would never be hateful, Sam." Alice shortened her name, reaching for her hand. "Come with me. I saw those lovely bath crystals you unpacked; even sniffed them. What you need is a long soak in the tub. Believe me, it's a tonic for weary bones. And if you go to sleep, I'll come and scrub you like a baby."

Like an obedient child, Samantha followed. She could only sink on to the commode while Alice ran the water and was conscious the tub was full when the fragrance of the bath crystals rose to assuage her nostrils. She heard Alice say, "Strip." Then she left the room and closed the door. "I'll have your plate ready by the time you've finished." Laughter sounded through the door. "Leftovers, Hon. I didn't cook."

Stepping free of the grimy shorts, the smelly halter and damp panties that clung to her skin, Samantha sank into the water, it's warmth closing around her until she felt her body begin to relax. The truth of the matter was, she was worn out both physically and mentally from trying to understand why Landon King stayed in her thoughts. Why couldn't she quit thinking of him? Her mind was at war, between reality and emotion. This was no time to become infatuated with a man, especially a man as bold, mocking and assuming as him. She had experienced one bad relationship she did not need another and her feeling about Landon King was that he was dangerous. He would use up a woman and throw her away. But it nagged at her conscience he didn't seem to understand his own actions.

Sinking as low as she could, she let her hair soak in the water. How could she be so stupid? She had just evolved from beating herself to death over Blake. Reaching for the shampoo, she watched as gray suds oozed through her fingers. He must have considered her the dirtiest woman he'd ever kissed. Oh. She closed her eyes to see his face, the dark orbs watching her every move. Deliberately she sat about the task of scrubbing her skin. Rinsing her hair with a vengeance, she dared the emotions to flare but the resolve sapped her energy further. Ruthlessly she tried to purge her mind; it was the tiredness of mind and body betraying her.

Once she arrived at the table, Alice regarded her with motherly eyes. Grinning she said, "Same song, tonight, second course." The words were lost on Samantha, who was nearly asleep in her plate.

"What?"

"I said the men have made threats, the creepy ones," Alice replied. "They say they'll come out here and teach me what a man's all about, since I think I can fill their shoes."

"They wouldn't, would they?"

"I don't know, Honey. If it's necessary I'll make hens out of those roosters. The gun is on two nails above the door," Alice replied, her voice grim as she pointed to where it was.

"When did you put it there?"

"Today. Do you know how to shoot a gun?"

"Yes." Samantha yawned. "Expertly. My dad taught me."

"Good. I have to go in at midnight. I almost think the manager is in on the men's threat, why else would he sign me up to come in at night? Do you think you will be all right?"

"A herd of elephants wouldn't bother me."

Alice considered the dishes and silverware, two of each. "There are not many dishes. Let's leave them. You're dead on your feet and a couple hours sleep won't hurt me either, before I go in."

The last thing Samantha remembered was Alice saying, "You might should take a Tylenol to help you relax. I have a feeling when you lie down your body will go into over load and you'll be so stressed you can't rest." She brushed her teeth and took the pill and crawled into bed.

Alice peeked in on her a short while later. Moonlight streaming through the window revealed the outline of Samantha in peaceful slumber. Returning to the kitchen, Alice turned the tap and filled the sink with water. As late as it was when she finished the dishes she decided she needed to make a call. The phone was dialing the number.

Landon answered on the third ring. "Land, will you be making your routine check on the irrigation motors tonight? Would you drive by and check on my house guest?" She listened. "Yeah, she told me a truck nearly ran over her. She's dead tired and already in bed fast asleep. The thing is, there are a few creeps at work giving me a hard time; they've made threats about coming out here. With Samantha sound asleep, I'm afraid it would take a real commotion to waken her." She listened again. "I'll leave your number on the night stand. Come off of it, Land, she's a nice girl. Besides, this is your route, I see you checking the irrigation in the night." She chuckled. "Something tells me you can't sleep either."

The hackles rose on the back of Land's neck. With a hand rubbing where the pain gnawed between his shoulder blades, he wandered to the kitchen, searched the back of the shelves and found the bottle. At first, he filled a small glass, then turned the bottle up and gulped the liquid feeling it fire up his throat. Disgusted with himself, he pushed it to the back and closed the door. He'd given that up with the problem. He sat down at the table, staring at nothing. Why had he kissed her? Twice. As she reminded him and she was a good kisser. He groaned. He was no silly school boy. Unorthodox, she called it. He stared around the kitchen as if expecting food to jump out of the frig or the cabinets but he knew nothing was there. Not a thing to eat.

Nine o'clock and he had to check pumps in less than three hours. Sometimes they ran out of fuel in the night. What he needed was sleep and maybe a shower would help. He thought punishment would be a cold shower, it shot through him, waking him up but he was too tired. Turning the water past warm, letting it stream over his body, watching sweat literally disappear from his arms as he turned the faucet water as hot as he could stand. Amazed he considered his actions. What had gotten into him? He'd stared into those blue eyes nearly violet, what the hell? Mesmerized by her nearness, he'd given in to the physical. He clenched his fist until the knuckles turned white angry with himself. Finally with only a towel wrapped around his midsection, he was back in the kitchen, tipping the bottle again.

He hadn't needed the bottle since Lila's death; Lila of the brown hair, the flashing eyes and the torturing spirit, his wife. She haunted him. "Yes, Land, darling, I've found another man, one that makes me feel alive. Not some dirt farmer who spends more time with his hired men than his wife, but a gentleman with soft hands and money." He drained the bottle and threw it against the wall.

Were they all alike, wanting nothing but what a man could bring home to them? He had guarded his emotions since her death. What had it been, four, five years? He wondered if Alice told the McKinsey dame the sordid story how Lila died. He shivered, a chill penetrating his inner soul. Was he to blame? He'd tried to talk sense to her but she'd left, laughing and mocking him. "I'm leaving everything, Land, darling. No reminders. Call your mother, she'll explain."

Drugged he paced the floor, walking the rooms, coming at last to the bedroom. There, in the drawer he found Lila's picture. Long ago, on that painful night, he'd smashed it until the glass shattered in a million tiny pieces. Through a blur he studied Lila, his body heaving in a torrent of emotion, finally to throw the picture back into the drawer.

He'd kept the picture and the house she wanted with the French doors. Now he walked through them, out onto a small railed patio. A ragged sigh escaped his lips; the view should have been appeasing. The lawn had finally taken shape, the landscaping, the shrubs artistically arranged, were now lush in growth. Shouldn't he be as advanced as those shrubs? They'd gone through every stage to reach this point. All of it, bought for her and he'd done his best meeting her demands, even when money was scarce.

In the night shadows, he considered his life. It was meaningless because there was no one to share the good times and the bad. The price, Lila, his mind went on, relentless, we mortgaged everything to give you this house and where are you, what did you do? I thought we were going to lose it all when you left and it didn't matter then. But you left and I quit the project, your wants, your desires you said you needed. Now I'm here, walking the floors in living hell.

She wanted the house in town, but he was a farm boy. It was a grand house for the country lane. They'd agreed on nothing. The house was completed a month after she died in the accident with her doctor. He'd moved in with a bedroom suite, a sofa, table and chairs for the dining room and the meagerest supplies. All that Lila's hands touched was left behind. Only items ordered and delivered were there.

A wild profusion of laughter sounded in his ears, it was his. The bay window in the dining room had no curtains, the breakfast room had no table until he found one by the side of the road and brought it home. It appeared to have fallen off a truck, damaged the top and someone left it. His gain. Once, he'd accepted her dreams and looked forward to the house being finished but Lila had changed course in the middle of their plan. Carrying his child, she met her doctor and left him.

He sank onto the bed, letting fatigue take over. The towel fell from his body as he reached for the clock and set it, and fell into deep sleep. It was not Lila's face haunted him this night but the face of a stranger, thin, full breast, and blue eyes staring at him puzzled as a strand of her hair wrapped around his face. He was in his truck, speeding from one field to another when he ran over something. The sound brought chills to his body, a big thump. He left the truck to check it out and found her laying on the ground a great gash on her head, her body flat. "Do you kill the women in your life?" The ringing of the clock brought him out of the dream before he could answer her question. Confused, he searched for the button to turn it off. It was time to check the levies and the motors.

Staggering into the bathroom, he searched for a clean pair of jeans and a shirt. Bone-weary he pulled on his clothes left the house and crawled in his truck. By the time he checked the fields to be sure the levies of the rice field hadn't broken or a fox dug a hole through them and the motors were all running, he was more alert. Begrudgingly, he headed toward Alice's house. Bouncing along the country roads he was thinking the fields would be watered within the next twelve hours if nothing went wrong.

Reaching the lane, thinking not to disturb the house if she was asleep, he turned off his lights, surprised when lights came on from the house area. Quickly he pulled into a stand of trees by the roadside and cut the motor. A jeep passed by, open top down revealing three male heads whooping and hollering once they thought they'd cleared hearing distance. Damn, he swore under his breath, it looked like Jess Lassity's jeep. If it was Lassity's kid driving, it would be Leon, the trouble maker of the bunch. Never worth a minutes work to his father, Landon heard the boy had finally gone to work at the plant.

So Alice was right, whether the men were making idle threats or not, their kids had no right to trespass the property. Alice knew her way around but the Lassity boy wouldn't like any means of reprimand. Lan had seen Lassity's wife, a string of a woman cowered by both father and son. She looked as if she carried the burdens of the world, if she'd pick up a two by four and bash them in the head a time or two… then again, they'd probably kill her and band together to lie out of it.

Good. They hadn't seen him, yet. He watched. If they left without making much trouble he'd talk to their dad tomorrow. Maybe attention from outside the family might turn the boy around. He left his truck, circled the drive in the shadows and started walking toward the porch. Something in the path made him stumble and fall to his knees. He felt something warm and sticky on his fingers. Blood. It was a dog, he was sure of it, a dead dog but it hadn't been dead long. Alice didn't have a dog. He was stunned, trying to search for a reason.

They would do that? Kill a dog for no reason? Drop it on Alice's doorstep? Suddenly his body was pumping adrenalin and his brain was set on alarm. What if they'd heard him coming and they left because they'd done more? On his feet, he was running, up to the door. It was locked. He tapped on the window he thought belonged to the daughter's room. Nothing. He came to a water hydrant. They had been close. A stream of water was running through the grass. He let it splash over his hands. Quickly he turned off the water. Now he banged his fist on the door. Frustration was rising. There wasn't a light on in the house.

Where did she leave the key? With trembling fingers he searched the supporting posts of the porch. Finding the key he dropped it, scrambled for it and finally slipped it into the door lock. Moonlight streamed behind as he walked through the door into the room. "Not a step farther." He knew the sound of metal against metal.

He jerked and would have turned but he felt the familiar sound of the safety on the gun released and the barrel pressing in the small of his back. "It's me, Landon King."

"What are you doing here?"

"Alice sent me." Was that a sigh of relief he heard. "How long have you been awake?"

"Someone was pounding on the door. Alice is at work." Her voice came, methodical. "I didn't know what else to do."

"You did fine," Landon replied, softly. "Put the gun down."

"Why are you here, really?"

"I saw three men in a jeep leaving the drive." He saw her reaction and the possibility she could have been in harm's way. She didn't seem overly concerned, as she yawned and looked toward the bedroom.

"Oh." Samantha lowered the gun and removed her trembling finger from the trigger and started back toward the kitchen as Lan reached the front door and pushed it firmly shut and slid the bolt. Just like that she accepted his explanation, going to the door, rising up as far as she could to replace the gun. It was a wonder she could reach it. He was by her side in a second, his hand on the stock to push it back.

She didn't resist when his hand landed on top of hers, nor when their shoulders bumped. Something wasn't quite right. She seemed in a zombie state. Alice said she was tired and had advised her to take a sleeping pill in order to get some rest. Good Lord, did she think this was all a dream? He almost believed she did because of her near state of undress. She was making no effort to pull her top together and without a word she was headed toward one of the leather rockers. Tucking her feet beneath her bottom like a child she sat rocking and staring.

"Are you all right?" He bent and peered into her face.

"Yes." She kept her eyes on him, after all, she had been dreaming of him. How she got in the kitchen holding a gun on him, she had no idea.

Without a word, he reached for her hand, pulling her free of the rocker and led her back to her room, motioned for her to get in the bed and brought the sheet up to her arms and stepped back to think.

"Go home," she said as she closed her eyes and was gone.

What was he supposed to do? Something settled inside him as he listened to her steady breathing. How could you leave someone who slept so soundly and especially with the Lassity's running loose? That boy had a reputation for nothing good. Drinking and staying out all night were but a part of who he was. The old saying, an apple doesn't fall far from the tree applied here. What if they returned?

Along with the brooding uneasiness concerning Leon Lassity, he suddenly felt paralyzed to stand by the bed studying her sleeping form. Something tightened in his chest. He took a deep breath.

Trying to tamp out the memory of holding her, he glanced across the room to where his reflection scowled back from a floor length mirror. In the moonlight her skin took on a silvery sheen. Hair fanned across the pillow, soft skin, the clean floral fragrance of her wafted up. He tried to tell himself, as any man he'd been attracted to a pretty girl that was all. But he knew it wasn't. She wasn't Lila, but he'd fight her with his last breath. He never intended to be taken in to a woman's whims again.

After Lila he'd vowed no woman would claim his heart and his body only when need and occasion presented its self. Here, then, was occasion, an inner being suggested. Disgusted with himself, Lan stooped to tuck the sheet more firmly about her body.

Snuggling deeper in sleep, a sigh audible as the purr of a kitten issued from Samantha's lips as one hand roamed the covers. She found the hand, let her fingers trace along the arm and drew him near. What a lovely dream she was having. She was a child again, sitting in the sun with her dad as he read the paper.

He stopped the groan before it reached his lips as he sank onto the bed beside her. A cloud passed and moonlight outlined her body. Her arm went around his waist and he lay down beside her, feeling her breath warm on his face as she closed the space between them. He felt the heat in his body, the escalation of his heart as her arms slid up to his neck. Dear Lord, she was lovely, warm and sweet she smelled better than anything he remembered. She looked like an angel but when he remembered the fire that usually smoldered in her eyes when she saw him, he chuckled. She was a fire angel.

Groaning aloud, he wondered how in the world this happened. She was some dame from the city. No one he should associate with, a hell cat, again he chuckled, a fire angel, he'd bet always, from the way she flung sarcastic remarks his way. Who did that? But right now he was in awe of this fire angel with her softness and gentle touch.

The touch of a woman was different and the whole thing threw him off balance. Like a child with fevered brow, he'd missed that.

Now the mirrored reflection stared with uncertainty. Surely he was above ogling a woman in sleep. He would feel better if she awakened and smacked him between the eyes. What had lain dormant was alive and well at the moment. Raging was more like it. He lift one hand and drew a finger across her lips. What harm in one kiss? Gently he brushed his lips across the softness of hers. Sweet. The second kiss was not so gentle, drinking deeper of her warmth, seeking acceptance without realizing it.

For a second her eyes opened. What was she doing? The dream seemed so real but it was a cross between now and Landon King or back then with Dad and the dog, Sleep had never been that good.

Every sense in his body was alive, but his conscience was at war, one encouraging the other. "Lady." He whispered, "If I were any other man and you any other woman…" Landon King was a lonely man but he was not a man to press himself on anyone and certainly not an unconscious woman. It would be easy, the demon on his left shoulder mocked but the man he needed to be, saw himself in the mirror across the room, lonely, vulnerable and shaken that this woman could make him forget the torment of the past.

He held her, listening to her even breathing. Whatever she'd taken had left one hell of a dent in her consciousness. Maybe he'd find out and try it himself on one of those nights he badly needed rest. He almost believed he had lost some of the bitterness as he slipped away from her, sitting on the edge of the bed his head in his hands thinking. If he was ever to love another woman he must forgive Lila. The pessimism and hardness of his heart would take longer but right now he felt they would go. The uncertainty of what he felt at this moment could turn into a positive, wasn't that what his mother always said? Dear God, he didn't know if he had the courage or patience to try again. Dead, Lila ruled his heart in a way she had been unable to while alive. The idea of someone else hurting him made his blood run cold.

When morning light pierced the sky, he rose up to leave, first studying the woman on the bed, a wisp of hair across one cheek, the fringe of lash covering the deep blue eyes that could flare so quickly in rage. He had pulled the sheet, tucking it under her arms, much as one would an infant. Her left arm was drawn onto the pillow, palm up. He drew a quick breath. A row of large and raw blisters ran almost a solid line the width of her hand. And now that it was daylight he could see scratches on her inner arms and no doubt the rest of her body, from carrying brush she'd cut.

Feisty little wench, and brave to tackle Jade and old man Jessup's granddaughter about the barn. He almost chuckled. As unexpectedly as before, feelings claimed his body. He wanted to touch her, remove the strand of hair from her cheek and watch those magnificent eyes widen in surprise or perhaps appreciation. Whatever, his little fire angel wanted, if it was help, or someone to count on, this moment he wanted to be there for her and that was a major statement coming from his terrible past, a past he'd hinged on bitterness that he deserved better and he would make a life pleasing to himself where no woman had a say.

On that thought he was able to pull himself away, the day was dawning, Alice would be home soon and there was a dead dog to bury. She would never remember he was there.

CHAPTER 7

$\mathscr{S}$HE AWOKE EVERY muscle in her body crying out in pain and the palms of her hands throbbed with blisters circled in redness. Standing was another cruel joke but she made herself straighten the sheets and pull the spread over the pillows neatly. Impressions of a dream invaded her thoughts. She couldn't remember. That would never happen, her dad and Landon King together in a dream. Whatever made her dream such wild dreams. She wasn't sure she rested as even now an encounter with Alice's gun crossed her mind. She hurried into the kitchen, relieved to see if it was still hanging above the door.

She was gone when Alice arrived home from work. Leaving by the back door, Samantha didn't see the pool of blood on the porch. Alice heard her phone ringing and answered. Evidently the man had no use for formalities. "Warren's Rental, here, I was given your number, Miss Jessup. That woman from Flint, Samantha, hasn't checked in. I need to be sure she hasn't run away with my equipment."

"Really, Mr. Warren?" Alice was tired and frustrated over what she'd seen on the porch. "She's working herself to death. You could have given her a larger tractor." Besides this man on the phone, the Lassity kid had tried to run her off the road.

"You don't rent large equipment to women who have never driven anything larger than a lawnmower. She could kill herself."

Samantha hadn't explained the complete wilderness she was undertaking. "At least we agree on that," Alice replied. "Sorry I was sharp with you, I just finished an all night shift." She yawned. "I'll tell her you called."

She was ready to hang up when he said, "You get some rest, Miss Jessup. Next time you're in town, drop by and I'll take you to lunch."

"Are you married?" Seemed to her he came on rather quick to have had irritation in his voice earlier.

She heard laughter. "No, if I were my wife would kill me, wouldn't she? She's been gone seven years."

"I'll think about it," Alice replied. "Right now I'm dead tired. I don't want to think. Period."

Making a note, she stuck it on the frig where Samantha would find it. She was waking up, a call to Lan might make her feel better. She pressed the name on her cell and waited for him to answer but he didn't. Wide awake by now, she headed back out to the jeep and drove the round of farms Land rented, passing by her grandfather's place she chuckled as she gave Samantha credit for being organized. There were small orange flags dotting the landscape. She'd have to ask their purpose. Last stop was Land's shed. Three of his men looked up from their work as she entered.

"How's it going, Jimmy?"

"Sleepy, otherwise fit as a fiddle."

"Just off from work, huh? If you're looking for the boss, he's somewhere close to the combine."

"Little early, for that, isn't it?"

"Nah, you know the boss, he wants everything ready to go. So we start early."

She saw the backside of Land going around the building. "Hey, Landon King. Wait up."

"What're you doing out here, taking your morning drive?"

"There was a pool of blood on the porch when I got home." She hesitated. "Well, it looked like blood."

"It was. I was checking motors and saw Leon's jeep coming out of your drive. I found it and buried it."

"You mean?" Alice blanched. He was nodding. "Does Samantha know?"

"I doubt it. I wouldn't know if I hadn't taken you serious and checked on your house last night."

"That Lassity boy." It made her dizzy too think he'd killed something. "What was it?"

"A dog."

"Yeah, it was still warm to the touch. I ought to know, I fell over it."

"Kimberly always said he was weird. He had a crush on her, once. I don't know if he connects me with the plant and his problem or what. I heard they fired him. Maybe he saw Samantha from a distance and thought Kimberly was home."

"You said he caused trouble."

"But a dead dog?" A worried frown crossed her brow. "If it's true what I heard, he's been suspended for some kind of job hazard at the plant."

"Can you handle it?"

"Yeah, but I can't complain to the plant authority."

"You sure the job's worth it?"

"No, have you got one handy?" She shook her head in dismay. "Where else can I make that much an hour? With Jade's bills and having to eat…you get the picture?"

"I'll put a word in with the sheriff. A kid with his nose out of joint doesn't stop with one incident."

"Fine, but I doubt he'll check out the Lassity kid, besides he tired of me when Jade was running wild"

"Still," Landon looked her in the eye. "In the event he showed up with intent to harm?"

"Don't even think about it." Alice closed her eyes. "I can't handle any more problems, Land." She turned to leave. "I got to get some shut eye. By the way, Samantha is a terrific cook. Would you like to have supper with us one night? I'll have a few days off when my shift changes. We could have a sort of official meeting on friendly turf."

"We've met," he replied. "Why tempt fate?"

Alice left, laughing. Once in her car, however, she drove around the shop and stopped by the combine. "What you need Land King is to find yourself a wife and get some curtains on the windows of that house."

"People who live in glass houses shouldn't throw rocks."

"Meaning?"

"You're a fine one to talk. I suppose if you get desperate, we could pool our miseries." He stooped down by the jeep, his head level with the open window.

A flush of color heightened Alice face. "I'd consider if it wasn't for the fact I'm old enough to be your mother."

"Child bride, huh?" Land grinned. "What, ten or twelve years older than me? That's what I need, a woman to mother me."

"Lot of good stuff going to waste, Lan, gentleness and caring, not to mention a superb body. Hard work's keeping you lean and mean."

"Yeah, I'm a tethered stud waiting for the right filly to unleash the fury of my powers. So why act like a sister, we'll get together some time."

"Darn." Alice grinned. "We always could flirt good together." She yawned. "It's because you consider me harmless. After Jade Collier, I'd think long and hard before I took on another man." Her eyes narrowed, "but Lila's been gone five years now. Why don't you date again, Lan? You're a good man and I hate to see you wasted."

Land groaned. "Come off it, Alice. Who'd want me? I'm set in my ways, now."

"What about Amy?"

Land stood. "She's fine."

Alice saw the line had been drawn, invisibly clear. "We used to have some nice talks, Lan. I miss them."

"Yeah, me too." He sighed. "Maybe after the McKinsey dame leaves your house."

"She's no threat to you, Lan. Actually, she's a very nice girl."

Watching Alice's jeep disappear in a cloud of dust, Land thought, if you only knew.

❋ ❋ ❋ ❋ ❋

On Saturday, Samantha rose to find Alice dressed and waiting. "I'm going with you, remember? I said I'd help."

"But you don't have to." Samantha shook her head, smiling sadly. "I wish we could have a holiday from work." She studied her hands. "I've got blisters, sore muscles and peeling skin, not to mention I've barely made a dent in the job I've started but supplies will be arriving and I've got to be ready for them."

"Did you call Mr. Warren?"

"Yes, and he said you lamblasted him for sending a woman to do a man's job. Truth is, Alice, I didn't tell him the condition of the barn lot or he'd never have gone along with renting me any equipment."

"I kind of suspected that." Alice grinned. "I've already apologized. Kind of and almost got a date out of it."

"Maybe he's like Carlos, not used to a woman telling him what to do now that his daughter married Blake."

"Give me a mental description of Carlos."

"Umm, fiftyish, five ten, dark skinned from too much fishing on weekends. But what do you expect, he lives near the great lakes." She sighed as she shrugged, "He's sophisticated, as behooves a rich man."

Alice studied her, eyebrows raised, questioning. "Do I sense a mite attraction going Carlos way?"

"Sure, I'm always trying to replace my father, though it never happens, Sam was quite a man and no one ever measures up."

"Does Carlos have a wife, a girlfriend, a mistress?" Alice tilt her head to one side, "Let's face it, rich men have advantages."

"Yeah, but should money be the advantage, so much for attraction, passion and the need to be together." She considered the question. "His wife remarried and from that they have one very spoiled daughter, now Blake's wife. She was the center of his life. Tell you what I'll introduce you to Carlos. You can decide what kind of man he is." She grinned mischievously, "But then there's Mr. Warren. Right?"

"So what's the deadline to have everything in place and Carlos make the grand tour?"

"I hope by last of September, then first of November have an early Christmas opening. The grand tour."

"You're kidding?"

"Nope." Samantha eyed the calendar on the wall. "Next week the industrial equipment arrives. Surely you didn't think I planned to clear the pasture all by myself. No offense but it's pretty bad."

"I wondered," Alice replied. "I admit I did," she giggled. "For heavens' sakes what are those little orange flags sticking up all over the place?"

"Your husbands junk spots," Samantha replied, dryly. "If I find them it saves dollars and no damage to the equipment. Mr. Warren said if a tire is ruined I have to pay for it. A man coming out to check for the junk, your husband's buried treasure said it would have cost me five hundred."

"That's disgusting."

"Changing from the small equipment to large doubled the price. That's life."

"I'm in the wrong business." Alice stared hard at Samantha, "Changing the subject but I don't think I have told you about the night the Lassity kid went on a tear, now I find out he is working at the plant again, having been reinstated and makes two dollars an hour more than me. Why is that?"

"Either union or he's a man?" Samantha guessed. "Really I got no idea. But…we need to be going."

"I noticed Lan's got the lane blocked." She eyed Samantha's halter, "I was thinking of working on my tan." Alice lift her shirt to reveal she was prepared for a few minutes in the sun."

"No one will bother us back there," Samantha replied. "Who would want to…we will get so dirty."

With Alice helping the morning passed quickly. When noon arrived they paused for a light lunch. Alice surveyed the wood lot. "I always loved this place and hoped someday to build a home here."

"It's not too late."

"I think it is." Alice stretched her bare arms across the hood of the car where they'd spread lunch after finding too many fire ants to sit on the ground under a lone tree. "I had a lot of dreams with Jade Collier. In the beginning we were happy living in an old run down house that leaked when it rained and dust blew in other times. But when Jade started fooling around, there were things I couldn't put back together again. I lasted as long as I could…and I had Kimberly to take care of."

"You're not so old, Alice, you're one of those women could lie about your age and no one ever know, except you are an honest woman and that's beyond your mind set. What people see is what they get."

"I thank you for that."

"You need to find time to meet new men, decent ones'." Samantha's eyes twinkled mischievously.

"How do I do that? I work with them and the ones I thought decent are catering to the Lassity kid. Kind of like you must have felt passed over by Blake for the boss's daughter. The last cabbage in the bin."

Samantha laughed. "I hadn't thought about that, Alice." Astonished, she tilt her head, "I haven't mourned over Blake since I've been here. There's hope for me yet. This hay field may be my salvation."

"Do you think about that, Sam?" Alice slipped easily into a new name for Samantha. "Do you believe in God and church and all that stuff?"

"Do I believe?" Sam threw her head back and laughed. "Am I Tessia's granddaughter? She would disown me if I didn't. That was part of the training she gave me as a child. We did not miss Sunday School or worship hour, any Sunday of the month, and Tessia was the one who played piano for church services…do you? At times

I wondered if my training held me back in life but I've decided it helped."

"You know," Alice stared up to the sky, "I've owned every thought a person could have on that subject. When things went well, I became complacent and forgot to thank God and praise him as I was taught, then when my life was falling apart I called on him as though I'd been faithful all the way. And I hadn't. I put him on the back shelf, so to speak. Then when Jade hurt me so badly, I became angry with God that he wouldn't whip Jade into submission as though that would make everything better." She dropped her head to study the ground. "Then some terrible things happened and it broke me. When you're broken in spirit there's nowhere else to go and that's when I learned who God really is."

"Who is He, Alice?" Samantha asked softly.

"He's the one that is there when everyone else fails you, Sam. When you don't know where the next meal is coming from, your baby needs milk and diapers or your kid in college may have to drop out and you don't want to tell her what a terrible parent you are, you can't even take care of your kid's needs."

"This is getting pretty deep, isn't it?" Samantha hugged Alice, "but we both recognize because of Him," she pointed up toward the heavens. "We are making it. My broken heart really wasn't as broke as I thought. God knew I didn't need Blake and I didn't have to go against my principles to please Blake…and you, my dear found friend may build a home for you and some old geezer right out here next to Grampa Jessup's barn."

"Was it a man woman thing, Samantha? He pressured you to do things his way?"

"It was always, if you love me….and you know the rest, so do you think you could build a home here?"

"The houses in Riverdale are nice…but where your Grandmother lives, they are magnificent." She glanced across the fields, "I'll probably stay right where I am. You can't see Land King's house from the field, but up in the barn, you can. It's nearly lost in that line of trees; most people forget it's there. Lila wanted it that way for privacy since Land wouldn't build in town. The trees conceal the farm shop."

"Who's Lila?" They were walking across the field, looking for pot holes and buried equipment.

"His wife."

Samanatha blanched. "I didn't know he had a wife." She stared at her feet, trying to make them move faster, and wondering why. Strange and crazy thoughts raced through her mind. "I would never have guessed."

Curious at Samantha's turning away and turning quiet, Alice decided to take her into confidence. "Lila died in an automobile accident five years ago." She was increasing her stride to keep up with Sam."It wasn't a pretty situation, Lila dying, and it turned Land's way of thinking from the man he used to be."

Looking away, beyond the line of trees barely visible on the horizon, Samantha felt a burden settle around her heart as her eyes mist in disappointment, so that was why he had no use for women. He still loved his wife, there would be no replacement. What had she expected and why had she even encountered the thought? For some stupid twist of her own heart she pictured his hands, he had touched her, his lips sought hers and he dared to settle in her dreams. How dare he? Perhaps it was a dream. Did he mock other women as a replacement to chastise his wife who replaced him and then died?

She berated herself, wasting hours wondering about him as she worked and it made the work easier. Now, she realized what a fool she had been. No man stayed single in today's world that looked as handsome as Landon King, other women would have noticed. "Was she pretty?" The words escaped before she could stop them. Not how did she die, nothing but "was she pretty."

"Yes, she was beautiful." Anger crept into Alice's voice. "But I'll tell you this, but don't let him know I told you. She wasn't good enough for him." Unconsciously, Alice picked up a piece of metal and finding another of Jade's sinkholes threw the piece in with a vengeance. "Lila was having an affair with her doctor. Being pregnant the first month of marriage to Landon wasn't part of Lila's plan. Not at all. Then she met the good doctor and couldn't wait for those appointments with him. It appeared he had more than Landon, her very good and handsome farmer; Lila went after the doctor and he was smitten. She confided in a mutual friend of hers and Land's and it was her plan to leave with the doctor as soon as the baby was born and what irritates me is no, she wasn't going to take the baby."

"How do you know this, Alice?" Samantha felt troubled hearing and yet, she'd found Alice fair.

"I filled in a few months for the doctor's receptionist when her baby was born. I heard them talking and their plans. But how do you tell a friend his wife, that's expecting his baby, is having an affair?"

"What did you do?"

"Nothing," Alice replied quietly. "The accident happened and I felt Lan's pride would be hurt even more if he thought I knew. After Lila's death, he began hitting the bottle, I suppose that was his way of dealing with it, or maybe he thought he'd wash it out of his mind. Who knows? He'd come to talk to me, then." Alice lips trembled. "Sober, Lan doesn't talk much, but drinking he can't seem to keep all those dark secrets in…he said she came home that day and told him she was leaving and he asked her to stay and they'd work it out. There's more but I'm not sure Lan knows what all he told me, so if you don't mind…"

Samantha nodded as she slid off the flat bed of the trailer. "Don't blame yourself. There was nothing you could do. Sounds to me like you've been a real friend."

"It's Amy that has suffered."

Samantha's blood ran cold. "Are you telling me, he, too, had another woman?"

Alice gave a feeble laugh, "I guess I'm thinking of Kimberly again. When her father left, Kimberly hurt but she was wonderful, too. But Amy probably doesn't understand to this day what happened."

"Who is Amy?" Samantha nearly shouted.

Surprised, Alice's head shot up, her eyes narrowing. "Why, Amy is Land's little girl; their baby."

Wearily, Samantha sank down on the trailer. "Tell me."

"I haven't seen Amy in a long time. Lila had left Amy with Land's mother that day she and her lover planned on leaving. I don't think to this day Amy has been in her daddy's house."

"Land King has a mother who takes care of his little girl?" Incredible findings worked through her mind. Was there anything else she should learn about this man who made havoc in her mind? It was much the same as walking down a long hall of doors, knowing there was something in one of the rooms she needed but she didn't know which door to open. She wanted to hide in the shadows, think things over.

"Alice, I have this incredible urge to sweep the barn."

Completely bewildered, Alice stared toward the barn. "Forgive my wandering, Sam; I didn't expect you to care for him as I do." Alice shoulders slumped. "I guess it's the mothering instinct in me."

Irritated that he'd claimed her time, Samantha yanked a hoe and broom from the trailer. "You know," she said, "I'm supposed to visit my grandmother this evening. Shall we make a start with the barn and then call it quits early this afternoon?"

Alice blinked uncertain. "What's the hoe for?"

"Snakes." Samantha grimaced and pressed on down the path. Soon she was sweeping the floor with a vengeance, "It's a good sign, isn't it," she muttered, "If a snake didn't attack me coming through the wilderness there shouldn't be any in here." Her thoughts returned of their own will to considering Land King. The pieces of the puzzle were beginning to fit together. The mocking way he stared at her, his flippant way of taking her lightly. She wondered that she bothered to think of him at all. In light of Alice's story, perhaps it would ease her sleeping hours considerably and relieve her of Land King invading her dreams.

She was putting the broom away when she heard a plopping noise behind her; something had fallen from overhead of her make-shift closet, a few boards stacked around a lift of some sort that came down from the barn roof. She turned; it was a soft thud on the boards, what could possibly have fallen?

Not two feet from where she stood, a black snake she guessed at least six feet long was drawing its body into a round of sorts, its eyes on her. Stifling the second yell that spewed in the back of her throat she grabbed the broom and slapped at the snake, now sliding across the floor in escape mode. She followed, beating the boards, sometimes hitting and more often missing.

"What in the world?" Land King towered over her, yanking the broom from her hand, tossing it aside, steading her as she shook. "Let it go, it's a king snake, a good snake; they take care of the bad ones."

Teeth chattering, she pushed away from him, nearly falling, and his hands were on her again. "The only snakes I want to see are the dead kind." She was out of breath, her voice raspy and tears were threatening to spill out and she was doing her best not to let him see her cry, when what she wanted to do was bawl her eyes out.

"I stopped by to tell Alice Kimberly's home and the keys gone. She said she'd see you at home."

That was it. Tears were running down her cheeks faster than she could control them. Now she had no bed to sleep in, maybe no place to stay with Kimberly home. She felt herself crumbling down. It had been a long day and she just as well let go and cry it all out.

"What?" Land was staring at this weeping woman. She looked like someone she loved had died. Now she was blubbering, her head seemed to have fallen forward of its own accord and had his hands' not been on her she would have fallen to the floor. He pulled her into his arms and pressed her head against his chest. "Lady, I've never seen such crying, if it's the snake, you didn't hurt it."

"I wanted to," she sobbed. "I hate snakes. I am afraid of them. They scare me to death." Every word was rounded by a sob of heart breaking depth. "And there are places in this barn I don't know what they're for."

He found himself smoothing her hair. "Then why in the world are you tackling this old barn and a lot full of weeds?"

"I have to," Her words were broken by a heave in between to breathe. "It's the perfect place for my business." She felt him stiffen. He swallowed a remark he knew would turn her into a raging shrew.

With every ounce of strength he could sum up, Land laid his hands on her shoulders and pushed her an arm's length away, her hair was a mess, an obvious gray of eyeshadow ran river lets below her eyes. "Your, uh, your make up or whatever you call it is running down your cheeks."

"I didn't wear any makeup. It's either that black stuff off the floor or a bit left over from yesterday."

"How would bat…" he searched for a word, "dung," get on your face?"

"Sweeping." She was scrubbing away at her cheeks. He laid a finger higher, just under her eye. She gave him a scorching glare as she scrubbed at the spot he'd pointed out.

He shrugged and turned toward the door. "You must have been sweeping with a frenzy, then."

She felt desolate and deserted with him leaving but she wasn't about to cry out stay to him.

Slamming the door on the way out, Land let out a deep breath, "Women." As long as he lived he would never understand what they were about. That's why he'd sworn after Lila, there'd be no other. But, he sighed, there was something about holding a woman in your arms, even that fire angel. He didn't know whether to laugh or cry. She was a mess, all right. But he'd recognized by now, what you saw was what you got, that one didn't put on airs. No, sir, she was a worker, that one, but she was one stubborn gal. Once more he decided he'd best keep his distance from her. Something in him wanted to slow her down; she was going to burn herself out. No one could tell her and least of all him. Glancing at his watch he headed back to where the men would be closing up to go home.

Samantha was worn to the bone. She still had to get a bath and make the drive to see her grandmother. Being the only living relative bore responsibility, she had to check on Tessia, there was no one else.

Half asleep and tired to the bone, she drove back to Alice house. Stepping inside the kitchen, she found mother and daughter sitting at the table. "Join us," Alice offered.

A good bath was what she needed. "I have to clean up to go to my grandmothers."

"Oh, hon, that's right. Now Kimberly will only be here tonight so don't worry."

"I won't, but I will stay at a hotel in Grandview after we visit awhile and give you two time together."

The sun was a red ball sinking in the west when she finally drove into Grandview's city limits. She found her grandmother sitting in the screened area that was usually filled with those who smoked. By now, they would be watching television and most of them nodding off as they sat in their chairs, but not Tessia Cleveland.

"Samantha, Child," her grandmother's eyes lit up. "I've been waiting for you."

"Sorry I'm late, Grandmother. Alice helped me today. Together we made quite a showing."

Tessia patted her grandaughter's knee. "Tell me. What's next?"

"Oh, I wish you could see it, the walls are wonderful." Instantly quiet, she recovered to say, "You can. When it's finished, I'll drive in for you and we'll spend the day together. Supplies start arriving next week."

"Really," Surprise shone in Tessia's eyes. "You are a worker, aren't you? I understand it's quite an undertaking."

"And who would tell you such stories?" Taking a minute, Samantha rose to stare out the window. "Are you happy here?" She turned to face her grandmother. "Because if you aren't, you can come live with me, once everything's in place."

Tessia sighed. "Sweetheart, I'm an old woman. Too old to climb stairs to the top floor of your barn."

"How did you know that's where I'll sit up housekeeping?"

Expertly, Tessia changed the subject. "I had hoped you might want to live in my old house, someday."

"Oh, that's too much house for me. Maybe you'll go back to it, or maybe someday I will want to."

"It's fully furnished, if you take everything out of storage, that is." Tessia reached for her hand. "Where is your father's furniture? Did you give it away?"

"Not on your life, it will arrive as soon as the upstairs is finished and they start on it next week. So where is yours?"

"Remember old Mary?" Tessia smiled. "I couldn't part with the first home Mr. Petite and I lived in, so Mary needed a home big enough for all those youngsters her own children produced and I moved her in. There's still a bedroom suite and my heavy oak table stored if you need them."

"Why you sneaky little thing, you never said a thing all these years and I thought you sold that house with the farm." Her grandmother was laughing. "What?"

"I never sold the farm, either." Samantha sank back into her chair. "I was twelve years old the last time I was there. Isn't it more near where I'm building my business than...than Grandview. Somehow I've been driving by this place that makes me think of it but it can't be, can it?"

"Maybe." Tessia's smile widened. "No one seemed interested in an old lady keeping her farm so I didn't talk about it. John Granger has been farming it all these years and the two houses are still there."

"He must be eighty if he's a day, by now." Outside the shadows were creeping in, soon it would be dark.

"Well, yes, he is and he tells me he can't farm it next year, so I've been interviewing young farmers and if I'm lucky I'll find one good enough to take his place. A man has a right to retire before he dies, doesn't he?"

"Is Mr. Granger dying?"

"Heavens, no, but he wants to travel before he does. His wife died a few years back and it's been difficult."

"Travel alone?" They listened as a bell rang. "Dinner time?" Tessia shook her head. "Not the last bell."

"Who said John will be alone?" Tessia laughed until tears were rolling down her cheek. "He ask if I was interested. We had quite a chuckle over that. John's spry. I told him I'd just slow him down."

"You amaze me. You are just a wealth of information. Here I thought you were on your last leg, and you are sitting here doing business."

"Did you think I came here to die?" Tessia examined Samantha's clothing deciding to remain silent.

"Well, no, but to settle down. You seem to enjoy the people and playing the piano for them."

"That's true but I've been thinking about our last talk. Maybe I'm not ready to stay here. We'll see."

As usual, their conversation skipped from one subject to the next and they laughed together. Then The last dinner bell rang, Samantha walked the hall toward the dining room with Tessia and said goodbye. "I'll be back soon, for you. I promise, so have your walking shoes on and your climbing pants."

"Slow down, Sweetheart," were her parting words. "Life needs to be shared. Find a nice young man." She turned toward the dining room. "Dear, when you dress to go out in public, pay more attention."

CHAPTER 8

SHE FOUND SHE was starving and pulled into a roadside restaurant circled in by trucks, which reminded her it was a rural area, no matter if Grandview was considered "posh." That meant the farmers around would know if it served good food and from all the pickup trucks she surmised it did. A young lady led her to a high backed booth, secluded as one table could be from another, and took her order.

"Here you go, Ma'am." A dark eyed boy, possibly in his twenties brought her drink, and leaned down to talk a minute. "What brings you to Grandview, don't think I've seen you around." He gave her a broad smile, taking the liberty to reach down and move a strand of hair that had strayed onto her cheek. "A fellow remembers someone as pretty as you. Even with all these teams in here tonight.

"So, you attend the nearest college, working as a waiter, to make a bit of spending money, and out of hundreds of beautiful young girls you don't remember seeing me, before?" She smiled and pulled her hand back as he moved his own to cover hers. "Jim," she read the name tag on the pocket of his shirt. "Jim, you are much too young for me." She wished he wouldn't linger, she was getting jittery from hunger. "Why are there so many wearing uniforms and cheerleader suits?"

"Honey, I'm much more grown up than you will ever realize." He was leaning in to the booth, she could feel his breath on her face. "Tournaments are going on, lot of schools in town this weekend.

If you are alone and lonely, hang around and I'll show you the town after I'm through here."

"You move a little too quick for me, College boy. I'm afraid I could never keep up with you. Now if you don't mind, just serve my dinner and I'll be on my way and you won't have to remember me, again."

"Oh, did I offend you?" Jim moved into the seat opposite her. "I may have come on too fast, but there's things you need to see here and I'm just the man to show you…" His words ended rather abrupt as he paused to look down to collect his next word, but stared first at the boots, leather, rough scrubbed and worn but expensive and on up to the shirt, faded but clean and the lean chest, where he knew there were hard muscles from hard work, right on up to the stern face of one tall dude wearing a cowboy hat. He swallowed. "Excuse me, miss. I 'll bring your dinner."

"Don't stump your toe." Land King peered down at Samantha, removing the hat. "Mind if I join you?" He took her nod as acceptance and slid into the booth across from her, taking up considerably more space than the college boy had as he placed his hat on the seat. "I couldn't help but over hear, I was sitting in the booth right behind you."

"He was harmless, just a bit mouthy." She took a moment to take in her unexpected dinner companion. Tanned to the hilt, his shirt open at the top button, she noticed it hadn't been ironed and who cared? She caught her breath. A bit alarmed that he had been there a moment and already she felt out of breath. What was there about this man that put her on alert, but more than that muddled her mind?

"You finished?" His eyes shone with amusement as his mouth settled into a describable smirk. "My turn." Tilting his head just so, he studied her for a time and then shook his head as though acknowledging some world piece of news and then reached for her glass and took a sip. "Is that tea?"

"I don't drink." They stared at each other across the table; as usual a match to see who would blink first. "You seemed to have a question, but didn't ask it. May I ask why?"

"I was just wondering, do you always wear your blouse wrong side out?"

She glanced down. So that was what Tessia meant, she had wondered. *Pay more attention.* Although she was certain her face turned beet red she had to smile at her grandmother's old fashioned tact. "What if I said it was made that way, supposed to be...what tipped you off?" He was silent. "You are pretty observant, aren't you?"

"Yeah, I am." He averted his eyes, staring across the room. "In a crowd of women, you're hard to miss."

His voice, little more than a whisper, she needed no explanation and started to rise. His hand came across the table. "I mean no harm. Any man in this room would be proud to have dinner with you."

"Is that what we are doing, having dinner together when we wreak havoc on each other every encounter?" Frustration brought animosity into her voice to cover up any feeling she might have.

"Look," his eyes held hers, stern and unbending. "We've both had a rough week. Why don't we bury the hatchet for a couple hours and act normal, besides I need to talk to you about something, since you're here?"

"Then don't placate me with your useless, not to mention, insincere compliments, when you don't mean them." She arose. "I'm going to correct my blouse and if you're here when I return, it's up to you." She seriously doubted he would stay. But he did and she slid back into her side of the booth, mollified.

The waiter arrived with their food, and it wasn't Jim. When they saw him he was on the other side.

"Very interesting," Land observed. "We ordered the same thing."

"I'm starving. If you are expecting some little underfed darling, put them out to pasture and let them fill holes, pull weeds and chase snakes and see if they're hungry." She hadn't meant to retort so mean.

He held up both hands. "Forgive me, if I implied you were a heavyweight eater. I'm glad."

"Now I'm a heavy weight?" She glared across the table. "Just don't offer any more of your jewels."

"My jewels?" He looked confused. "Whatever that means, I like a girl to be a hearty eater."

"Forget it," she snapped. "It's been a long day. I'm hungry. I'm tired and I have to find a room."

Someone put quarters in the Juke Box, unknown to the spender, a calming influence on some. She found the momentum of her fork slowing, as the food fed her jittery body. What she had needed was food. "Do those songs go together? She listened. "Unforgettable, that's what you are?" She dipped into the last of mashed potatoes. "Oh, my goodness, I have made a happy plate. What's that new song?"

"A relief. If a person has to tear their heart out, why not have a little energy in it." He asked. "Well, I've only heard the intro, but my guess it's Since I Met You Baby, You're Always on MY mind."

"As you say," she elaborated, "If someone tries to run over you in a ten acre pasture, you do give that person some thought." He was shaking his head again, rising as she spoke and ready to leave. She glanced to where people were taking to the floor, dancing. But he wasn't leaving. Holding out his hand, he was waiting for her to join him.

Uncertain, of his intentions she took his hand. "What are we doing?"

"We are dancing. It's one way I think you will stop talking and maybe, just maybe, breathe."

"First, I was jittery from hunger, then frustrated by your insults and now, just tired and we are dancing?"

"Just lay your hand on my shoulder, your head against it if you wish and follow my lead. It will be soothing."

She couldn't believe this. "You tried to kill me. Run over me with your truck. You want me to dance with you."

"Shh." He laid a finger against her lips. "Now listen to this and be quiet."

"I can't believe…" He leaned back, not taking a hand away this time and gave her a stern look. She hushed as his arm tightened around her, his hand holding hers firm. She closed her eyes. Her mouth was straight lines, displeasure at its utmost; as he pulled her closer and she thought she heard him whisper, relax.

"That's Ivory Joe Hunter singing, hear the piano? That's what he played. Now he was an early one to sing the song in the fifties, but Sonny James came along later in the late sixties and recorded it. I know because I had to practice that song for a recital about a million times."

She listened as he whispered in her ear, but couldn't resist asking, "You play the piano?"

"Yeah, I do, what do you play?"

She almost giggled. "Piano. In high school band I signed up for the reeds and wasn't bad. Sat in the first chair until I became a majorette and then it was either practice the routines for marching or the Clarinet for the wind section but I'm not bad on the piano." She didn't mention her piano teacher.

"I wanted to play football. My Mom said it was dangerous, but I persisted. Sneaked practice until one day she was suspicious and kept me home. Of course the coach called to bawl me out. My mother bawled him out. He told her what a good player I was and that the team needed me." He sighed and was silent awhile. The song ended and another began immediately. They were on the far side of the room; he pulled her close again and tilt his head to look down into her eyes. "You aren't a bad dancer for a girl who wears her clothes wrong side out and likes food."

She almost smiled. "What happened, did you play football?"

"Yeah, but my mom made a deal I had to honor. I would take piano lessons again, just pick up where I left off when I was ten, and she'd haul me around until I got my driver license, but she said, "You will learn the piano. Few are beneficial to their community with a football background but who knows if I keep you in church, you might help out there."

"You attend church?"

"I could almost squirm the way you said that. I did attend church. Faithfully as a teenager, and fair while in college but when I began farming I turned loose of that ritual and later there were bad things…"

"Why is it a ritual?" Samantha could hear her grandmother, always encouraging her to stay in church.

"It's important to you?" He questioned. The song ended and they were near their booth. The plates had been removed but their drinks remained.

"I believe it is, if I can get the business on its feet, I plan to find a church for weekly attendance. My grandmother instilled the importance in me. But now, she says I have to find it for myself. I've strayed."

"Me too." He sighed, leaning away from the table letting his shoulders press against the back of the booth. "I don't know how you've held up, all that stooping and bending you've done clearing the place." She was leaning into her hands, elbows on the table propping her up. "You are too tired to talk, aren't you?"

She yawned. "I've got to find a room." She was ready to pass out.

"Let me go with you. I'll find a way back to my truck. The town's overrun tonight and you're tired." He offered a hand. "Come on, sit in my truck with me for now and I'll make a few calls. This town has three fair Inns and one run down so reasonable rated it makes you wonder why."

She was hesitant but the tiredness of a week claimed her. "I'm really in no shape to drive. I am so sleepy. That's the way it always happens…when all else fails, meaning energy, I go to sleep and recover."

"You have a heck of stamina. I've seen you work and wondered when you'd drop." He was making an entry from his phone directory and then shaking his head. "Not one room?" He pressed the next entry. "Do you have an available room? Not one? What's going on?" He listened. "Tournaments and other schools came to Grandview? Hmm. Filled every room? That's good business for you. Thanks." With a slight shrug he pressed the next number, "I really hate for you to stay in this one, it does have a bed though." Someone answered.

"Do you have a room…." He was interrupted. "Nothing?" He closed the phone. "There's nothing. Could you sleep on Alice couch?"

"Their time together is short; I was trying to stay out of the way and come to think of it, there's no sofa."

For a minute he sat there, almost in a facial grimace. "I have a room. It's not been used for years. A lady comes once a month to clean and your guess is as good as mine whether she even enters that room."

"Oh, I couldn't. That would be a perfect way to be branded, compromising shop dealer stayed at Land King's home before she opened for business. I would be ruined before I started."

He laughed. "No one would ever know. Who knows, it might help business." He noticed she was running her fingers through her hair, stressed he supposed and wondering how life had dealt this one. "If it's me you're worried about, I promise I won't bother you. Have I overstepped that invisible boundary you threw up, tonight?"

"How did I do that? I thought I did very well, considering. And you're appearance was a complete surprise." Resolved, she said, "Take me to my car, I'll go to the barn; there's a place I can park and sleep in the car."

"No. That's not smart. Jack the Ripper could break in." He put the truck in reverse and backed out of the parking lot. "You are spending the night at my house and there's a lock on that door." His chin was set.

She saw that obstinate body, tensed as if ready for combat, the chin jutting forward, no need to reply. She hunkered down, pulled her sweater tighter and as if on cue, went to sleep. Let him deal with it.

"All right, we're here." He went around to the passenger side, opened the door and waited. She was sleeping, curled into a ball, clutching the front of her sweater. "Come on, get out." She didn't move. He doubted she heard. "Lady, wake up. Come on, let's go." When she didn't respond, he heaved a deep sigh, his eyes rolled as he reached in to try to pull her from the seat into his arms, and when he did, he said to empty air, "That was no easy feat." Once he shifted her in his arms, he headed for the door. For all the build he'd observed being around her, she wasn't that heavy but asleep she was dead weight.

Pleasantly surprised, he found the room acceptable with a clean smell and wondered at the fragrance. After an awkward struggle of turning back the covers he laid her on the bed, removed her shoes and pulled the cover up to her chin. Nothing more was needed, but she looked so vulnerable he leaned down and kissed her.

"G'nite Blake."

Who the heck was Blake? Not even stopping for a drink, he stomped into his room and fell across the bed. So she had someone. For one minute he considered his dislike for the opposite sex, but seeing her work ethics he had begun to have a respect of sorts for her. Now he placed her back on that deniable shelf determined no matter what the future presented she was off limits. He'd never seen a person sleep such a deep sleep. Living alone with that problem could be dangerous.

She awoke to the smell of bacon and coffee lingering in the background. Funny, she didn't remember going inside the hotel and why was she still in her clothes? Glancing around, she found it was a pleasant room, the walls were bird egg gray, the windows curtain less, with nicely painted white trim. The coverlet was a quilted material in pink and the covered seat by the window and the lamp base also matched. Definitely a girls room…maybe intended for a little girl. What?

She jumped out of bed. How did she get here and was she where she thought? She glanced out the window, grain bins in a row, shining in the day light. Adrenalin was flowing, rushing through her veins. She had to think. She was at the restaurant, he was there, they ate together, and they danced. What? They danced? A smile curled its pattern across her face; her eyes became dreamy as she savored the moment. *Since I met you baby. He plays piano. He can't be so bad, can he?* Slipping into her shoes she followed her nose. He was standing at the stove, breaking eggs into a pan.

"Good morning and thank you." The smile fell from her face when he turned to face her. He looked grumpy. "Thank you for a place to stay last night. I hope sometime I can repay your kindness."

He gave her a once over, his expression remaining stern. "I'm sure we can work that out."

She felt a nervous shudder working its way in. "Ummm, could I help you?"

"Sit." She sat. "There's orange juice, coffee, milk. Which do you prefer?"

"Either." His glance was withering. "Did I do something last night that made you angry?" She shrugged. "I mean, it was your idea we dance and evidently, though I don't remember, you brought me here."

"Eat." He commanded, taking the seat opposite her. "Then, I'll drive you to pick up your car."

"Thank you." She tasted the coffee. "Umm. Next she forked a bit of eggs and bacon together. "Ummm."

Elbows on the table, he paused to stare at her. Eyes closed, she appeared in pure bliss tasting the food. "Is that what makes you happy mornings? Food?"

She opened her eyes to return the stare. "Doesn't it please you? It's delicious. You are a good cook. What makes you happy, mornings?"

A wicked smile replaced the scowl. "A warm body next to mine, maybe making love to that person."

With great precision she laid down the fork, pushed back her plate and looked him in the eye. "Is that why you are grumpy? I wasn't in your bed? My warm body thanking you for being a gentleman, except it appears you aren't." She pushed away from the table. "I'll be going. Surely someone will pick me up."

"Sit down. Finish breakfast. I only said that to get a rise out of you." He saw her hesitate. "Seriously, I was trying you to see what you'd say."

"I take it you have women in your home on a regular basis, warm bodies…." Her words trailed off.

"There have been no women in my home. You are the first."

"Oh, well, I'm honored," she said sarcastically. "Then we understand each other, but why me?" She eased back to the table. "Why are you so grumpy?"

"Whose Blake?"

Startled, she gave him a troubled look. "Did you go through my phone? I thought I deleted his name. Why would you ask?"

"I'll be honest, you looked so vulnerable last night, I leaned down and kissed you. You said, good night, Blake."

"You kissed me?"

"As one would a child."

"I don't know what to say." Anger was lashing through her mind, consuming her and she wondered why. "I'm sorry I went to sleep. I do that anymore. I'm so tired from all the physical work. No one wants to work and I have a dead line to meet." She stared across the room. "Someone's coming to put the inside of the barn in place… but it's the outside will determine whether anyone stops and I'm trying to get everything cleaned up." Tears stung her eyes but she would not let him see her cry. "Then there's you asking about my ex-boyfriend who is no longer in my life. And you kissed me when I was asleep. Who does that?" She swiped her hand across the tears spilling onto her cheeks. "And making it seem like a kiss for a child, who believes that?"

He rose up from the table and come to stand reaching distance of her chair. "Do you remember the kiss?"

"Of course not."

"Stand up." He was waiting. She stood. Suddenly he pulled her close, kissed her. At first she resist but he held tight, the kiss lasting while she did her best to remain unaffected but there was that magnetism she felt the first time she met him. He took her breath away. "Now," he said finished and sitting back down to the table as though he had only reached for the coffee pot. "Maybe you didn't remember last night's kiss for someone who looked vulnerable, tired and in need of help, but I think you will remember this kiss. It's different. It tells you I'm interested in you and I haven't been interested in a woman since Lila died. The next time you will want me to kiss you, but I won't. You will kiss me."

"Try not to stop breathing, because it simply will not happen."

He closed the distance, not six inches between their bodies as he smiled. His eyes warm as honey, the smile inviting. She studied his lips. He studied hers. The smile faded, replaced by a sultry half lidded look, his head tilted staring down on her. "Yes?" She shook her head. He grinned. "You will; because I want you to kiss me."

She shrugged loose, picked up her plate and cup and walked to the sink. "You should hurry if you are going to take me for my car. I have work to do." He laughed and she turned to give him a dirty look. "You really don't endear yourself to anyone, do you? You just want to pick a fight. There's something wrong with you."

"I realized that, last night, and I wasn't happy. You, with your independent sassy ways, could drive a man crazy. I've decided to keep tabs on you. You're in my radar, like it or not."

"I didn't ask for this."

"Neither did I," he quipped softly. "Neither did I. Now I'm just waiting to see if the feeling lasts."

CHAPTER 9

THE CARPENTERS ARRIVED early Monday morning. She showed them her sketches and told them her deadline. "The trucks are set to arrive the next Monday. The drivers have agreed to help shelve the orders and I can't let that pass, as I'm running on thin ice as it is. My body can't take much more."

"Then we'll be bringing in our second crew. What would have taken us two weeks; we might all together finish by your deadline. It's a close call." To say the barn was teeming with activity was an understatement. For the most part she stayed out of the way.

Ten o'clock brought more excitement. Two large tractors pulled into the drive, followed by a pickup truck. Two men embarked and began scouring the lot for Jade's hidden treasure. By four o'clock, the plot of ground that was once a pasture had taken on a freshly mowed appearance, the tractors that had filled the holes and rolled the earth solid were pulling out the drive with the men in the pickup following. Not once had Land King shown his face but she knew it was he that made the clean-up happen.

He called that night. "I hear you were dressed decent and didn't set any of the men in heat."

"That's a terrible remark. What are you a deacon?"

"I was, once."

"I thought you were the piano player." She threw a challenge in the works. "I need to find a church, don't suppose you'd darken the door of one, the mighty Land King?"

He took the bait. "Yeah, I can stand the heat about as well as the next man. But I was just checking in. Glad you didn't work in front of all those men wearing those shorts and halter."

Before she could tell him to mind his own business, he hung up. "The nerve." She felt her face grow warm. "So my choice of clothes on the back lot was a worry. What in the world will he complain about next?" The adrenalin saw her through sweeping saw dust and pieces of wood left by the carpenters.

Then it was day for the trucks to arrive. The carpenters smiled at her nervousness. "We're down to the small stuff," the main guy explained. "Toilet paper and paper towel holders; Lights hanging over the stalls that no longer resemble stalls." He grinned "Those nooks as you call them will make individual displays stand out. I like your ideas. I have a feeling you've done this before."

"But not for my own business."

"You'll do just fine." He patted her shoulder and continued installing plates over the electric outlets.

Perhaps Providence had a hand in the trucks rolling onto the lot as the carpenters stowed their tools in the back of their own and drove out, leaving the barn and all its newly acquired trim to Samantha and her new helpers. It would have been chaos if she hadn't had a plan, which she gave to each driver that was now helping unload and place merchandise. It was midnight when the truck doors were closed and the drivers said goodbye, headed for the nearest motel to rest before returning to Michigan the next day.

Samantha had the foresight to call Alice and tell her if there was a place she would spend the night in the barn. "Are you sure? That sounds scary. You remember, watch out for that Lassity kid."

Samantha laughed. "Don't say that. I'm going to live here."

She pulled a chaise lounge into a secluded corner and covered herself with the blanket she kept year round in her car. Her body was distraught from the day's happenings and sleep wouldn't come. She thought of her father and longed to talk to him. "Daddy, if you could just see this place. If I could just talk to you, Daddy," she whispered, "I don't know why I continue to think about this man. I made such a mistake with Blake, I'm afraid I could do the same thing again."

He hadn't called and she wondered if he would. She lay on the chaise until her legs hurt and her body was all atremble from trying to sleep. When she saw a flash of light on the window she rose up to see who was outside but it was pitch dark. Then she heard the banging at the ground level door. Cell phone in hand, she crept down the three stairs rather than walk the ramp which led directly to the door. Her heart hit bottom when she saw it was unlocked and a hand, the fingers curled around the wood was ready to open it. Picking up a left over two by four she swung at the door, but she missed the target.

"Lord's sake, woman. Be careful. You could have broken my fingers." Land King opened the door fast enough to grab her by the wrist and turn it enough she dropped the two by four. "Your door was unlocked. You can't do this. If you plan to have a business, every night you check each entrance."

She was shaking. "You scared me to death; all I saw was a hand and thought someone was trying to come inside." Her knees buckled. He caught her before she fell.

Land saw the tremble but more importantly he felt her body quaking with fear or relief he wasn't sure which. He pulled her into his arms, his chin resting on her hair, as he felt her sag against him. It must have been five minutes they stood there. Then she took him by the hand and led him to the chaise. "Thank you. I couldn't sleep. My bodies too keyed up, I guess, from a long days work."

"Is that a matching rocker?" He pointed to the piece still wrapped in paper. "Whatever this is we're sitting on, it's too low for these long legs." He was making short work of pulling the paper away, and then sit down in it. "Well, that's better...but it's a rocker. Come here." She gave him a puzzled look. "Come here." He pat his knee. "Come on."

"We'll break the rocker, both of us in it."

"Then it's not worth selling, is it?" He reached for her hand and pulled her onto his lap. "Shh."

"But I need to thank you for the men's working here today with your tractors."

He laid one finger across her lips. "Shh." Tucking her to his body he began to rock. "If that's your bed for the night you won't rest, that's for sure."

"I have a bed but we ran out of time before we could put it together." She was yawning. "Tomorrow...."

She awakened before day break the next morning, lying on the bed she'd ordered complete with box spring and mattress, something one hardly ever accomplished, all in one. The lilac sheet set covered the mattress, pillow cases were on the pillows and the floral quilt was over her. She giggled. How had he done it by himself? And she wondered if he had placed the extra quilted mattress cover beneath the bottom sheet. Sitting up she leaned over and pulled the sheet free, another giggle escaping as she saw it was there. She had slept like a baby. "It must have been quite a feat carrying me up those six steps."

"It was." He was leaning up from the bottom, one foot on the first step. "I couldn't leave you here alone to wake up and forget where you were and fall down the stairs."

"Steps. Six steps." She swallowed her surprise. "Where did you sleep?"

"Not on that chaise as you called it. I slept on the floor where I could stretch out."

"Oh, my goodness, I'm sorry. You should have gone home. But, thank you."

"I was proving my gentlemanship." He sighed, a certain gleam in his eye. "If you only knew. I did not bother you the night I carried you in and put you to bed at my house, nor last night when we were alone."

"I'm sorry. You are a gentleman."

"It may not last."

"Why?"

"You try my patience?"

"I owe you."

"Yes, you do." He stepped closer; the second step creaked beneath his weight. "What do you have in mind?"

"I was thinking once the kitchen is in order, I'll cook a meal and have you over for dinner."

He groaned. "That wasn't what I had in mind."

She gave him a wicked smile. "We twain may never meet on that road."

Yawning, he turned to leave. "It will be daylight soon. I parked the truck out of sight, so no passer-by could question your character, nor mine, though by now they seldom give me any thought at all."

"I bet," she said softly. Climbing off the bed she walked to the steps and started down, her hand outstretched intending to thank him but he turned, taking her hand and pulled her to his body.

Resolved not to bend, she merely stared up into his questioning eyes. The question had no need to be asked. "I intended to shake your hand and say thank you for everything." She heard his deep sigh.

He brought his head down to within an inch; their lips could touch so easily. His eyes held that lazy daring expression, "It's your turn," he said. "Tell me you don't want to kiss me."

"I keep remembering you telling me all those other things that weren't sweet nothings in my ear."

"Like what?" His hold tightened, bringing her as close as he could to his body and still see her face.

"You said you wanted to see if the feeling last. Has it, or are you toying with my emotions?"

"I don't think you have emotions. You tease with your way of dress, the shorts and the halters…"

"You mentioned that, no one was supposed to be on the back area and it can't be seen from the road, and no one expected you to come barreling down through the road making dust clouds that covered everything."

"This is farming country, lady. The sooner you realize that, the quicker you'll fit in."

She struggled to be loose. He was looking dangerous now. "I have work to do," she said.

His laugh was a strangle of sound as he bent his head and claimed her lips. She closed her eyes. Let him make a fool of himself, but the fact he had stayed with her when she couldn't sleep, had rocked her on his lap like a baby, her heart softened. Who was he? All those pent up emotions over losing his wife to another man, she couldn't handle that and if she allowed herself to fall for him he would toss her aside. But the fact he was kissing her...she felt resolve fly right out the window. She kissed him back and when she did he turned her loose.

"I told you, you would kiss me."

"But you were kissing me." Her eyes squinted; she rubbed her lips as if to erase the kiss. "Why are you being so childish? You cut me down for clothes I wore when I was burning up in the heat. You don't see me wearing anything indecent around people. What people for that matter, why would you care?"

"I told you. I'm interested."

"Then don't toy with me." She wished her voice wasn't so shaky.

"Is that what I'm doing? Staying here all night on a hard cold floor. Any other woman would have invited me into her bed."

"I'm not any other woman," she screamed. "I like the feel of your body against mine. I like your arms around me, but my love comes with a price and it's not going to drop to hop into bed with you. Do you get that? Do you understand?"

He tipped his hat before putting it on. "So you like the feel of our bodies together?" His face was void of expression now. "I'll think on that. It's good to know there's something warm about you. I'll be leaving now. You are going to want to see me...but it's going to be awhile. Call me, or come to me."

"Don't come back until you can act normal." She nearly fell as she flounced down the steps behind him and slammed the door. "What is normal?" Her words bounced against the hollow spaces as she leaned against the door, totally exhausted. What was it with them; they couldn't spend an hour together without feuding unless she was asleep. Hands to her face, she closed her eyes and could see him, tall, standing over her mocking, expecting her to fall at his feet. No, that wasn't true; he had shown caring in holding her when her body was in a state of exhaustion. Twice he had put her to bed and done nothing wrong. He was a gentleman. He was handsome and any other woman would want him. Hanging her head she wondered, they had both been burned, scorned in being second place to another; was that why they were wasting precious time casting ridiculous blame on each other, things that didn't matter.

Alice stopped by after work that evening. Without a word she began to help Samantha place items on the shelves. That went on for an hour, when she finally asked, "What's going on with you? Are you worried or just totally exhausted?"

Samantha pushed her hair up, reclasp a large Barrett and let out a sigh that stirred the tendrils escaping around her forehead. "I think it's a little bit of everything. Going early till late, I think I see headway then there are a dozen jobs needing attention."

Alice leaned against one of the counters. "Did you do all this? The assembling?"

"The drivers were good to unload and then they helped. I guess took pity on me."

Alice leaned over to push up a strand of hair that already escaped the barrette. "Your hair is getting long. Are you going to have it cut?"

"No, cooler weather is around the corner and I want it long so I can wear it appropriately when there's holiday and I wear the costumes," she met Alice inquiring look, "long dresses and such."

"Hmm. Interesting." Tilting her head to one side and pursing her lips, Alice said, "I can't turn this loose. I feel there's something else. Do you want me to mind my own business or would you like to share? You seem troubled."

"You know I visited my grandmother. Then when I had dinner at this restaurant, there were couples and I remembered once asking my grandmother how you would really know you were in love or if someone loves you." She looked down, so as not to allow Alice to see she was leaving something out.

"What did she say?" Alice reached for her hand and led her to the chaise where they both sat down.

"She said if you think of that person all the time, that's a pretty good sign unless it's someone you're obsessed with because you hate them, and she laughed and asked why would anyone waste their energy?"

"Are you reliving times with Blake? Maybe all this," she spread her hands toward the shelves, "maybe it is reminding you of happier times and you're feeling a bit melancholy."

"How was it for you, Alice?"

Alice closed her eyes. "It was wonderful. Even when it turned bad, I admit in the beginning it was good." She opened her eyes and there was a twinkle as she replied, "Your grandmother is right. I was obsessed with Jade. If I could have looked in a crystal ball and known through time he was going to be hard to live with, at that time I'm certain I loved him so much I would have thought I could change him." She sighed. "In the beginning, he was a gentleman, well, he was risqué, Jade had a certain flair for the dramatic, but that's what made him interesting. We were magic."

"What happened?"

"He wasn't cut out to farm. Jade was a born salesman. He could talk the arm off a person, make them open their pocket book and buy things they didn't need, but farming is a down to earth responsible art."

"So where is he now?"

"Few people know this, Samantha. Jade is in prison. It's not something we are proud of and we don't spread it around, because it hurts Kimberly. If you stayed with us long enough you would have known."

"I'm sorry." Her eyes were sad as she considered this bit of information. "Will he be gone long?"

"His time is almost up and then where will he go? We were already divorced when he got in trouble." She squeezed Samantha's hand. "We all have troubles, girl. What do you do when your daughter's daddy needs a place to stay, has to get a job because it's what we all have to do but most of all he won't have a penny to his name?"

"He has asked to come back to you?"

99

"Yes."

They were silent, thinking. "For Kimberly's sake, how could you not take in her daddy?"

"Circumstance." Alice stared at the floor. "I don't want to put either of us through the same, again."

"Maybe he's changed."

"Maybe I'm afraid that old magnetism we had in the beginning will come back and then he'll leave." She took a deep breath. "Samantha, when you meet someone that you feel drawn to and your mind seems to forget how to work and your body won't take commands, you'll know what I mean."

"Magic?" Without saying it, Samantha believed she knew what Alice meant.

"Worse." They laughed together.

Samantha gave an inner sigh of relief. She had a feeling if Alice saw her and Land King doing verbal battle she might read something in to it; and she wasn't ready for anyone to make assumptions. She had been thinking of one of her and Tessia's past conversations.

"Samantha, when the time comes that you find your young man, you better talk to God about it because the Lord knows even with his blessing on a marriage there's always hard times ahead."

"You're smiling."

"Yeah." She shared her grandmother's words of wisdom. "I think I need to get back in church."

"I'll go with you."

CHAPTER 10

EVIDENTLY HE WAS as good as his word. Two weeks passed and two more. Samantha and Alice attended the community church the third week. The shop was in order. The sign hung by the highway and Samantha's living quarters were furnished and appealing enough to keep her there. The carpenter insisted a strong door between the shop and those quarters be installed. "Metal," he said, "with double locks. You never know whose going to turn crazy these days, besides we have some questionable characters in this neighborhood. I'm just telling you like I'd tell my own daughter."

The official opening had arrived. Alice was ready to help after work hours if needed and one of the Carpenter's son's had asked for a job. "I'll call if we need you," she said, sizing him up.

The first day the curious trickled by, but word of mouth brought more in each day. Samantha was relieved. Carlos would be arriving to check out Samantha's hand work and plan of organization. He was tough but he was fair.

Huge combines used the highways for access to lumber across the fields. Often Samantha glimpsed a familiar face thinking of Land King behind the wheel of numerous white pick-up trucks. Once, it was him and he gave the old familiar salute that mocked her. It was his way of recognition and she wondered if she meant no more than that. Seeing him was enough to set her blood racing and she could hear her heart beat in her ears. That was no heat wave, she thought, putting Tessia's words of wisdom to rest.

She decided he was an impossibly private man that expected the same from a woman. In view of Alice's story and what she thought she knew about him, the inner workings of the man intrigued her. Nights she lay in bed considering the meaning behind the man. What she didn't know haunted her dreams. More than once she awoke, sweating, thinking he was holding her and then she wondered about the little girl named Amy, remembering how lonely she was when her mother left. Sniggering reminders came, in spite of Sam and Clarissa's problems, that her childhood had been good in spite of the divorce.

She had a bed but no supporting furniture. It was time to take a look at Tessia Cleveland's stored furniture saved for her granddaughter. Her plan was to use Carlos truck while he was taking inventory. Little did she know her plans would change? Instead of the pickup he arrived in a low slung sports car, shiny black and an eye catcher parked in front of the shop. Dressed to the nines, his presence brought the curious once more and among them Land King, scowling, big as life in his faded denim shirt and jeans with eyes on no one but her. Carlos, gray hair at the temples, dark olive skin, white teeth and six feet tall belied his age. He had lost weight and was fit. Could that possibly be the reason Land King finally decided to visit? She was on the phone, trying to find a truck to haul furniture. "Thanks, yes, I understand. No, I thought my boss would help with the furniture but he came in his car."

Carlos had stepped in the back to answer a call.

"Can I help you?" He towered over her, as usual, his mouth stern, eyes half closed and questioning. "Is there something on your mind?"

"Who's he?"

"My boss."

"He doesn't look like a boss."

"Really?" She leaned against the counter, so close she could smell him. Earthy. Masculine. There were perfume makers would die for that formula. "What does a boss look like?"

He relaxed a bit. "I wondered. I saw the Michigan tags."

"So, after a month's absence, you marched right in to protect me. I'm not buying it."

Disgusted, he slid an arm around her waist and pulled her to him. His lips were on hers, searching at first, and then demanding. She pushed away. "MY Boss is here," She hissed through closed teeth.

He tipped his head, gave her a smoldering look and headed for the door. "I hear you are attending church now, better work on a few things."

She rolled her eyes. "You can do better than that."

"First Sunday it rains, save me a seat." The laugh he gave as he went out the door did not resemble church material.

Yeah, she thought. I'll believe that when I see it. His kiss had left her a bit unnerved. She wanted to hide in the closet and savor it, see if she could still taste his lips on hers. She shook her head, so he got to her; trying not to read anything in to it she thought he's a loose cannon or someone would've caught him.

Carlos returned, tucking his cell phone in his shirt pocket. "You okay, Sam? You look a bit ruffled."

"I'm fine." She realized Carlos thought of himself as the father figure in her life. "Relax, Boss, I've been really busy, trying to have everything done by the time you arrived."

Carlos smiled. "And you have exceeded. Now there's one thing I want installed so you will be fine." Taking the cell out of his pocket, he checked the number; they will give you all the info when they come." He slid onto the tall cabinet, letting his feet swing like they always did. "Don't protest. It will be the best five hundred I've spent." He was studying her again. "You sure nothing's wrong? Well, something is that's apparent." He checked his watch. "It's five after. Let's close these doors and eat at that new grill down the road. Ruthie's or Rosie's?"

She removed the old fashioned apron she was wearing, combed her hair, down onto her shoulders and applied lipstick. They laughed climbing into Carlos low to the ground Sports car, 'I may be going thru some phase of life, I had taken the old Buick in for repairs when I saw this little darling and just had to have her. Might have been frivolous, but I've enjoyed every minute driving. "Now let's go and have a luscious meal."

It had rained during the night. Samantha arose long before opening hours to tell Carlos goodbye. He kissed her on the forehead, like a dutiful father and looked into her eyes. "I wish you would tell me what's bothering you." He sighed. "You have a right to privacy, but after the Blake episode I worry about you."

"Blake's your son in law," she scolded.

"Don't remind me," he whispered. "Be glad he's gone."

She didn't think of Blake these days. A tall scowling bad boy taunted her by day and tormented her dreams by night. She was growing older by the moment. One last wave to Carlos and she picked up her phone. "Drydon's Delivery? Yeah, I do. I need belongings brought to the barn and the person who has my furniture in his grips, languishes in a nearby swimming pool and I'm reminding myself in three weeks we will bring him down."

A hand came out of nowhere as a voice said "put down the phone. I'm your man for the day."

Jolted at first, "I thought I was alone," she said. "What did you do, tiptoe?"

"Actually, I banged on the door; of course you were busy lying to the owner of Drydon's Delivery. You couldn't hear me could you?" She shook her head.

"I didn't intend to lie, but he said tell me a story and make it good. I might help you. You can even lie. I liked him. He said he was listening intently to me, something it seems you never do, and I got caught up in the moment...oh, well, I don't know why I did that.... not for you."

"Too bad," he said, as his hand closed around hers. "Now go get yourself ready for an adventure." He backed up, to lean against one of the support poles of the barn. "I heard you the last time I was here, saying you needed furniture moved." His eyes were in that noncommittal mode, she couldn't tell his attitude. "You were on the phone. Your boss was here. Now, are you ready to go?"

"Only on the condition you don't bait me for bad choices of words when you talk to me."

"Truce," he said, holding his hand palm up. She touched hers to his. "I'd like that."

She returned, wearing denims, an orange T-shirt and an oversized big shirt in case it was needed.

His eyes wore the look of a man examining a fine piece of equipment, his mouth pursed as if he would say something.

"What?"

"You told me not to say anything…bait you, I believe were your words, when I talk to you."

She heaved a sigh and walked past him. If she only knew, behind her, he mimicked her walk.

"I came in the old truck," he said, "for a reason."

"Not to scratch up the newer one?" She questioned. "I understand."

"No, you don't. I came in this one with no console so you could sit close to me and its larger."

"You want me close to you?"

"Yeah, all that warm body stuff you spout. If it doesn't put you out too much, scoot over here."

He was smiling. "We are friends, today?" She smiled. "I can do that. But don't get ideas."

"Makes me feel fifteen again, driving down the road with sweet Millie Chambers next to me."

"You were making out?"

"Heck no, we were green and embarrassed. I did finally hold her hand though."

"That was exciting."

"It was," he admitted, sober faced and watching the road. "I nearly peed my pants."

"You didn't."

"Nah, I stopped at the filling station to save myself."

They laughed. "We're doing better," she said. He reached for her hand, brought it up to his lips and kissed it.

"Yeah, we are. I like this."

There was only once things got a bit sticky. The furniture was loaded; she was signing her name accepting responsibility for removing items from the storage unit. "Cleveland," the owner of the units said. "Contessa Cleveland's relative?" She nodded and hand him back his pen. "My grandmother."

She saw Land turn his head suddenly from adjusting a tie down over the furniture but she forgot to ask why. She remembered later, for a time as they drove down the road he seemed in deep thought. "You're tired." He shook his head. "But you've grown quiet. Have I done something wrong?"

"No, I just remembered an errand I forgot to do, regarding the farm."

"Great. I thought moving furniture was more than a tall strong farmer could handle."

"Or, a little head strong, hell bent, barn keeper, maybe?"

"The real struggle is getting it up those stairs, past the six steps."

"Who thought of the metal door at the top of the steps?"

"The head carpenter." She smiled. "He said he'd want the same for his daughter. I liked that."

"You didn't do away with the trap door in the barn attic did you? There's a lift there, as I recall that Alice's dad used to hoist bales of hay on up to the wasted space of the roof line, what you call attic."

"Is that what that is?" She gave an embarrassed laugh, "I hate to say it but I wondered if it was some sort of medieval piece of antiquity."

"Antiquity, huh?" He shook his head. "Where do you come up with such words?"

"Where do you come up with your moods? On the drive over you were teasing and almost happy but something changed and I don't think it was forgetting an errand."

"Why didn't you tell me you were related to Contessa Cleveland?"

"Why would that be important to you?"

"Because I just met with her, the night you and I had dinner together in Grandview." She was wearing a puzzled expression. "She has land, Samantha. Six hundred twenty acres to be exact and the farmer who had it last year is a good friend of my family, actually John Granger and my dad were childhood friends. He called me to say he was quitting and he had set up an appointment for me with Mrs. Cleveland to see if I might possibly rent her land."

"That's strange, she didn't mention meeting with you, but then of course she doesn't know we have met." Releasing the seat belt, she moved to the center of the truck, remembering it was his earlier preference she sit there. "Now, why would that ruffle your feathers that I'm her granddaughter?"

"I don't know." He appeared angry; he wasn't sure why he felt the way he did. "She was nice to me but made no commitment and when I heard the guy say your grandmother's name, I suddenly put two and two together and wondered, no, I thought for sure, you had told her how difficult our getting to know each other has been. Hasn't it?

"Interesting or difficult?" She peered up into his face. "Why so tense, why the jaw set like steel? Why?"

"She probably formed an opinion of me according to what you think and now I lose the opportunity."

"Whoa." Samantha's ire was rising. "My grandmother is the most reliable example of someone who would weigh a matter and come up with the right answer of anyone you or I will ever know" She took a deep breath. "My grandmother is unaware you and I have even met, unless your friend, and hers, Mr. Granger had something to tell, so don't get all antsy with me over something I had nothing to do with, and when we arrive at the barn, just put on your nice white hat and ride away on your nice white horse. Thank you for today's service, when you've cooled down in two or three weeks come around for a home cooked meal and we shall bury the hatchet again." She had worked herself into a controlled frenzy, only her eyes gave way the anger that boiled up inside her. "I should realize you and I are like oil and water. We have nothing in common and we cannot get along." She flounced back to the passenger side of the truck nearly sitting on the door handle."

"If I may explain one thing to you, land is precious. There will only be x amount of acres for miles around here and when a piece of ground comes available, through some farmer dying or retiring, everyone for miles around vies for it. We are up and in the running. Do you want to know why? Because it is such an expensive endeavor, this business of farming, we need certain acreage to justify buying any piece of equipment. And we have to satisfy our banker, the lawyer, the…" he threw his hands up in the air, "the lolly pop maker, it's that simple."

"Want me to put in a good word for you?" She asked sweetly. "As if that would help."

He grit his teeth. "That…is the last thing in the world I want you to do. Forget the home cooked meal and assure me you won't mention knowing me to your grandmother. Should she choose me, I want it to be on my own merit and certainly not what a barn keeper could tell her."

"If we were any closer to the barn," she emphasized the word, "I would get out right here and walk."

He laughed and pressed his foot to the gas pedal.

They spent two hours jockeying the lift as he called it, a floor of sorts that raised up and down by chains from one area to the next and with the skill of a magician the bedroom furniture, a fireplace mantel, and Tessia's heavy oak table and chairs were placed on the home floor, the magical lift was stored for future use and Landon King gave his familiar salute, placed the white hat on his head and drove away in the larger older farm truck he had chosen to use that day.

Watching from the shop window, Samantha kicked the huge iron pot she used for a door stopper and limped into the backroom to do damage control on herself. Pulling off the soft soled boot and then her sock, her big toe was already turning purple. She taped it, put the sock back on and tried to forget the pain. While the toe throbbed, she berated herself, she had fallen again, into the malaise of thinking possibly Land King could be prince charming on a white horse…when today all she could think was she made terrible judgement concerning men. He wasn't Blake of the fickle heart, he had no heart.

By nine o'clock that night she had wiped down the furniture, decided which drawer of the dresser would hold her clothes and the bedroom was complete but she was relieved they had sit the table and chairs where they were meant to be. When the phone rang, she thought it would be Land. But it was Alice.

"Are we on for church tomorrow morning?" She replied. "Okay, I'll see you there." Alice hung up.

She spent a restless night. Not only her toe ached but her heart was running a race. She raked through the box of shoes she'd kept and found one pair wide toe'd and chunky heeled. Even the wide toe left her limping, but she managed to dress and drive to church. Alice was waiting in her car. "What in the world?" She eyed Samantha, "aren't you about the most pitiful sight I've ever seen. What happened?"

"I kicked something I shouldn't have and it didn't move. I think I broke my toe."

Alice found a seat mid-way and went in first, leaving Samantha the outer seat by the aisle. It was on the second verse of Amazing Grace, she felt someone touching her elbow. "Move on down, please." Surprised, she glanced up to find Land King standing in the aisle. "I told you I'd join you first time it rained and I'm keeping my word."

"I'm sure my grandmother would think highly of you."

He felt animosity, as intended by her words, his face color heightening as he stepped up beside her and began to sing. She listened. Of course he would sing and he could play. Yes, her boy was adept at many things. There were other songs but Samantha was lost in listening to him sing.. When the service ended, he leaned in close, his eyes on her while his hand reached for Alice's and ask the two if they would enjoy having lunch with him. Alice seemed tongue in cheek, watching them, her eyes relaying the message that she had figured it all out.

"I take it you two know each other pretty well?"

They both tried to answer. "Actually, we don't know each other." Samantha denied. "At all."

"We don't seem to like each other," Lan answered honestly.

"Well, in that case, yes, I'll have lunch with the two of you. We'll ride with you and leave our vehicles here." She saw the stubborn streak rear its head in Samantha and taking her hand tucked it between her arm and body to lead her to LAN's truck. All the while the people in attendance were welcoming them and making friendly conversation with Land King. Alice climbed in the back. "I'll chaperone the two of you in the front," she said.

"We're going to my Mom's." Lan gave Alice a glance by way of the visor mirror. "You know my Mom."

"Yeah, I do," Alice replied dryly. "Something tells me you've been avoiding her and she has summoned you."

He laughed. "I've been busy." He avoided drawing Samantha into conversation. "I told her I was bringing company. That way she won't be on me too heavy."

"How old are you?" Alice laughed. "You'll always be Momma's little boy, won't you?"

"I can't figure that one out." He and Alice reminisced over shared times in the community while Samantha sat quietly. By way of the mirror he and Alice seemed quite capable of enjoying their conversation. It was a twenty minutes' drive until they drove into a tree lined lane that led to a white shiplap siding house, Samantha thought built in the forties. A wide front porch held bamboo chairs and table and a bright red scarf adorned the table's top. The porch looked scrubbed clean and she knew already it was a reflection of what they'd find inside. A white haired lady came to meet them.

"Mother." Land bent to hug her warmly and kiss her cheek. "You remember Alice?" The two hugged like old friends. "And this is Samantha McKinsey, the owner of the shop she's building inside Mr. Jessup's old barn." He turned to Samantha, "This is my Mother, Samantha, Olivia King."

She would remember later, their moment of sizing each other up. Olivia Land was the master builder of her own life; no one interfered, firm, resolute, taking care of what ever needed doing, without a quibble. "Samanatha," she said, taking Samantha's hands in her own, staring into the young woman's eyes, liking what she saw. There was no flinching or hanging back, instead an honest return of evaluating her, Land's mother. She did not reveal the inner ticking of her mind or heart, she seemed to be recording the moment, possibly considering whether she wanted to be part of such, but Olivia was careful to not jump ahead. "Welcome to my home. I am pleased to meet you."

"You have a beautiful home. I'm wondering if it is designed after one of Sear's Craftsman homes?"

Pleased, Olivia smiled, "Yes, it is. My husband's parents ordered it and hired two men to assemble it piece by piece and you know what?" The smile widened, as she lay a hand on Samantha's arm. "All the pieces arrived. Think of that, a whole house mail ordered." They all laughed. "Quite a feat, wasn't it?"

"Come, now," she led them to a dining room, complete with white damask table cloth, sparkling china, white with a silver band and silver goblets. "I know you don't like for me to use cloth napkins, Lan, but it's my only time to shine and I'm the one has to launder and iron them again," she laughed, "So I did"

Samanatha picked up a fork and guessed before she turned the piece over. "Your silverware pattern is Rose Garland by Rogers, I'm guessing."

Olivia clapped her hands. "You are exactly right. Alice sit by me, Land at the head of the table and we will put you to his right, Samantha." She waited until they were all seated and bowed her head. "Dear Lord, thank you for a beautiful day after the rain we received this week. We thank you Lord for allowing us to share this meal together. Thank you for food and shelter and love and laughter around this table today. Bless those less fortunate as we love and praise you. "Amen. They all said, "Amen."

"Alice, if you will, please pass the rolls, and I will serve casserole from the large bowl. It is too hot to pass. Samantha, may I serve you first." The next moments were caught up in the art of handing plates, the ladle and Olivia's witty talk to fill the moments as she expertly served them. "Now, taste and tell me."

"It's delicious, Olvia."Alice held her fork up, studying the contents. "Chicken, pene' pasta, a bit of broccoli and what else makes this so tasty?"

"I think," Olivia replied with a twinkle in her eye, "the can of celery soup keeps it moist while it bakes, and there's cheese sprinkled between each layer. You know I attend the church at Bird's Corner, and I can have this in the oven on warm, a bowl of green beans and a salad and a meal ready when I return."

"Umm, and did you make these rolls?" Olivia nodded. "Oh, my goodness you are so talented. I've never cooked like this. I wouldn't dare try." Alice laid her fork down to butter a roll. "Do you cook, Samantha?"

Before she could answer, Lan spoke up. "I'll let you know in a couple of weeks. I helped Samantha move some furniture and she promised a home cooked meal as my reward, didn't you?"

What could she do? Samantha managed a smile, wanting to say I thought we tabled that for my silence. Instead she allowed the light to come into her eyes as she smiled and replied, "Indeed, I did." She knew Alice was aware of the undertow and hoped Land's mother was none the wiser. One thing Samantha was finding difficult was, where was Land's little girl, but that would be rude to ask. If they wanted her to know they would tell her.

Samantha carried dishes to the adjoining kitchen, while Alice scrapped into the garbage disposal any leftovers and Olivia stacked the dish washer. LAN collected napkins, shook the table cloth and sit a tall vase of flowers back in the middle of the table. Once he had pushed the chairs into place under the table, he said, "I'm finished here, Mother. What's next?"

"If you girls will excuse me, I need to talk to Landon a moment."

Alice gave Samantha a knowing look. "Landon," she mouthed, and then as Olivia left the room, she whispered, "It's momma-son time, I'm sure it is about Amy."

She had only finished the sentence when a car pulled into the drive, two little girls climbed out of the back seat and a mommy person walked them to the porch. Once Amy was inside the mommy person and little girl returned to their car. "Nana," Amy called out. She hadn't seen Alice and Samantha, yet. "Nana, I'm home."

Alice stepped from the kitchen to the dining room, "Hey, Amy, come in here and meet someone." Olivia and Land were returning. Land seemed under pressure, the color in his face had heightened to a rosy red while his mother was walking with very crisp steps, her head high and a no nonsense expression on her face that melted to rearrange its self into a beautiful smile for Amy. She opened her arms and Amy ran into them.

"We have company."

"I see them."

"And your daddy."

Amy turned to stare at Landon King.

"These nice ladies want to meet you. There's Alice, remember her? And Samantha, your daddy and Alice's new friend."

After hugging Alice, Amy stood in front of Samantha, staring. "Are you my daddy's girlfriend?"

Samantha stooped down, bringing herself level with Amy, "I can honestly say I am not."

"But he likes you."

"Why would you think that?"

"Because he's not taking his eyes off of you."

"Well, I like you. Why don't we sit over in that corner and you can tell me all about yourself."

"I have a book. You want to come to my room? We can sit in there." Samantha raised her eyes to Olivia.

"That would be wonderful for Amy." Olivia reached down for Amy's hand and then Samantha's and placed them together. "There you are, now you're friends." She stooped to place a kiss on Amy's head.

"So what did you think of Amy's room?" Samantha had changed places with Alice and was sitting in back as they drove home. His eyes held hers by way of the mirror. "My mother said she decorated it in the colors Amy wanted."

"Have you not seen it?" She rolled her eyes when he shook his head no. "It's sweet, pink and crème with a touch of bright blue in pillows and a special little dressing table just her size."

"All right, Lan," Alice turned to speak directly to him. "Are you going to tell what your mother had to say?" She grinned. "I saw your face turn three shades of red." Then she laughed. "You are squirming."

"She is going to travel this winter with John Granger. You know he was Dad's school mate."

"Does that bother you?" Alice questioned. "Good heavens, Lan, he's ten years older than your mother. I truly doubt there are clandestine motives. They have known each other all their lives."

"It's not that. She said they would have separate rooms, she has never traveled abroad."

"My goodness, they are traveling." Her voice was serious when she ask the next question. "So, if you aren't worried your mother will be off doing immoral things, what is bothering you?"

He gave a deep sigh, "It's painful to say. She said Amy is to come live with me, that it is time she gets to know her daddy." His eyes searched for Samantha's understanding but she wouldn't look up. "It is time, but I don't know how to do it. You saw how quiet and aloof she is with me. I doubt she even likes me."

"Lan she's your flesh and blood, she loves you, she's part of you." Alice reached across to pat his hand.

Reaching the church, they parted ways, each in his own vehicle. Samantha waved bye to Alice and drove out first. "What's going on, Lan. Here I didn't know you two had been around each other two minutes and you invite us to lunch with your mother. That's a little odd, don't you think?"

He stretched, muscles rippling beneath the shirt. "So I'm odd, Alice. That about says it, I feel like a fifth wheel. If I open my mouth around her she takes offense. Usually I storm off mad."

"Who are you mad at? Yourself, Lila or Samantha. I assure you, the two are nothing alike. This one's all right, Lan, but as the song goes, maybe you should try a little tenderness, you are always pretty staunch."

"If you only knew."

"Tell me." She waited. "So it's like that, you hold your misery close to your heart and your feelings locked away." She paused and then said, "I'm going to tell you something Samantha doesn't even know. A letter came to the house for her; it was open and hanging out of the envelope. I shouldn't but I read it when I saw the name of her ex-boyfriend on it. He's not happy with the bosses' daughter and the boss is the last to know. He's sending this Blake person down with a load of inventory to stay three days and help put it in stock or on shelves. I'm telling you, if you want her to have feelings for you, then get to work on it because I have a feeling troubles coming." She put a hand up. "I sealed the envelope; she should receive the news this week. You might want to have that dinner with her soon."

"I can't play the game the way you women play."

"I didn't see Samantha playing any games and she had a kindness that was genuine to your daughter."

"She said it best, we are like oil and water and it doesn't mix."

"There's another saying that opposites attract. You are both fine people. You're just coming out of grieving but you can't decide if you want to punish all women for what Lila did or let it go. Try letting go, on the one hand you hate the way Lila treated you; you are almost treating Samantha with contempt."

"What about her?"

"She told me she made a mistake in trusting this Blake, they were engaged. He promised marriage, then broke the engagement. She doesn't intend for that to happen again. But the way you reel her in then push her away is confusing her."

"It's not like we've been in bed, together."

"No, but you wanted to, didn't you?"

"Alice, I'm shocked." He opened his arms wide, "And here we stand on church property."

Laughing, Alice put the key in the ignition and started the Jeep.

"If I didn't know better, I'd say you've got it pretty bad, but you are in denial and you are waiting for her to come to you, which she won't. Talk about stubborn. Remember, Blake is coming, don't you wonder why?"

CHAPTER 11

THERE WAS NOTHING interested him on t.v. He roamed the house, walked outside checked the rain gauge and knew it would be Tuesday before they were able to get back in the fields. He wanted to get in the truck and go see her, but if he did what would he say? "I'm sorry I act like an ass?" No, he couldn't say that. She was refined. He used to be. He slammed himself onto the bed. He had a problem and he had better deal with it. If her ex was coming, there was a good reason. As Alice said, he had better get his act together if he was interested in her. He had given up goodness for drinkin', cussin' and hatefulness.

He blew out a batch of hot air, his stomach was in turmoil. She blamed him for his daughter never being in his home, her own daddy's house. Touché. Was she always right? His thoughts turned to the two nights he had stood by her bed, gazing at her asleep, innocent to his wandering thoughts, he wanted her and he could have taken her, possibly the same fire ran in her veins as his, but he couldn't do that to her, not if he wanted a chance down the road. He truly couldn't figure out if she'd been with her Blake.

Why was he drawn to her? Because she was everything Lila had never been. Now he faced the fact, he had never trust Lila and yet he was the one always trying to prove to her he was good enough for her. She'd had someone from the beginning. Flirtations turned to conquest and conquest to one night stays in Grandview hotels. "Did you really think I'd give these folks around here something to talk about?"

By the time she was slipping around with the doctor, he believed he despised her, but mourning her death he realized just because someone hurts you doesn't mean you quit loving them. Then, at the funeral he stared at her in the casket and determined he would never love another woman. He might speak to them with all civility but they were mere chattels he could do without. Why, then was he so drawn to Samantha McKinsey? Women were a dime a dozen in Riverdale and Titusville. But they weren't her caliber. Her caliber? He laughed, a bitter effort, she was brazen defiant and completely unbendable. She cared. He knew and she knew, so why not get it over with, go ask her.

There was possibly a half hour before dark fell. She would lock up soon. He drove as frenzied as his nerves felt inside. Let the local cop stop him, he was in a mood and he didn't care. She'd parked her car crossways in the lane to her house. Now, was that a calculated move? He was hot. Pulling his t-shirt over his head, he let it settle around his shoulders. Maybe someone was with her, the reason the car sat crossways. With a scowl on his face he strode through the lane, covering the distance to the barn and grabbed the handle to the door and yanked it open. Gleaming with sweat and muscles rippling in his chest, he stood there staring at her as she whirled around. "Samantha, we need to talk."

"You idiot," she screamed. "You scared me to death and now I'm having visitors and you…you can explain why you've upset me."

"I'm afraid I had no idea. I didn't know you were expecting visitors." He shrugged. "Does it matter?"

Disgusted, she gave him a withering look. "How long has it been since anything mattered to you?"

"You matter." Watching her had a calming effect on him as she folded cloth items. "Come here."

"You startled me. I was lost in thought and had everything tuned out, then there's this madman…"

"Come here."

"No." Tears were in her eyes. "You can't be so brusque all the time and then expect me to…"

"Then, I will come to you." Wiping the sweat off his body with the T-shirt, he crossed the room. "I came to apologize. Grant me that."

She stared at him. "How long will your apology last?"

"That's up to you. I'm turning over a new leaf. I'm really going to try." He gave a laugh of sorts. "I have to; in a few days Amy will come to stay while my mother is away." He reached for her hand. "Truce?"

"You surprise me." She accepted his hand. Hers in his, she said, "I can't believe you came all the way across town for this."

"I didn't. I surprise myself." Now the tension had left his body. He grinned. "I had a lot more in mind."

She blushed as a beam of light came into the room and headlights crossed the path to the house.

"Saved by the arrival of guests," he murmured. "I'll be going. Leave you to your…uh…wanderings."

"Whatever that means," she muttered. They both heard a door to a vehicle shut, then someone crossing the path, finally to unlatch the door to the steps. "Sam. Sam." A man's voice was calling. Samantha smiled and went forward as the door opened.

The two embraced. The man kissed her on the cheek. All this, Land observed. On a woman's scale of one to ten, he supposed this man was a ten on appearance. Performance was good now, but what about the past and he grimaced, what about the future. Why was her old ex here?

"Let me introduce you two." She said but it was little more than a nod they gave each other.

"I would kiss you," he said, daring her to protest, "But I'm too blame sweaty." Her expression was hard to read. "On second thought," he stepped back, leaned down and kissed her, staking his territory to the new guy. For some strange reason, he thought he felt response. "Honey," he said. "Let's not be shy in front of your friend." He kissed her again, suddenly to cry out. "Damn." She was laughing. "You bit my lip." So much for marking his territory.

"New leaf," she said. "Remember?" Land was leaving wiping blood from his lip on his pants.

"New boyfriend?" Blake was studying her. "Lovers quarrel, I'd guess. He's a tall dude."

"He is that," Samantha agreed, trying to shift back to the present, Blake standing before her. "Now," she said, "Why are you here?"

"Carlos sent me."

"You are newly married to his dearest little girl, isn't that what he calls her? He would not send you."

"He did. My dear little wife bailed." Blowing out a breath of frustration, he sank onto the chaise. "I never dreamed she had a thing for that guy who delivers from Seattle; you know where the greenhouse supply comes from. It's been going on for years."

"That would make her a child. What? Fourteen or fifteen?"

"Exactly."

She sat opposite him. "Now the shoe is on the other foot, isn't it?"

"I loved her. She completely..."

"Betrayed you?" Her eyes were glued to him. "Now you know how it feels."

"She's gone for good. She told her father she will not come back. Would ...will you take me back?"

"No. I won't and please tell me Carlos is not a part of this."

"But he is."

"I give you no hope as far as the two of us getting together. I have difficulty sitting here with you as though nothing happened. You hurt me, Blake. I cannot go through that again. Go home."

"Where is home?" His eyes were sad and his shoulders drooped, this man who took such pride in himself. "Can't I stay here with you?"

"No. This is where I intend to put down roots. I can't let what would look like...like I let a man move in with me happen." She saw his sadness. Perhaps it was real, but he no longer affected her. In the past she was taken in by his stories. "Not just for myself, either. My grandmother is near I can do this for her…do you understand? I can't live two different standards. I'm trying hard, Blake."

"What shall I do?"

"There's a nice hotel about thirty minutes from here. I suggest you go there."

"Tonight?"

"Yes." She saw the first flash of temper, as his eyes flared and he started to say something.

"I didn't ask you here, Blake. We have nothing to say to each other. It's all in the past."

"It's the tall dude, isn't it? I saw the way he looked at you. Why was he half dressed?"

Samantha laughed. "I hadn't registered that. He's a farmer. Who knows? They're different."

Blake left. She wished him well and admitted she was over him. That cleared the way.

❋ ❋ ❋ ❋ ❋

On Monday she had a surprise visitor. Lan's mother arrived with Amy. "I want to see your shop," she said. Amy turned loose her grandmother's hand and hugged Samantha.

"How are you, Amy? Want to see my art nook? It's where I keep pencils and paints, things I might need to touch up any item that might be scratched in delivery."

"I like your nook," Amy exclaimed. Her eyes lit up seeing the colored markers. "May I use them?"

"Not those, they aren't washable, but," Samantha smiled, 'Behind this door of the cabinet are the ones' especially for little girls like you. Here's paper and you can sit in front of the window and draw us a picture. And while you do, I'll talk with your grandmother."

"She wants to tell you about Mrs. Lassity and she wants you to run an ad in the newspaper for help."

Enlightened, Samantha asked, "Was there anything in particular you were looking for, Mrs. King?"

Olivia turned and gave her a warm smile that reminded Samantha of Lan."I came for a reason; dear, and I hope you won't think I'm interfering. You have really nice collections, but you don't have any of the local people's work. There are some very talented people in this area. If you used them, think about it; that would draw their friends in making the endeavor beneficial to everyone."

"Tell me more." They found a place to sit by the window. Olivia gave her a list of names.

"These are very talented people who take pride in their work and they need the income."

Two weeks passed. She arrived at church the next Sunday to sit by Alice half expecting him to arrive. "He's chafing," Alice offered. "Oh, yes, I've seen him. When he's hurting, Lan roams iike a hungry lion. He's crossed my path twice. I knew he wouldn't be in church." She sighed. "Did you know he is an ordained deacon to this very church? It happened around the time Lila his wife began to see the doctor. The time to select deacons was near and hearing Lan's wife was expecting a baby, the lot meant to reward him. He was faithful in attendance and where Land King goes other men follow, though they knew nothing of the ordeal he was going through, his name was submitted and he was chosen."

"You are saying he reneged on that too, not only his child but his church, too."

The third Sunday he appeared, slipping into the seat by her side as though life was normal. "Where's your boyfriend," he whispered. He chuckled when she moved a whole inch away from him, all the space she could find. "Let's have lunch together and discuss it."

She shook her head. "No, he's not your boyfriend or no you won't have lunch with me?"

"Both." She was aware Alice could hear their discussion. Leaning in, Alice said, "Don't refrain because of me. I have to meet my sister in Grandview." In spite of the turmoil, Samantha tried to listen to the sermon. With Lan King on one side and Alice on the other, she wondered that the world outside could be so misguided that people felt the need to meet on Sunday to hear God's word. Like her, they felt the pull. The upbringing she received under her grandmother's care had stayed with her through the years. She made a few notes hoping to apply them to her life. When the benediction ended Land slipped out of the pew, Samantha felt relieved she wouldn't have to encounter him again. Alice grinned and wiggled two fingers at her in goodbye. No need to hurry, she lingered speaking a moment with two women.

✻ ✻ ✻ ✻ ✻

Land had not left, his truck was parked by her car and he stood holding the door open. "Get in."

"I'm not going to fight with you, Lan." She glanced around to see who was in hearing distance.

"Then get in, because you don't want these people to see the new proprietor in town having a hot discussion with single Mr. King." He bowed and waited, grinning when she cleared the running board and he could shut the door.

"Why would these people, who attend church care one whit about what I do?"

"I saw where you ran an ad in the newspaper for people willing to put their handwork on consignment with your shop." He read her expression. "Why would I even find the ad? My mother stopped by with Amy to look at Amy's room and she told me. Mother's sending Mrs. Lassity to see you, next week."

"The mother of the boy who killed the dog on Alice's porch?"

He nodded. "That's the one, his mother. I hope Olivia hasn't talked you into something that ends up a problem."

"I doubt that happening." She changed the subject. "How did Amy like her room?"

He took longer than needed to answer. "Mother said it is a cold room. Now why would she put it in those words?" He glanced her way. "As for Amy, she's quiet. I can't tell. Maybe she doesn't like me."

"You said that before." She wondered if he was troubled over the matter. "You will have time to know each other and if you are willing to do the little things together, I'm sure you'll both be wrapped around each other's finger in no time at all."

"What are the little things?"

"I don't think it matters but its spending time with her."

"You mean, like reading a story to her, or taking her out to the shop to count bolts." They had driven thirty miles, sometimes talking, and then sitting in great lapse of silence. Now he seemed genuinely interested in doing right by Amy.

"You have bolts that need counting?" He was pulling into the restaurant parking lot.

"Yes, I do. I want to know whatever we do it won't be counted against me." He gripped the steering wheel with both hands. "You saw the room. What does it need?"

"Tell you what, after lunch, let's go to one or two stores and see what we can find to help." He visibly relaxed but was quieter than usual as they entered the restaurant. Something was on his mind.

"Did you notice I've not been around in a while?"

"Three weeks. I figured you forgot me." He just looked at her.

When they left the restaurant he helped her into the truck. "It is definitely getting colder. I don't think that coat is heavy enough."

"It's wool," she replied. "Warmth without weight."

"It's pretty on you." Starting the truck, he sat there a moment, and then turned to her, his expression as sober as if his life depended on whatever he would say. "Samantha, what about the boyfriend?"

The question came unexpected. "There was no boyfriend. If you mean Blake, he left for home that night."

"I didn't know. I tried not to come up the lane, since we've been trying to get all crop out I've had other responsibilities." Putting the truck into reverse, he finished, "But it never left my mind. I'm sorry."

"Nothing for you to be sorry about; He left our relationship for the boss's daughter to find out she's had a thing for one of the delivery men since she was fourteen years old. That means Blake is out in the cold and Daddy's dearest little girl has run to the delivery person. I finally realized how fickle Blake was. It took this long for me to realize he was a jerk."

"Like me," Lan said quietly. "You think there's no hope for me? Sometimes I'm not sure either."

"Hey, there's Caroline's." He pulled in to the front of the store's parking spot.

"And who is Caroline?"

Samantha laughed. "A new line. It's somewhere between the ten cent stores and the new supply. We can find a few items to warm up Amy's room. Are you game?" She chose two pillows with bright polka dots. "What do you think; will that shade of blue suffice?"

After hand turning some kind of item he found interesting, He hand her the box. "This I understand, the rest I don't." She eyed the object, "it's old, isn't it? Antiquity."

He grinned, "They come and go. Aren't you curious what it might be?"

"No, I mean yes I'm finding this side of you to be most interesting and now let's go to where children's toys are and you are going to buy Amy the most wonderful doll, ever, aren't you?"

"I am." He grinned, pulling himself up right, no slouch to the body. "Carry on, I'll follow and by the way, it's a Jack in the Box. You don't know what you missed."

"Oh, daddy, dearest," she crooned. "Having this little girl is going to be the best thing in your life."

"You're sure?" He was looming over her. "I was beginning to think maybe you were...I mean, are."

She knew, he was getting ready to kiss her; she tried to move but his lips were already on hers.

"Uh, HMMM. People get thrown out of stores for less than this," a deep voice warned.

"Alice." Land shook his head. "I know your voice, even the bass one." Samantha was blushing.

"You didn't even look up. How'd you know it was me?" She laid an arm around Samantha's shoulder. "He was dying to kiss you in church when you two were wasting your energy sparring."

"He wasn't."

"I was." Land grinned, peering down at her, winking at Alice. "She's tough."

"Looks like you've met on hallowed ground, things for Amy, I bet. Am I right?"

The rest of the evening was a blur to Samantha. They were perhaps a mile out of town, heading home, when he pat the console between them, "These things are a hindrance. Could you at least let me hold your hand?" He reached across and waited until she placed her hand in his. They were silent and then Land heard the softest pearl of breathing. He groaned. "Asleep again?"

Arriving at the barn, he pulled as close to the entrance as possible, turned off the ignition, went around to the passenger side and opened the door. Gathering her into his arms, he gave the door a push with his hip and carried her in. Going up the six steps was considerably harder, but he made it, the next step was putting her to bed, clothes on, including the warmth without weight coat which made him smile but he removed her shoes. "This is getting harder each time," he said aloud, winded and laying down beside her for a moment. As if from out of the air, the radio came on, a song lilting through the air and he lay there listening wondering why she had the radio set for that hour of the evening.

What was he to do now? If he left, the alarm needed to be set but how was that done if he was out and the alarm in? He lay their comprehending the next step and why she went to sleep so easily. Unaware he kicked off his shoes or that he curled around her sleeping body he considered the alarm.

The room was dark, the hands on the clock lighted to eleven o'clock when he opened his eyes. Someone or something was pummeling his chest and a voice saying, "Wake up. Wake up. Do you hear me?"

"What? What?" He tried to jump up from the bed but he was tangled in something. Samantha was leaning over him and then he remembered. "I carried you in and was winded when I came up those stairs. I only needed a minute to catch my breath."

"Steps." She corrected, laying back on the bed, taking him with her.

"Steps. I lay back to think how to turn on your alarm and I must have gone to sleep." For the longest they stared at each other in an almost pitch black room, their faces lit by luminous hands of the clock. He was certain she would throw him out, maybe not physically but verbally for sure. Then, she began to laugh and as time stood still her laughter increased and he was laughing with her.

She laid her head on his chest. "Why are you wearing my coat? Now we are friends, for sure."

"What?" At that moment his cell rang and he felt around his pockets trying to find it. Samantha handed it to him, from beneath the coat. "Hello," he said. "Tell me." He listened and when the call ended, he pushed aside the coat, leaned over and kissed her before standing to put his shoes on. "Bad wreck out near the farm, Sheriff called to see if I would bring a tractor down to get one of the cars out of the ditch, the other, he said is demolished." Shaking his head at the turn of events, "Hold that thought about us being friends and I'll try to explain to you why I'm concerned over you." He kissed her again and was gone, halting on the last step, to call back, "Turn on your alarm so I won't have to worry more."

CHAPTER 12

ONDAY WAS A busy day. A tour bus passing by saw the sign by the road and the driver was kind enough to grant his passengers forty five minutes. "We'll call it a rest room break," he told Samantha. "Do you have a restroom for the public?"

"One," she replied.

"Don't worry," he said. "Some of them are coming in to look, but three or four are born shoppers."

Needless to say, the rest room got a work out but the cash register did too. She thanked the bus driver as he walked behind the ladies on the way to the bus. Their stop would pay the month's rent. She sighed, happily content as she went to look for the plunger to work on the commode in the public rest room.

Preparing to close the doors, Samantha heard the hum of another vehicle coming up the lane. If she hurried and closed the shutters no one would suspect she was there but the battered appearance of the old truck drew her interest and she lingered. Probably someone had taken a wrong turn and needed directions. She smiled. She was the least likely to give directions from her new address.

She watched as a woman climbed down from the truck, pulled a child across the seat and to the ground and clasp the child's hand. The woman wore her hair short, clinging to her forehead, hanging straight to the sides. Words of instruction drift in, "Now you be good. You hear?" The child nodded.

They came through the door together. "You," her eyes on Samantha, she questioned, "You the woman willing to sell other people's things?"

"Well, yes, depending on what you have and if there's a market for it. What do you have?"

"Wait right here, Anna Marie, while I go get the paintings."

Samanatha stared after the woman, her hard body, the sound of her voice, somewhere between exhaustion and giving up, she'd guess; eyes the color of summer's hazy sky, neither silver nor blue, a palid in between. What could she offer? Samantha glanced at the little girl, the girl stared back. The woman made quick and returned.

"If you can use them, I need the money." She was spreading sheet after sheet of water color paintings on the counter.

Momentarily taken back, Samantha stared at the charm of each sheet, curious as to the display of skill. "Where did you learn to paint?" She did not ask why the paintings were limited to certain colors.

"I always liked to draw, then Leon, my boy gave me a few lessons one Christian, he learned in school." A sad smile flit across her face. "Made the money to buy them all by himself. He knew it would make his daddy mad but he said I needed to know because I was good." The smile dawned for a brief second. "He said once he taught me what he knew no one could ever take them away."

"The medium used is water color?"

"Yes'm, oils are too expensive.""

"The paper?" Samantha smiled a peculiar gentling smile. "This son of yours must love you very much."

The woman's face tightened and then seemed to fall apart in front of Samantha's eyes. "Yes'm." Tears pooled to run down her cheeks. "But he's in bad shape right now, an accident. That's why if you can take them, any of them, I need the money. He's in the hospital."

"I'm sorry, Mrs.?"

"Lassity."

The two regarded each other. "Your son had an accident." Samantha shivered, this woman's son who loved her so much it sounded as though he had given her a gift, someone else would have denied. The name made Samantha wonder if it were the same boy that ran her off the road. "How is he?"

The woman's head fell to her chest as she suppressed a moan, so dire was her concern, her mouth trembled as she looked up to Samantha and her body seemed ready to collapse. "They don't know if he will make it."

Reaching out to touch Mrs. Lassity, she felt the woman stiffen and pull back. She was like a string, ready to break, fumbling now for a piece of cloth she pulled from her pocket as the little girl stepped near and clasp her arms around the woman as roughened hands gently stroked the little one's hair.

"I can't use too many water colors, Mrs. Lassity." She saw the woman raise one hand to clutch the edge of the counter she stood by and those knuckles of that hand turned white as she held on so tightly. "But I'm happy to take five of them and ask you if I supply the oils would you be willing to paint landscapes and bring to me unframed." She saw the slightest smidge of hope lighten the woman's eyes. "Now with oil, you do not use as generously as with acrylics or water colors. Oil paints go a long way. But you will master the art as you progress. Come with me, I'll pay you for the five watercolors and fix you up with what you need to do the landscapes."

Mrs. Lassity's stare was fixed on Samantha, despair covered her face as strength so deeply engrained in her very being fought its way toward hope until finally the gray listless eyes held the tiniest spark of light, her small breast rose and fell as she breathed and made a decision. "I'd be ever so grateful. I'm near going crazy with waiting to hear how my boy's doing." She hung her head. "My man, he says I'm not to see Leon." She brought her arms up to hug her own thin body and in doing so, the welts of deep purple bruises on her arms were evident to Samantha's frank gaze.

"Oh," unintended a slight gasp came from Samantha. "How have you hurt yourself?" Without thinking she grimaced and reached out to touch the woman but Mrs. Lassity's eyes narrowed as she stepped back. "It's nothing."

Samantha boxed up the oil paints with three canvases and handed money over to Mrs. Lassity. "You must go see your son," she encouraged. Again, the woman turned away, calling Anna Marie to follow.

Reaching the door she turned. "I'm forbidden to see my son. Thank you for the supplies. I'll be back."

It was the day after Mrs. Lassity's visit, Samantha saw two trucks at the end of the lane, one parked on the highway, and the other headed her direction. Flipping the light switch, she dispelled any thought of a power outage and went about her business. When she stopped at noon to glance out the window, she saw a sign shining in the aftermath of rain that was turning into icy sleet, a crowd had gathered but the two trucks were missing. Finding a pair of binoculars given to her by her dad she decided to see if their strength went that far. A chuckle formed in her chest, until soon she was rocking back and forth, back and forth, holding her sides. Come tour Samantha's Barn, 'the sign read. If you have ideas, let Samantha help you with them." As the sign turned, Landon King stood in the crowd watching her. Carlos had gone above and beyond being her boss. The other side read, Interior Designs available by Samantha.

She turned on the auxiliary heat, fearing without it the waterworks in the restrooms would freeze. Now was as good a time as any to thank the Lord for all the good works being done for her. Opening the computer she listened to the quiet in the next room, thinking of Landon King. Probably he was sitting in heavy silence contemplating the day of arrival for his child. If it ever happens, she thought. That day must be special. She hoped he wrapped his arms around the little girl and shushed away any hidden insecurities. She smiled remembering the doll and his saying, "You looked good holding that doll."

Iced in, she chuckled. No one could get up the lane and she had no reason to go out. However, the lull in business hurt as much as if the weather was personally directed at her. Three days passed, cars slowed on the main highway, but seeing the lane covered over now with snow and ice dumped unceremoniously off of power lines, she knew the weekend would be without incident. No need to make candy or popcorn. She was alone. This early ice and snow storm out wagered any she had experienced in the Northern state of Michigan. She kept watch on the faucets, all she needed was one to burst, then, what would she do?

The place was in shape, meticulous. She was too antsy to go to bed and although it was dark outside it was only eight o'clock. She heard the drone and at first thought a plane was flying low, or perhaps the sound came from a helicopter, but no, there was no wopping sound of the blades hitting the air. Glancing out the window she saw one large beamed light moving fast across the field, fascinated she watched as it dodged one of Jade's more prestigious junk piles, now covered with snow and beneath that at least two feet of dirt to conceal the rusting objects Jade had left behind. What in the world? And then the driver passed beneath the overhang of the Jessup barn. She laughed, whether relieved it was someone she knew or the fact anyone would dispel the loneliness of the past three days being alone.

Land was knocking on the side door, entering with a blast of wind when she threw the lock. Dressed in slick material snow suit, complete with hood and goggles, he was unzipping, pushing his feet from the confines of cloth and hanging it on one of the pegs by the door. His eyes met hers, "I hoped you could do with a little company and too, I wanted to be sure your heat was working properly."

"Thus far, I believe everything is working." He had removed the heavy suit. "Are you staying awhile? I mean, would you like to sit down?" She had gone tongue tied, always at a loss to what mood he was in. "With the weather, your men won't be working tomorrow, will they?"

He shook his head. "No, they can't be going in and out to the equipment and to tell you the truth this kind of weather brings out the talk; they wouldn't get anything done, anyway." He grinned. "Last year when we had the snow storm, they ended up playing.

They're just boys at heart. You have never seen such a snow man. Ten feet tall." He sat opposite her. She had claimed the rocking chair. He had the sofa.

"What's going on with you? And where did you get the snowmobile?" They were both staring into the flames of the gas log. "I mean, it takes some doing to brave this cold and no one made you get out in it."

"I guess you heard about the Lassity kid? The one Alice said was a problem at work? That troubles me."

"You mean the accident?" She nodded. "His mother brought in watercolor paintings."

His voice dropped low. "He's so young, I can't understand his recklessness. I know his dad's a problem. There were always whispers that the old man beat on the kids, Lord knows about the other, whether he's good to his wife, or not."

"I saw the bruises on her arms." Samantha shuddered. "She said she was not allowed to visit him in the hospital, forbidden to visit him, were her words." She moved across to sit by him on the sofa. "She said they need the money. She loves her son and he loves her, he's the one encourages her to paint. I think there's even a problem there. I could feel her sadness."

"It's worse now," he said. Samantha studied on that a moment. "Why is her sadness worse?"

"The boy died. Young as he is, there was a blood clot. That's the story I heard. That's what killed him."

"Oh, no." Samantha's response recalled all the despair she'd seen in the mother, but most of all the small beam of light that came in to her lifeless eyes when she spoke of her son. "That seems so unfair."

"It has bothered me ever since I heard. Billy called me, he said there's one less old Lassity won't be hittin' on." He sit there trying to decide what he should tell her as she waited for him to finish.

"Yeah, I've never been one to pass on talk, but Leon dying, something don't seem right." He leaned forward looking down as if he were studying the floor. "They had a girl, pretty girl. Pearl probably looked like her when she was young but marrying Jess, I don't know if he's as mean as the grapevine says or people like to talk and a tale builds as it goes around."

"Mrs. Lassity didn't mention a girl, only Leon and he was her pride and joy. That's why I don't understand her not visiting her son. Now this." She was trying to take it all in. "Where does the girl live?"

"Did Pearl have a little girl with her?" Samantha nodded. "That's her granddaughter."

"Where is her mother?"

"Supposedly on the West Coast, all according to Jess, but she never comes home to see her daughter, little Anna Marie."

Samantha felt her heart hit the bottom of her stomach. She couldn't perceive an adult would hurt one of their own. "She would feel she had to leave. Surely the mother wouldn't lead her wrong direction; a mother would have stood strongly against the girl's daddy. Still, I haven't met him."

"Believe me, you don't want to." He reached for her hand. "Have you ever met someone that looked you in the eye and you knew they were evaluating who you were?" He was making circles on the palm of her hand. "Jess sometimes has that look a person does when he's come unglued. Avoid him."

"You think something happened to the girl?" Samantha shuddered. "What if I hired Mrs. Lassity, so she can do what she does best and make a little money while doing it?" He drew her closer to his side.

"You have your gun ready?" He was dead serious, "No one knows about it?"

"No." She shook her head. "You're scaring me. Are you trying to tell me the girl's daddy may have killed her and now Leon is gone? Just tell me his daddy wasn't visiting him when it happened." She was near tears.

"All I know is what Billy told me. Leon's mother left the house where Jess was drinking and she did sneak in to see her boy, but when she returned home Jess was gone. The nurses said the boy's daddy visited him, they heard raised voices then it was quiet because the daddy left. It's a small town and no one wants to make enemies. Our little hospital struggles to make ends meet, but there's word, too, the parent company is stepping in and plans are up for making it large enough to serve the county."

"Oh, my goodness. Here I am, alone and you're telling me, I think you are saying Jess Lassity is a mean person when he drinks and if he's killed his children the whole town is letting him get by with it."

"I think most of us don't want to have to watch our back because we angered the town drunk. Samantha, you are shaking. Should I not have told you? I didn't want you facing him unarmed."

She settled into the safe feeling of his arm around her. They sat without conversation, the flames comforting as the glow on their faces. She had the fleeting thought when he was telling her about the boy and his father that she wouldn't sleep that night, but now the warmth was overtaking her. She must have fallen asleep, for the next thing she awakened to him saying, "Do you always fall asleep when a man puts his arms around you?"

"I'm sorry." She yawned. "Maybe I'm not aware of it, but I don't sleep well, yet, and I explain it to myself that I'm not used to living alone in a country setting. But I thought rural America was safe."

He pulled her close. "I like it. I think I dozed off too. It's been a long time since I've held a woman. Do we have to end here?"

She should have known. She had let down her guard. What else was he to think?

His hold tightened as he searched her eyes. "I know we share this feeling."

She moved away, the distance between them was not great but his expression changed. "I know you do." He reached for her hand, his fingers entwined with hers, as he seemed to peer straight into her soul. "I feel you care…"

Tears filled her eyes. "Yes," she whispered. "But I'm not going to make that mistake."

"I'm a mistake. Two adults finding comfort in each other."

"Things matter." How could she explain after Blake, she learned there's no taking anything for granted?

"Why does it matter?"

"For me, there's a price." She would have continued but he broke in, his body had changed, he was tense. She felt him stiffen, angry with her words. "One day I want what every woman wants."

"Oh," he drew a deep breath, his voice turning sarcastic, "So you are like the others, after all?"

"Should I be flattered," she questioned. "Others?" Angrily she wiped away the tears. "You and I are not on the same page, you want instant gratification, I'm old enough to think down the road I will want the right person and a family. If it's sex you want, then go find your others."

"It's more than sex. You know it is."

Her eyes held his, unwavering. "Then prove it."

He responded with a dubious stare. "How?"

"Treat me right." It was a wistful whisper. "I'm worth it," she struggled to explain, "my self-worth, what I think." A crazy laugh came from the back of his throat as he stared at her his eyes accusing.

"I saw the look on your old boyfriend's face. Who are you trying to fool?"

She rose up to go to the rocking chair. He looked insulted. "Do you think I'm crazy?" He stood and began pacing. "What are you thinking? What is your ridiculous plan? Shall I leave and never come back?"

"I have no say over what you will do." She struggled for words. "I'm not sure why you are like you are...like I said, I've made mistakes, too but I'm not going to jump into bed with you, no matter how much I'm attracted to you." She stopped. "Why do I have to explain?"

"Who does that in this day and age?" He kicked the big iron kettle setting by the fireplace. "I think I'm way beyond that." He jerked her up out of the chair, against his body. "I am a man. I need you."

She felt torn between yielding and denial. In truth, she quaked beneath his touch. His breath was hot on her face as she jerked away. "I don't want a bull in heat," between nervousness and her anger that he stated his wants, her words were more hiss and ravage than civility. "You want?" Now she gained strength in her anger. "What about what I want? Why does a man think a woman should swoon over him every time he has a need?" She rose up on her tiptoe, staring him in the face. "Women become mothers of little children to teach them right from wrong, what do men grow up to be?" She swallowed. Sanity was returning and she wondered that she had bowed to his level. "Go home, Land King."

He headed toward the door, "Let me tell you something, little fire angel, that's what you are, women like you lead men like me on, and then you back off."

"I never led you anywhere. Your arrogance led you to think you could come in here and wipe me out, and then wipe me off your list. Well, it didn't work. I don't mess with a man's feelings. That's on him."

He yanked the newly installed door knob so hard it came off in his hand. The rage he felt was shaking the inside of his body. He had been willing to commit himself and she rejected him. And on the heels of rejection came self-loathing whether he admitted it or not, he had performed poorly, anger and expectation robbed him; she thought he'd come to make advance, when he'd come to see if she was all right and to warn her about old man Lassity. But then, he had ruined it all hadn't he? He had bared his soul to her. He was a grown man acting like a spoiled boy who wanted his way.

He stood there watching her, his eyes half slits, while a sick yearning claimed his body, his mind, his spirit. He felt physically wiped out. He was sick of himself. He came to conclusion, she'd met him head on, she was worth more than the usual female that flirt with him and he knew they were easy, but he had not partaken of them. If she rejected him, again, he would never come back. "Will you go out with me, Saturday night? Somewhere?" The irony of what he would say next twist his lips into a sarcastic grin. "So we can become acquainted?" He didn't realize he was screaming until she screamed back.

"Yes." The tears were streaming down her face and dripping on the floor. She watched him walk out the door, stride to the snowmobile, to return without a word put on his waterproof suit, hood and gloves and leave again. The snowmobile started with the turn of the key and he was gone. Then the laughter boiled up, pouring out of her system, as she eyed the door swinging open, void of knob because of this man who had come to protect her, to warn her…she laughed as she collected the screw driver and replaced the screws, tighter than before she hoped, then she threw the double locks, and went around checking that all windows were latched down and the other doors secure. "Why, he's a madman," she whispered out loud as a shiver passed through her body, her knees buckled in sudden weakness as she reached for the bannister and sank down on the stairwell. This one, she won, but winning had a price.

The next morning the phone rang. She saw on caller ID it was him; she was half a mind to ignore it but that would worry him and for some reason he was like a high strung animal. She answered. "Why did you take so long?" He asked. "You knew it was me, didn't you?" She didn't answer. "It took me awhile to remember…I left you without a door knob on your door."

"Yeah, I fixed it."

"I got a call about the Lassity kid. They don't have money to bury him. They can't afford a preacher." He sighed. "It's about as sad as it gets. I kind of hate to tell you this…because you'll laugh." Silence came across the line as she waited. "They want to have a memorial service for Leon….. Pearl wants to."

"That sounds reasonable." Here they were talking as though the previous scene had not happened.

"Yeah, I know, but they want someone to sing and play the piano. They want a normal service Pearl said, but they aren't well liked and because of that they want to do this in my shop."

"Can you do that, I mean is it lawful?"

"I checked it out. It is, but I can't provide the music and sing…" he heaved a heavy sigh. "and say a few words. You understand me?"

"How did you get in on this? I thought they stayed to themselves."

"They lived on my property a number of years back. I couldn't keep them on because his work ethics have never been the best and he couldn't take instruction." He was quiet again, until he said, "Samantha, you said you play the piano. Do you sing?"

"I wondered why you called."

He groaned. "Will you help me out? I was wrong last night and I'm sorry. So will you help me out?"

"Lan you and I know there are a dozen people at least who know this family; they don't need a stranger."

"I need. The town has collected money for expenses but they draw the line at helping with the funeral."

"Why, Lan?" Her eyes were troubled. "Isn't that pretty heartless not to mention unchristian?"

"They've begged bought and stolen from nearly every family around and wouldn't work to boot."

She felt his troubled spirit. "I don't know how to put a funeral together. God help me, I don't." She heard the desperation. "Lila's funeral was a time of my being so bitter I really couldn't focus on what God wanted for me. I thought life was over. There was no future, no blessing, and no way to endure. I wanted to die and be buried beside her and then the pastor pointed out, although God allowed the accident, it was not God who orchestrated the accident."

"Say that, Lan, speak from your heart."

"I'm so unworthy. I have no business being in front of Pearl as she grieves over her son's death."

"But, they chose you. Someone has enough faith in you to trust you to say the right words; you will speak over their dearest possession." A thought came to her mind. "Where will he be buried?"

❋ ❋ ❋ ❋ ❋

It was eight o'clock, day of Leon Lassity's funeral. Samantha decided not to open the shop that day.

When the pounding on the door began, she hurried to open it, thinking something was wrong. Pearl Lassity stood on the outside steps, her features told of heart break, her eyes were pools of sadness. Stepping aside, Samantha motioned her inside.

"Here," she thrust the three new canvasses into Samantha's hands. "I spent all night on them; I'm sorry to bother you today but I need pay if you can manage, so I can buy Leon clothes to be buried in." She saw Samantha's startled look. "Yes'sm, I'm sorry to bother you, but his daddy burned his clothes 'ceptin what he was wearin.' Now, I got to find something suitable. Turning full circle, as if looking for something, she finally asked. "Those red flowers were here, that day I was but there gone. He loved red, my boy did," her lips began to tremble, "He's got to have red flowers, ma'am." Her body began to shake.

Fighting to stay composed, herself, Samantha nodded. She wanted to wrap her arms around this thin, sad woman who had lost her son. Instead, she led Pearl Lassity up the six steps to her personal space. On the low table in front of the fireplace she had set the red flowers. "They're yours, Mrs. Lassity. We can use them as part of the payment for the canvasses if you will accept. The woman claimed the flowers, holding them to her breast as great tears ran down her cheeks and a suppressed sob trickled out. The moan that followed, Samantha would never forget. It wasn't the flowers the woman was holding, it was her son. The boy who would never come back to brag on his mother, never say he was sorry what his father put her though and all the times he acted terrible to keep the old man off his mother, that was who she held in her arms at this moment. That one that had no decent clothes to be buried in was embedded in her mind's eye and she was sorry, sorry she'd birthed him into the hardship of dealing with his father; sorry he'd seen her beaten to a pulp before his and Anne Marie's eyes and he'd remained silent knowing his interference would only make worse the beating.

The terrible sobs gained momentum as Pearl's body swayed on those trembling legs and Samantha feared she would fall or die of heartbreak, or disappointments, but nothing compared to this. Wrapping her arms around Pearl Lassity, feeling Pearl's resistance she held on tight, while her own tears mixed with the grieving mother and then in that one moment when she could, Samantha pulled them both to the chaise lounge she had drug up from the bottom floor. It was dirty and encrusted with bat dung and wrapped in spider webs but she'd cleaned it up and brought it to her own personal space where she laid soft pillows on the seat and the back.

There on that ancient piece that had belonged to Granpa Jessup she crooned comfort to one whose arms were empty, until they were face to face, foreheads together with Samantha staring into those hollow eyes. "We are going to Grandview. I'm driving so you can rest a moment before the funeral. That's where we'll find clothes for Leon and come hell or high water I am standing with you today. No more pushing away, you understand. We're friends."

Eleven o'clock arrived with the Lassity family filing in, subdued but determined. Most were dressed in their best to honor Leon. "That boy was a dresser," his aunt said. She was Pearl's sister and she was avoiding her brother in law. "Thank you for standin' with my sister." She squeezed Samantha's hand. "She needs someone but we're all too scared to do what you're doin'. He's got a terrible temper and Leon dyin' ain't gonna change a thing." She gave the little girl by her side a nudge forward. "Go on."

Anne Marie climbed up on the casket and no one stopped her as she pressed lose to Leon to kiss his cheek and lay her head on his shoulder. "That 'un, she gonna miss him something terrible." Pearl's mother said. "We all are. He was the one between my Pearl and that bastard she married." She stared across the room daring Jess Lassity to look at her and when he did she made a fist, pumped it in the air two hard yanks seeming to invite him up front. "He aint' even looked at his own boy. He can't."

Samantha was relieved when Lan came to her side. "These are the three most miserable hours I've ever spent," she whispered. He only lowered his eyelids and stared at the floor. "Does that mean, you, too?" They watched Pearl move to the head of the casket as a more level headed group of family mourners claimed her. Lan produced a tall stool. "Sit, Pearl," he commanded, "before you fall." As he returned he motioned to Samantha they move a short distance away close to the key board he'd set up earlier.

"How did you know Pearl?" She was physically and emotionally drained and wished for another stool.

"For a short while Pearl kept house for me. She needed the money and I needed help but Jess put an end to that, too. She said he was jealous and we both had a laugh. I was over women." He nodded toward the keyboard. "What do you plan to sing? I'll play for you and after I speak while the family passes by the casket, you play. Now, what have you got?"

"Pearl ask for two and then if needed there's one I found. Just be sure I know when to sing."

He placed the sheet music on the bench and sit down. "It's nearly time, they need to be seated and prepare themselves." He began to play as all eyes were on the huge work clock at the front of the shed. At one o'clock he nodded and Samantha stepped in front of the rows of chairs.

"I only know Leon and his family through Pearl," she began. "You see, Pearl has a wonderful gift. She can paint on canvass what we would like to say in words and Leon had that gift. He was Pearl's encourager. In these last moments we spend with Leon let us remember the spirit of his personality, the love he had for his mother and our own sadness of his leaving life this soon in life. I choose to think of his painting, as his special way of communicating with our heavenly father. If you will all sing with me, now."

"Amazing Grace, how sweet the sound, that saved a wretch like me." One by one they began to sing and the sound was beautifully stirring for they sang from the heart. "Twas grace that taught, my heart to fear and grace my fears relieved..." Samantha led right on into Will The Circle Be Unbroken. "In the sky Lord in the sky. There's a better place a waiting."

Lan stood before them, some had worked for him, a few were his age and he'd known them longer. "Thank you for coming, you honor Leon's life by being here. In the Bible, in the book of Job, chapter one and verse twenty one, terrible things have happened to Job. Job speaks and says "Naked I came out of my mother's womb and naked I shall return thither. The Lord giveth and the Lord taketh away, blessed be the name of the Lord. Now there are different versions but this one serves our purpose today. Some would say Leon was a rowdy boy, and he was, but often the spirit of a person is governed by what God allows; what takes place in our lives has a bearing on who we are, the strength and the personal hardships form who we are. When we love our mother that explains a lot to the world; that's where we see honor, reverence, kindness and caring. What better explanation of a person? You might read that scripture in Job and ask did the Lord cause Job's problems? Because it reads the Lord giveth and the Lord taketh away. Did the Lord give Leon life? Did he take life away? If so, was there good in that life? I'd say yes. Was God good to Leon, did he know Leon? More importantly, did Leon know him?"

"Jeremiah, Chapter twenty nine, eleven reads, "For I know the plans I have for you, declares the Lord; plans to prosper you and not to harm you, plans to give you a future." That tells me, God wanted only the best for Leon. What we will find at the end of our life's journey will be better than what we experience here on earth." I would say to the family. "Let Leon's passing bring something good into your life. I feel Leon has seen the streets of gold, the warmth of heaven, but until he went, Leon was just like you and me, taking each day as it comes, compared to now being wrapped in the Savior's love. Maybe Leon didn't know he was thinking of Jeremiah twenty nine, verse eleven, he just knew it worked for him." Lan stood there, thinking, willing them in the silence to consider the Bible scripture, but he was relieved when Samantha stepped by his side. He returned to the keyboard.

"This is a song I wrote when my father died and I felt alone with no one to share the burdens of life." She listened to Lan play the introduction. "When our heart aches until we think it will break and we have sadness with nothing to gain..." She saw Pearl lift her head. "In the midst of pain, you don't have to...stand alone, you have nothing to prove and you never have to ask...no matter the things you don't know, in this my friend, when you have nowhere to go...remember me, I'm your friend, you will not lose, ...You never have to stand alone...." Pearl's eyes were on her and Samantha nodded..."We have nothing to lose...when our heart aches and we think it will break, we are not our own...." Samantha spoke the last lines ..."when you think no one cares...Jesus has spoken He's there, you don't have to stand alone."

Lan came to Pearl and reached for her hand to lead her to the head of the casket. His men stepped up to usher the family forward. One by one they filed by. When only Pearl, her mother and sister, Anne Marie and Jess remained, Leon's daddy was shaking uncontrollably. "Jess, you have a task before you, no man should have to bear," were Lan's words. To Pearl, he said, "You will never forget his face, his voice or his love for you. Now say good bye and let me know when you're ready." Understanding Pearl touched her son's face, leaned in to kiss his cheek, and then her eyes met Lan's. "I'm ready."

One of Lan's men was immediately there, offering his arm and ushering her to the old truck. When Jess was too stricken to take his place under the steering wheel, the young man helped him to the passenger side, and then went around to slide in and drive. At the cemetery was the most traumatic time, as the casket was lowered, Jess's uncontrollable shaking took him to his knees while Pearl's whimpering stirred their hearts and Pearl's mother commented, "It's his conscience botherin' him and it won't quit."

They left the cemetery with Lan's men shoveling dirt onto the casket. She knew Lan had taken responsibility for any cost that arose. Leon was buried in the presence of family love and friends respect. The red flowers had been laid at the head of the grave. Samantha wondered if she should leave Pearl without saying a word, and Land seeming to know her thoughts took her hand in his.

Samantha was physically and emotionally drained. Privately unsure why they were stopping by Lan's house she withheld any questions, taking his offered hand and following him inside. The house was spacious but sparse of furniture. He motioned for her to sit while he searched the lower shelves of the kitchen cabinets to produce a half empty bottle of whiskey which he thrust towards her. She shook her head.

He swallowed a hasty burning mouthful, replaced the lid onto the bottle and pushed it back to where he found it. Again he reached for her hand and led her to the living room to pull her down by his side on the one piece of furniture. First he thrust his legs out in front; laying his head on the back of the sofa, but that didn't ease his restlessness. Sitting forward, head in his hands staring down at the floor, he began. "That was the hardest thing I've faced since Lila died. Maybe it was remembering the farce of her funeral when the minister portrayed her as the loving wife, when really she was having an affair with her doctor. That very hour, listening to the minister, I began to wonder if she was having an affair with him. The whole world knew she was seen with other men and there he stood singing her praises as the best wife in the world. I quit church and I hadn't been in one since, until I came to stand by you that day. That preacher left before two months and I was glad." Tears ran down his cheeks. "I didn't cry when we buried Lila and I don't understand why I'm crying now. Do you? It's like something broke inside of me."

"My father cried the night my mother left us. I awoke to hear the broken sound of sobbing and it took a while for me to realize it was my father. He lost the person dearest to him and there was nothing he could do about it." She was helpless to explain her father. "Maybe you should have grieved over her death you would not have married her if you hadn't cared. I'm sure you expected it to last a life time."

The ache around his heart had lessened and the lump of despair that had settled in the pit of his stomach didn't feel quite as heavy. "You make sense, Samantha McKinsey." He squeezed her hand and for the first time he was a true gentleman. The bitterness that spewed poison when he thought of Lila might go away some day. Understanding was seeping into his tired brain; he had tried to punish other women for the sin that belonged to Lila. Resentment and scorn had created someone he never intended to be. "I've been so wrong," he said. With gentleness he took her into his arms.

Samantha later wondered if that day they had reached an understanding of sort, but only the future would tell. Perhaps now, there could be a beginning, leaving behind previous disastrous encounters.

CHAPTER 13

$\mathcal{T}$RUE TO HER word, Olivia stopped in. There was an embarrassing quietness between them until finally Samantha asked, "Mrs. King, have I done something to displease or trouble you?"

Olivia looked quickly to where Amy was busy exploring the children's corner. Pressing a hand to her forehead, Olivia said, "It's Amy. You remember I'm going on that trip with John and leaving Amy with her father, but she's never stayed with him and that worries me." Tears welled up in the older woman's eyes. "Please." She laid a hand on Samantha's arm. "Would you be so kind as to keep in touch with Amy? I've bought her a phone and told her I would ask this of you. I hope you don't mind."

"I'm pleased. Why don't you give me Amy's number and in the next few days we will set a pattern of calling? I'm quite honored you would think of me."

Olivia called Amy. "Dear," she said, "Samantha likes our little plan. What do you say?"

"Thank you. May I call you each night?"

The nightly calls began. Amy was bubbly and bright in the beginning and then became subdued. "How are you?" Samanatha

145

asked. "Good. We drove everywhere looking at Daddy's dirt." Samantha laughed. Another night the reply was, "I'm tired. Daddy counted bolts and separated them today. I don't like them." Then it was the weekend. "What did you do today?" Samantha asked. "There was a giggle. "I sit on daddy's lap and drove the tractor. I love Daddy." The visit was working. Samantha relaxed, but for all the screaming she and Land had done that fateful night when he asked, "*will you go out with me this weekend*," it never happened.

Nearing the end of the second week, Samantha realized it had been several days since she and Amy had spoken, nor had she heard from Land. She tried to rationalize the silence between them. He was dealing with being a father. She wondered if perhaps he also realized the loss of Amy's mother was indistinguishable. Thanksgiving was upon them, busy in the shop she could not linger on personal longings. She did miss seeing Land and speaking with Amy each night. Then, Amy called. "How is your daddy?" Amy's reply brought tears. "Daddy's good. Today me and him and Kristen went to Grandview, shopping." Amy's giggles told the story but she had to ask. "Who is Kristin?" The reply hurt. "Kristin is my and daddy's friend. She's pretty. I want to be just like her when I grow up."

The last customer left the shop, going out into a light rain; "a damp thankless night," she complained. "I came for another painting by that woman you brought in, but I'm going home empty handed."

"Pearl's paintings sell as quickly as they arrive. Why don't I call you the next time she delivers?" She hadn't seen Pearl since the funeral. On second thought, how could the woman paint if she was without supplies? Checking for Pearl's address, she decided she would make a visit and take canvasses. Three canvasses, a tube of white paint and a little reprint of an encouraging poem and she was on her way.

She found entrance to the Lassity property, a graveled road with a sign posted and nailed to a tree that read Hell's Acre. She drove carefully up the lane, half expecting a bullet to whiz by her ear. There were no cars parked in the yard, in fact the place looked deserted. Still, she headed for the porch and front door. First she knocked timidly but hearing someone moving around inside she knocked forcefully. The door opened quickly.

Pearl stood there, a frightened and startled look on her face when she saw Samantha. "I thought you was him."

Slowly Samantha stepped into the room and closed the door behind her. "What happened?" She felt her blood pressure rising, probably to hit the top of her head. A buzz of adrenalin buzzed her veins. Pearl's left arm was in a sling. There were knot sized lumps purple colored and oozing that nearly blocked her vision, while scratches covered her forehead and whelps led down her throat and into her blouse.

Samantha stood accessing the mistreatment, the misery Pearl couldn't hide and she wondered if Jess Lassitiy deserved to be alive. Seeing Samantha's concern, Pearl's eyes welled with tears. She was mute as she began to rock slowly side to side. "He beat you? Your husband?" Pear nodded. "Do you want to leave him?" Pearl's eyes showed fear and terror that more would be forthcoming. "Is he expected back soon?" Pearl had become a hunted animal, her face turned white, her movements were jerky and she seemed unable to speak. "You need to get out of this mess, Pearl."

Traumatized, Pearl tried to speak and after several tries offered, "He said he'd kill me."

"Why did this happen?"

"I wanted to take the truck, go to Leon's grave." Her words came in jerks caused by the shaking of her body. "I was going even if he said no but he stopped me. He kicked me off the porch then drug me back up and that's when he battered my face and I think broke my arm. The pain is fierce."

"Where's Ann Marie?"

"I don't know. He said he had a good woman taking care of her and he won't tell me where she is."

"Was she here when he beat you?"

"No, she was at school. But he picked her up that day and took her somewhere I don't know."

"Go pack your bag. Get several changes of clothes, your toothbrush, your purse with identification and an extra pair of shoes. You are going home with me."

Pearl shook so violently she couldn't move. "I can't. He'll kill you too."

Samantha took over, gathering underwear, a gown, toothbrush and shoes. Almost everything she owns, she was thinking. "Now, grab your purse and let's go. This is for your own good. Next time he'll kill you."

Rooted to the spot, Pearl did not move. Samantha grasp the bag in one hand, Pearl in the other. Her own hands were shaking as she backed the car out of the drive and drove like demons were after them down the lane. "We are stopping at the cemetery. I think you need to feel Leon's love to get you through this."

Later, she had the fleeting thought she was glad it had not rained at the cemetery's location. Pearl practically bolted from the car and threw herself on the grave that was still bare of grass with its few straggly remains of flowers from those able to spend and place their offering on Leon's final resting place. Walking a distance away, Samantha stood vigilance while giving a mother time alone with her child but the sobs and incoherent rant of sorrow came often to her ears. "He beat me, son. He said he wished I was dead and he'd bury me on top of you, that I wasn't worth my own grave." Silence, when it came was deafening, those scant intervals between words. "I don't know where he's put Anne Grace. He said with a good woman. Son, you know how I've loved Anne Grace and took care of her."

When drops of rain began to pelt the ground, Samantha went to Pearl, reached down and took her hand. "Come on, it's time you eat something. I can tell you haven't eaten in days." Exhausted and subdued, Pearl walked beside Samantha, childlike and obedient. "A full belly, a warm bath and sleep, you will feel better in the morning." She heard Pearl murmur something. "What did you say, Pearl?"

"He will come after us."

"He has no idea where you are."

"He can track anything. What will we do when he comes?"

"I have a gun."

She made one stop at the Quick Shop for supplies for the next few days. She promised Pearl a meal but they couldn't be seen together in public. Pearl was as skittish as a new born colt and although Samantha was new to the area, Pearl's family was not. She told Pearl to stay in the car and sit low. Making fast work of finding what they needed, she scanned men who were loitering around the one table and was relieved when she had not encountered them before. For some reason it gave her false hope that Pearl's husband wouldn't come after her.

While Pearl soaked in the tub, Samantha tried rationally to think through a way to find Anne Marie. She was hesitant to call the local police or the Sheriff. Could she leave present differences alone and call Lan? If there was another woman in his life, he had lied about everything, his reluctance to trust a woman; had it all been a ruse to break her? Lan King wanted to play by his rules and she had her own. Still there was a child's welfare at stake. A child in the hands of a man who beat his wife didn't set well with her. What if she didn't seek help and something bad happened to Anne Marie? What kind of man beat his wife, anyway? What happened in his life to make him that way and for that matter what happened to Lan King that he had little respect for women?

Deciding to call, she pressed the cells directory and waited. A happy lilting voice came across, "Hey, this is Kristin, I'm answering for Lan King. You want, leave a message otherwise call him back. He's busy." Samantha could have cried...but there were things to do. Selecting the right size pan, she filled it with water and set it on the stove to boil where she would add spaghetti. She felt like fretting but who would benefit from that? She swiped angrily where tears ran down her cheeks. There would be no call back.

She had to think on this, how to find a child Jess Lassity said he had hidden away with a good woman. Sliding two slices of texas toast into the toaster, she called out, "Food's ready. Come on, let's eat." Pearl came into the kitchen wearing the robe Samantha had laid out. "This is it, spaghetti, salad and bread, eat up."

Tears ran down Pearl's cheeks. "Leon used to make spaghetti, he always said, "Dig in."

Samantha squeezed Pearl's hand. "I'm sure in the weeks to come there will be constant reminders of Leon. Is there any way we can make those happy memories rather than sad?"

"It's so real right now. I've been beaten. My son has died. My Anne is wherever he left her and I'm not in my own home because my husband has threatened to kill me if I don't do as he says. Could you be happy?"

"Your plate is full." Samantha sighed. "What takes your mind off of the evils of this world, is there anything?"

"When I paint, I lose consciousness of my surroundings," she whispered, "but I want to think about Leon."

"How about tomorrow we set you up in my bedroom by the window where there's the North light; maybe you can paint and loosen up a bit, anyway we'll know whether your husband storms the shop."

"You won't know he's here until he's standing over you." There was pain in her expression. "I know."

Samantha's fork paused midair. She was aware of Pearl's trembling but a shudder went through her own body. A warning, she thought, of utmost intent. She must stay on guard for both their sakes.

That night going in the room where Pearl slept, for something she needed, she felt she was trespassing Pearl's privacy, when she saw in the dim light the terrible bruises on her arms and the lumps around her cheekbones. God forgive her, she opened her phone and took pictures of the beaten woman asleep on the bed. There was no way of knowing if Jess Lassity planned to cause problems. She would have the film developed and hide the pictures just in case.

Olivia stopped by the next evening and it was not by chance, Olivia had something on her mind.

"How was the trip?" Samantha led her over to the chaise. "Have a seat." Amy brushed against her side and Samantha kissed the top of her head. "We missed our phone call last night, didn't we?" Satisfied, Samantha had noticed her, Amy went on over to the children's corner. "Your trip was good?"

Olivia nodded. "Yes but I'm a bit unsettled, Samantha. As you can see I'm taking Amy back home with me. I had hoped Lan would see the need for this child to have her parent in her life, but it isn't that way."

"I wish I could help with Amy but there's…" Samantha saw Olivia was making certain Amy was out of hearing range. "I thought the plan was to see how Amy and Lan's relationship developed, a trial run of sorts. Didn't Amy want to stay?"

A frown worked its way across Olivia's features. "She did and even cried but something is a little off kilter there, which I can't put my finger on and I thought perhaps you could enlighten me." When Samantha was quiet, thinking, Olivia continued, "Forgive me for coming right to the point of why I'm here today." Her skin flushed briefly, as she was determined to ask. "Is there anything going on between you and my son?" She fanned a handkerchief across her face. "I have worked up quite a sweat in order to ask that of you, Samantha, and I'm sorry to be rude."

"I'm still hung up on why Lan didn't keep Amy. We kept our nightly conversations, Amy and I, and she was always upbeat and happy and that made me happy for both of them. But, Lan and I aren't staying in touch."

Olivia's countenance fell. "I'm not getting any younger and Amy needs someone besides a seventy nine year old woman in charge of her life. I like you, Samantha, and I hoped Lan had finally found someone."

"I'm sure Amy doesn't realize age difference, Olivia, and if she did she is so blessed to have you."

"Well," Olivia rose up off the chaise, "I hope you won't give up on my son. One of these days he is going to turn loose that poisonous attitude his wife created before it destroys him. Surely he will." She turned to Amy, "Put things away, dear, we need to be on our way." A bit woeful, she shook her head. "He used to be such a lovely man, my son, but after Lila's betrayal he seems to trust no one. Sometimes I wonder if he even trusts me."

"You have his dearest possession, Olivia. Under all that brusque demeanor if he's anything like you, I'd say there's hope for Landon King."

"I pray you keep that opinion, dear, because my son's attitude wears me thin." Noticing Amy closing the books and putting away the crayons, Olivia leaned in closer to whisper, "Do you have Pearl?" Samantha nodded. "Words out, Jess is looking for her. His problem is he thinks she is his possession. Be alert." She lay a hand on Samantha's arm. "Don't hesitate to call the police if he comes here. Jess is a mean drunk. He does not control his temper. In fact, that temper sent him to prison once for a three year stay. That's the only reprieve Pearl ever had."

"Are you saying she has no say in whether he beats her or not?"

"I'm saying he will kill her one day if she doesn't move away. As long as he can find her she is in danger and if she is with you, you are in danger too." She gave Samantha another pat on the hand. "I don't blame you for helping her, dear. Lan didn't mention Pearl, so I'm guessing he doesn't know she's here."

Sunday's Samantha and Alice continued to attend the community church. Samantha glimpsed Lan standing at the back of the church several Sundays but by the time the last prayer was said he had left. *Alice* wore a pensive expression which said I want to know what's going *on* but I won't ask.

"Want to catch a burger?" Samantha nodded. "Ride with me, then and we'll come back for your car." Later, waiting for their meals, Alice leaned forward, elbows on the table. "Are you going to tell me?"

"There's nothing to tell. I helped Lan with Leon Lassity's funeral and haven't seen him since."

"He's sulking. I don't know why," Alice shrugged. "But I've known him a long time and he is."

"So he's said something to you?"

"No." Alice scooted back on the bench. "He's a mystery, always has been."

"Changing the subject, but have you heard anything about the little Lassity girl, Anne Marie?"

Puzzled, Alice asked, "Why would you be interested in Jess and Pearl's granddaughter?" Suddenly a light dawned in her eyes. "I did hear Jess is looking for his wife." Her voice took on awe. "That's it, isn't it? You are housing Pearl." She laughed. "Well God bless you," but then added. "God keep you safe."

Pearl was restless. She was standing at the window when Samantha returned. "I can't stay in the back room forever," she said. "My bruises are almost gone and the lumps on my face are fading too."

"And evidently the arm has healed which means it wasn't broken, or you would still be wearing the sling. But tell me this, truthfully if your husband finds you are here, what then?"

"He will come after me." She handed Samantha the canvasses she had completed.

Studying the oils, Samantha nodded, "Very good. Landscape and ocean tide. I like them. Now, is that what you want, him to come after you after nearly killing you?"

"No, not what I want but life in one room, painting, is not quite what God intended either, is it?"'

"You believe in God?" Samantha smiled. "I've thought it quite evident you communicate with him when you paint."

"I do and I've been praying you would take me to Leon's grave again and maybe I could go to church with you next Sunday." There was a wistful childlike expression on Pearl's face. "I hope you will agree."

Surprise dawned in Samantha's eyes. "How could I keep you from going to church? But first figure out a way to keep your husband away from us, unless you want us killed."

Sadness crossed Pearl's face. "He nearly killed me. I said as much but he says, no I know just when to stop." Pearl turned to her. "I got this really bad hurtin' to be near my boy; If you could take me to the cemetery, please."

"You will have to wear a hat or something that might disguise you." She glanced at the clock. "By six it will begin to grow dark, and we'll hurry. Pearl's face was pale to the point of white as they loaded into Samantha's vehicle. She was gripping the strap to her old purse as though it were her lifeline. They didn't speak a word and Samantha's own body was doing a silent shake as she could tell Pearl was near catatonic, which made her wonder why are we doing this, are we so anxious to flirt with death?

Knowing they were not far from Hell's Acre, Samantha pulled the car to the side of a growth of saplings, hoping no one would suspect any one being in a cemetery at this hour. Pearl hadn't thrown herself on Leon's grave but she was sitting on the ground talking to a bare stone less grave and Samantha wondered did she feel him, her son? She remembered trying hard to feel her father in his grave.

Time brought memories and doubts that she had pushed back in order to keep her mind focused on the shop and its customers, but now she could not hold them at bay. She had succumbed to the grief of a broken man's sorrow and now she must pay the price. They hadn't talked because she had nothing to say and he, she closed her eyes knowing he would revert to his old ways and taunt her for high standards. Foolishly she had begun to think those last week's there was hope for them beyond the magnetism so obvious when they touched. She had never felt such wonder or need with Blake; to be held in Lan King's arms was wonder and dread because she should curse the day she thought he changed.

Hearing the murmur of Pearl talking to her dead son, she reasoned she was not unlike Pearl. Her situation wasn't what she wanted any more than Pearl's need to be free, but then she was lying. She wanted Lan King but he was caught up in his world of vengeance toward all women because of his ex-wife. She was foolish, foolish to think he cared for her. Then there was Kristin, a name with no face. How quickly he had given up his words of truth and back slid into his world of emptiness.

Last night Amy had cried while they were on the phones. "I miss my daddy. I thought I was going to live with him, but Nan says she's sorry he sent me home, she doesn't know why. But I know he doesn't want me." Samantha felt a flush of anger speed through her system. How could he do that?

As though she had a built in timer, Pearl rose and walked to the car. Samantha backed down the narrow lane and headed home. They had entered city limits when the Police Station came into sight and Pearl said, "Stop here. I'm going in and see if I can get an ex-parte' against Jess, then I'm going to find Anne Marie. I simply cannot live my life in one room. How could I do that?" With those words she was out of the car hurrying up the sidewalk and within thirty minutes returned to say, "It's done and I ask them to find my Anne Marie."

"How does that work, Pearl. I don't understand." She peered into Pearl's changed countenance. The woman had made up her mind. "Aren't you afraid?"

"There's worse than fear, Samantha. I've thought and thought, cried and prayed, but I don't know where Anne Marie is and I've got to find her. She could end up living the same life I've led."

"But the ex parte', whatever you called it. What does that mean?"

"I was granted an ex parte' due to my being beaten. I guess they believed me based on Jess's record but for Anne Marie, Jess will have to respond and a judge will have to decide if there's due cause to find her and whether I get her back. They said I needed proof to prove my story to the judge, and ask did I have evidence or family to speak for me. Even though they knew, it gave me an opportunity to say I did not."

"But you have family. I met your mother and your sisters."

"I can't put them in danger. Jess would kill them. They've tried too many times and he turns the table on them. It's better I say there's no family. The Police have tackled with the Lassity's enough to leave it alone. I signed the papers even though I'm homeless, and I said I have no family to help."

Resolute, the two went to bed, each with their own thoughts but when morning dawned, Pearl was in the kitchen making coffee and breakfast was ready. "I'm going to help you in your shop today," she said. "I'm going to earn my keep."

Smiling, Samantha clapped her hands. "Bravo. I've wondered how we would do this, but today we will try. We are going to set an easel in that lighted corner, and hang several of your landscapes on the wall, we are going to make wine out of water, madam resident Artist. This is your debut."

The smile she wore due to Samantha's enthusiasm disappeared from Pearl's face as she became sober and tears welled in her eyes. "No one's ever thought I was worth anything." Wiping the tears away, she glanced around the shop. "Give me a list and I'll know what to do. I'll work my heart out for you."

By end of week they had sold all of Pearl's paintings. The shop was in excellent condition and Samantha was exuberant. Leading Pearl into her bedroom, she opened a large chest of drawers and began to pull several pieces of clothing from them. "These just may fit you, if they do; good wearing is all I can say." And there were the pictures she had taken, she handed them over to Pearl, "Now try on these clothes." She paused a moment and then said, "I hope you don't mind, but there's proof for your judge." But not realizing what Samantha was giving her, Pearl was caught up in the clothes handed to her,

"Not your style?" Pearl was pleased, her face glowing. "I've never had such finery. They're beautiful."

"My long lost mother sent them," Samantha explained. "You're her style. Not me. She failed me again."

"Tell me about your mother," Pearl said, but the shop door opened and a troop of ladies marched in.

❋ ❋ ❋ ❋ ❋

He waited until the people left. He had counted. He knew exactly how many were in there.

He was in throwing distance, according to his plan. Cupping his hands he hollered. "Pearl Lassity, this is your husband. I've come to take you home." He threw the first rock. It hit the door.

"Is that who I think it is?" Samantha was on her way to get the gun as Pearl nodded and began to wring her hands.

"I can go and there will be no problems."

"Come on out, honey. We need to go home, now, no need prolonging this." Jess fired a shot in the air.

"Jess Lassity, this is Samantha McKinsey. Your wife's employer. I have called the Police and I have a gun."

His laughter was bold, louder than when he called out. "But do you know how to use it?"

"See that branch hanging over you? Yeah, look up. Do you see that one gumball that's hanging on?" Samantha moved to the outer hall, where he could no longer hear her, but she had warned him. "Now I know why I didn't plug this hole," she muttered, moving a picture aside and then a metal plate. "If I'm lucky," she said, giving Pearl a do or die look as she placed the end of the rifle in the hole, shoved it through, steadied herself to see the gumball over the sight, closed one eye and pulled the trigger. The sound of the gun was loud as the gumball exploded and the limb remained intact.

Pearl watched from the front window, the Police Car came down the lane but Jess disappeared. Samantha was replacing the metal plate, hanging the picture and sliding the gun back over the door to her bedroom. Spasms of fear chased up and down Pearl's spine. She may have just signed her death warrant for sure. Jess Lassity scorned a woman who took charge and Samantha McKinsey just did.

CHAPTER 14

$\mathcal{A}$MY'S CALLS CONTINUED. "What did you do today, Samantha?"

"My question is, what did you do Miss Amy King?" They laughed together while Samantha listened. "So you don't know whether to draw a turkey or a picture of Santa Claus? Well, draw the one that makes you happy. That usually works. Have I seen your daddy? Well, no, I haven't. You haven't either? Maybe he's busy." Amy's voice was the wistful little girl she had been when Clarissa left. No child ever forgets their parent leaving, she thought. "I don't know what to say, Amy. He must be very busy because I know for a fact you are very special to him." Quiet for a moment, Amy finally replied. "Okay, Samantha, I love you." Samantha's heart ached. "I love you, too, Amy."

Tomorrow was church. It would be different. Pearl was going with her. Samantha wondered how Alice and Pearl would like each other. Life was becoming overwhelming. Amy floated in and out of her dreams, a little figure, sad and drawn trying to make the best of a situation she had not made. Awake, Samantha lay thinking of Amy, then of her own parents, an invitation for Clarissa to invade her dreams. "You turned me away, Samantha. You have been so unfair. Grow up." She tossed and turned all night and when morning come she would have stayed home from church but there was Pearl to consider.

It was Harvest Day, set aside each year after the crops were out for the agricultural area enabling the congregational members' better opportunity to give their tithe while a little extra money was in their pocket. *There shall be showers of blessing, showers of blessing of love.* The music was uplifting, the people sang their hearts out and thankfully the three sitting together knew every song. By the time the minister stood behind the pulpit each heart was either washed clean or waiting for absolution.

"Luke chapter six, verses thirty eight through forty two," the minister called out, leaning across the pulpit to stare them in the eye. "You may think this sermon is about giving but there's much much more to it. Not only is this a day to give your hard earned money but a day to give up your hard chosen view of others. Ask God to forgive you; that includes me, when we make assumption of other people's lives. We really don't know what our brother or sister suffers, now do we? Ours is an opinion. What is an opinion? The dictionary tells us it is a point of view, an attitude, a judgement. And who are we to judge? Do we like to be judged? Let us stand for the reading of the word."

"Give and it shall be given unto you; good measure, pressed down and shaken together and running over, shall men give into your bosom. For with the same measure that ye mete withal it shall be measured to you again. Jesus spoke a parable; Can the blind lead the blind? Shall they not both fall into the ditch? The disciple is not above his master, but every one that is perfect shall be as His master. And why beholdest the mote that is in thy brother's eye, but perceive not the beam that is in thine own eye? Either how canst thou say to thy brother, Brother, let me pull out the mote that is in thine eye, when thou thyself beholdest not the beam that is in thine own eye? Thou hypocrite, cast out first the beam out of thine own eye, and then shalt thou see clearly to pull out the mote that is in thy brother's eye."

"We could stop right there, but I'm going to give you the short version of what's important about these verses. I guarantee you; each of you will think I'm talking directly to you but as in my own case when I read this it is God speaking to each of us." He paused to study the scripture and then continued. "I don't think it's about money. I believe it is about attitude and forgiving others. Doesn't it remind you of the Golden Rule? Do unto others as you would have them do unto you? Otherwise, why would we be reading about the beam that is in our eye compared to the mote in our brother's eye?"

"In closing, think about your life, someone who has wronged you and you say, "Oh, no, I didn't do anything to them, it's all their fault. But where is the fault in that statement? Sometimes we don't know what's going on in our brother's world. Now let us stand." The music began as the pastor smiled and reminded the congregation, "First we reap for our Lord, human souls and then…" he laughed. "Then we'll ask you to empty your pockets. God bless you and bring you back is our prayer."

They declined invitation to join the church members in their Harvest dinner. Everyone was welcoming but the three gave each other an understanding look and left deciding on this Sunday, again, they would go to the local hamburger spot. Once they were seated, Alice asked, "What did you think of the sermon?"

Samantha grinned. "It covered a lot of territory, so what part, exactly, are you talking about?"

"The forgiving part and of course that's personal since Jade is definitely coming back to my house."

"That's interesting," Pearl was concentrating on opening a side salad. "How will that go?"

"Exactly." Alice gave a huff of built up air. "I have no idea."

"Maybe he's changed," Samantha offered. "By the way, how do you two know each other so well?"

"We were class mates," the two chorused. "Jade and Jess are a few years older. Except Jess played hookie more than he attended class." Pearl nodded in agreement. "About the forgiving I've been thinking about that, whether I could, ever since Jade asked to list his old address. It's like I'm picking up old baggage." She turned to Pearl. "So how's it going with Jess? Is he leaving you alone?" This time Pearl and Samantha exchanged glances with a roll of the eyes. Alice stared at the two. "Tell me everything."

"I'll give you the short version," Pearl said. "I was scared to death while Annie Oakley, here, got a gun."

Alice was shocked. "He came with a gun? And you had a gun, Samantha? What is this, Dodge?"

"How about your question concerning the forgiven part?" Samantha changed the subject of the gun. "I have my own agenda, on forgiveness." The two leaned forward. "Not that, I'm talking about my relationship with my mother."

"That can't be as bad as a husband who runs around on you," Alice offered.

"Or, threatens to kill you," Pearl added, softly. "There's always that hanging over your head?"

"Is that why you vied for the chair that faced the door?"

Pearl nodded, "Maybe we have missed the point of the sermon or maybe it's different for each of us."

"Sometimes," Samantha began, "I don't know what's going on in my mother's world, but after all these years its' easier to leave it alone than to do something about it."

Later, as they headed home, Pearl said, "Thank you, Samantha, for including me, today. It has been years since I've been so blessed. I never dreamed, back in high school I could fall into such a mess."

"I'm glad you were with us and it is nice that you and Alice already know each other. I just hope your husband doesn't take it upon himself to do something vile if he hears we were out together."

"He already knows, Samantha. The grapevine news in this community rivals our president's contacts."

That night as Samantha sat staring into the fireplace flames, Pearl excused herself to go to the room they had made for her, and furnished from the shop inventory. She was pleased with her surroundings. "It was a good day," she said, yawning. "I have the beginning of feeling peace in my heart."

Comforted by the warmth of the fire, her mind felt the loneliness of knowing she had decisions to make and for a moment her mind strayed to Lan, wondering what he filled his nights. Was the lady Amy described as beautiful always there and why against her own judgement had they experienced one night together when Leon was buried? Did he blame her for coming to grips with his wife's death when it was Leon's funeral that put everything into place and what about Amy? Did he never expect to take her needs more serious than his own?

They began decorating for Christmas; the barn took on an atmosphere of happiness with the red ribbons and snowmen she chose for accent. When Amy called, she ask, "would you like to come decorate with us on Saturday if your grandmother doesn't mind driving you over?" It was only seconds until Olivia was on the phone. "What do you think if I take her to church with me on Sunday and then bring her home that evening?" Amy was jubilant when she came back on the phone. "We will have fun, Amy. I can't wait to see you."

Saturday was full, Amy helped in the shop and when night came she and Samantha wore their long flannel gowns, ate popcorn and sat huddled together whispering about nothing in particular, satisfied.

The next morning they went to church as planned. Now the pastor's sermon was Christ love and hope for tomorrow. "Isn't that what we all long for?" He asked, leaning across the pulpit staring into their faces. The three women treated Amy to their favorite Sunday eating spot and made her feel special, but Alice and Pearl declined the invitation to join Amy's return home to her grandmother. Alice drove Pearl back to the barn and Samantha and Amy went on.

"Samantha, can I come to the children's Christmas Play with you?" She hadn't intended to go, but seeing the wistful look in Amy's eyes, she said, "Yes. But you mustn't let me forget when it is. I'll be busy in the shop, so I could forget, and your grandmother has to give her permission. "She will," Amy said, smiling. "Nana likes you."

"Where does time go and where are these women coming from?" Samantha whispered to Pearl in passing. The shop was alive with laughter and in the background the soft sound of Christmas carols. "I have begun to wonder if it's your special brand of eggnog, or the coffee you serve, because the coffee service is always empty." Pearl smiled. She had bloomed under Samantha's watchful eye. "Gracious, Pearl, you drive them crazy. Who knew you could create such a stir?" Soft laughter bubbled up from Pearl's chest. "Those wives will be watching their husbands," Samantha teased, "You have bloomed."

"I'm not sure it's me," Pearl replied. "Those single guys who drive their mother's over from Grandview keep asking if you have a husband and I tell them no, you're allergic to men." She stopped short, wheeling a huge box into the main room. "Are you saving yourself for Land King? Because if you are, I could put a word in for you. Believe it or not, Lan and I are pretty good friends and he needs a good woman. That's something he never had."

"Don't you dare speak to him about me?" Samantha's stubborn streak rose quickly. "I mean it."

"It must have been something pretty dire for the two of you to avoid each other like poison. I've been surprised he hasn't been around." Easing the wheels of the dolly onto the wood, Pearl wasn't watching Samantha. "Everyone speculates, you know, something happened." She waited. "Are you going to tell me?" Aware of Samantha's silence, she said, "I guess not. So, are we having company?" Her boss nodded.

It was the weekend and Amy was coming. She arrived to throw her arms around Samantha and then Pearl. "Where's your little girl?"

Amy asked, innocently. "You remember I played with her one time at Daddy's house." Samantha whisk Amy away to the big tree in the corner with the gingerbread house.

Pearl kept things to herself. The Police had found Anne Marie in a foster home. "You'll have to have a home and employment before you go to court and face the Judge," they said, "And proof your husband abused you would help in your case." Seeing she didn't understand, they said, "Do you have pictures of yourself after he beat you to show bruises or anything of that nature?" Sadly she nodded her head.

Samantha did not pry. Pearl would tell her what she wanted her to know, when she wanted her to know, matters of the heart ran deep. Her help was invaluable. A hard worker and a good person, Pearl was happy being included with Alice and Samantha on Sunday's. "This is a balm to my soul," she whispered once they were seated together although the sanctuary was filled to capacity. "I've not had a close friend since I graduated. When we first married, Jess was as good a man as I needed but when he started drinking the battering began. As time went on I lost say in everything and then when our daughter left," she paused, "leaving Anne Marie with us, it got worse. I didn't think it could, get worse, but it did." The sermon had been on brotherly love and Samantha thought it loosened the cobwebs in their souls. The three, little by little were piecing together knowledge and understanding of each other.

Amy was delighted when the children performed the Christmas Program. She watched each child say their part with a hunger of one wishing to be on stage with them and when the program ended with everyone joining in on the second verse to Jesus loves me, Amy's little voice sang straight from the heart as the three women clasp hands. There was truly a song in their hearts. Amy blessed their lives.

"Do you know why you are here?" The preacher had infinity for beginning his sermons with a question. He peered out into the congregation, his eyes seeming to pierce each person's soul. "You have found the scripture sinks into your heart, it touches that yearning you have to be the best person you can be. The prayers, the love and sharing, the caring you have for one another, brings healing in a cold world. The children have just sung Jesus Loves Me; those words are balm for broken hearts, the means to clear hearts and minds of unnecessary junk and to find the peace only He offers. As we enter the Holy Season, let your heart feel the anointing of His love. John three, sixteen, reminds us, For God so loved the world He gave his only begotten son, that whosoever believes in Him shall not perish but have ever lasting life." He paused; taking them in, his people; "whatever you do, let it be to His Glory as you accept His grace. Let us truly worship His Holy Name as we look toward the day of His birth."

Stress had robbed Samantha of sleep, her personal problem was ever in her mind but she found peace. Pearl's broken spirit rose up to find hope for tomorrow without having to look over her shoulder and Alice, with a tear in her eye, admitted she had fought within her spirit Jade's right to be forgiven, not by her rules but by the example of the Golden rule set before her by Christ himself. "Jade will be here, the day after Christmas," she said. "That means I can't be with you girls after church, unless you let him come too." Pearl and Samantha looked at each other. Alice laughed. "I feel the same way."

Samantha had the fleeting wonder, what would happen to Pearl in the future? Once she saved enough she would move to make a home for Anne Marie in order to meet the authorities requirements. Something else niggled at her mind, Jess had been too quiet and she feared what he was planning.

Interrupted by peals of laughter, Samantha set down the bowl of popcorn they planned to eat by the fireplace. Today they had come to Samantha's to enjoy Amy before she returned home, spreading a picnic lunch of sandwiches and chips, now they were finishing off before going separate ways. "Hey, what's going on, I don't want to miss the fun. I was popping corn in the kitchen."

"We were trying to put the star on top of the tree. Didn't you hear us singing Oh, Christmas Tree? We forgot the words and tried to make them up when it got out of hand, so we switched to Twinkle Twinkle Little Star." Alice waved the star in front of Samantha. The three had attached it to a long stick in order to reach the height but that hadn't worked either. "How does Oh, Christmas tree go, the lyrics?"

Samantha removed the cloth that covered the keyboard she'd had since childhood. Seeing Land play at Leon's funeral reminded her it was in storage. They were in full swing when Land King came pushing through the door, his eyes blazing and his mouth a straight line of displeasure. Their singing stopped, mid stanza. Amy not understanding his demeanor, ran to her father throwing her arms around his legs.

"What's she doing here?"

They heard Amy whimper as she moved back, her hand reaching as Samantha went down on her knees and pulled the child into her arms.

"Hello, Land," Alice stepped forward as though there was no awkward moment. "You were moving pretty fast there, friend. Were you in that great a hurry to see us?" She tried to smile. "Well, I think you scared Amy. So why don't you drop down, to her level," Alice practically hissed the last three words while smiling with her teeth clenched. "And make amends before Pearl and I take her outside to view the lights we strung around the barn door and that old wooden fence Grampa put up that refuses to fall down?" And though her mouth smiled, Alice was warning him he'd regret the day he was born if he didn't make amends with Amy.

He was caught between a rock and a hard place. "I didn't know you were here, Amy girl." A tear had welled up in Amy's eye to slide down her cheek as Land came down on one knee and opened his arms. Amy forgot the hurt she'd felt. To her delight, he crushed her to his body. "I'm sorry, baby girl, Daddy forgot his manners. I practically ran up the path, I guess I lost them on the way."

Amy's giggle was almost a sob. "You can't lose manners, Daddy." Her eyes were luminous. "It's all right."

The women were thinking if that doesn't touch his soul, nothing will, and they were relieved when he kissed her cheek. "Can I go with Alice and Pearl to see the lights, Daddy?" He nodded and in the blink of an eye the room cleared with Land and Samantha standing staring at each other.

"Why do you have my daughter?" His voice was not that of a friend.

"We are friends."

"Yeah," He rolled his eyes to a squint. "How did that happen?"

Samantha thought for a moment. "I guess it happened the day your mother stopped in."

"My mother?" He stormed around the room like a man who had come unglued. "Don't you have a mother of your own? Oh, wait," his eyes smoldered, "Did you or someone else tell me you and your mother are estranged. No doubt you are making all kinds of conclusions about me and my child when you can't stand your own mother. That's crazy. Wasn't the situation comparable, my wife died, your daddy died? Didn't you tell me that? Now," he thundered, "Leave my mother and my child alone."

"Why are you so mean?" She'd had enough questions. It was her time. "Are you crazy, frightening a child, your own daughter, as you just did? And for what reason to tell me you disagree with the daughter you neglect and ignore coming to be with friends that love her and enjoy her company? Are you crazy, honorable Land King?" She practically spat at him. "Isn't that what you want people to think, you neglect your child but you are honorable?"

"Oh, no you don't. Don't switch the tables on me. Crazy?" He gave his terrible laugh. "Crazy is shooting over Jess Lassity's head. Don't you know he will be back and without a thought to sanity he will rip your throat open and take his wife home where she belongs and torture her until she dies? All it takes is one hopeless drunken night. Now that's crazy."

"If he's that crazy, tell me why wonderful upright hardworking men of this community allow it, men like the honorable Land King?" She paced around him. Whose crazy now, she thought, circling him like a cougar ready to pounce. "You come in here to tell me she should be with him? Where she belongs? Is that how it is with women? Put them in a cage and let them out when you want something?" She was screaming. "Is that who you are? Thank God you have stayed away so I could forget you." Tears were streaming down her face. "Thank God I didn't fall for you. With your way of thinking I'd have to kill myself to escape your sadistic ways." Now she was backing him to the door. "You're surprised I feel this way? This disgust for a man, who asks for your help, acts grateful and then drops you like a hot potato. Haven't you heard, Mr. King? A woman scorned is something to deal with. Now, get out."

"I'm taking my daughter." His eyes matched hers, fire and blood pounding behind his temples.

Slamming the door, he came face to face with Alice. "That woman is a hell cat," he hissed. "What's wrong with her? We never have a decent conversation. We fight."

"Do you always storm through the door, Lan?"

He drew himself up. "That's beneath you, Alice. I'm taking my daughter."

"Lan." Alice reached out to touch him. He shoved her aside.

"Don't mess with me, Alice. She's mine and I'm taking her."

"And will you return her to your mother's later and explain why? And do you need her clothes, or shall we leave them here." Alice voice ground on smooth and unrelenting. "Then there's the popcorn we promised; just a Sunday afternoon after church with a little girl who is loved and loves back so generously. Can you top that, Lan?"

Some amount of reasoning was returning to his fogged brain. "I came here because I broke out in sweat when I heard about the gun incident. You know it's only time until Jess comes for Pearl." He wiped a hand across his face. "Lord, Alice, if he killed his daughter, what makes anyone think he won't again?"

Alice remained silent. She saw a troubled soul, a man fighting over one thing while thinking another.

"Why do we fight, Alice?"

"Maybe because you both care and you are both denying it."

"Who could care about that...that...fire angel? She's a spitfire," he corrected. "I've never met a woman so stubborn."

"No, Lan, you met a woman who betrayed you and now you're taking it out on one who loves you."

"What?" He stared at Alice. "You have got to be kidding. She hates me."

"You mean because she stands up to you and you've been burned and you're just not going to take it anymore? You need to think this through; you destroy something good because of the past."

"You're playing with me now, girl. Don't go there. I can't get three feet with that spitfire."

"For what it's worth, I believe she thinks you have another woman." Alice laughed. "Now that you've calmed down, do you want Amy's clothes or are you leaving her?" She turned to motion down the lane to Pearl that it was safe to bring Amy back.

"Why would she think that, Alice? Another woman?" His expression changed to a contrite medium. "I ask her to call me, that was after Leon's funeral. We, uh disagreed on something then, too."

"She did call, Lan, a woman answered. Amy and Samantha talk every night and Amy chatted about this woman. Beautiful she said, daddy's woman."

"I'll leave Amy," Lan was backing away. "I had no right to pull authority on that." So that was it, Amy told Samantha about Kirsten. This one was on him. It was time he left, what else could he do?

"Lan," Alice hollered after him. "Don't forget to tell Amy goodbye. Give her a hug and a kiss."

Samantha was sitting on the foot stool in front of the fire, her hair falling around her face as she stared at the floor. Amy's first thought was to run and throw her arms around Samantha. "Are you crying?" She pushed Samantha's hair out of the way. "I cry sometimes. Daddy made me cry when I couldn't stay with him. Is that what's wrong, you can't stay with him either?"

Crawling up on Samantha's lap, Amy nestled close, her head on Samantha's shoulder, her thumb in her mouth. "Why Amy, I didn't know you sucked your thumb." Amy grinned up at Samantha. "I did, too, when I was little when something made me scared but you know what? When I started to school, I noticed my friend's teeth were a little straighter than mine and I didn't want to be different."

"Nana says my teeth will stick out like the front of a train if I'm not careful. Do you think so?"

"Let me think, hmmm. Well, that is possible, but I don't think they'll be that big."

Amy giggled. "Do you feel better now? Daddy hurts my feelings, too, but you feel better?"

"I do. And it is time to take you home. Your Nana will be walking the floor, looking out the window and wondering where we are."

"I'm driving," Pearl said. "Alice and I decided we wanted to ride home with Amy. Isn't that special?"

While Amy made one last inspection of the Christmas tree, the gingerbread house and all the snow men, Samantha confided. "I am so sad Amy heard her dad and me fighting."

"She didn't. Pearl and I walked Amy down to the end of the lane to see the sign. Did you know Lan had the sign installed?"

"No." That bit of news caught her breath. "How do you know that? I thought Carlos did."

"Amy said when they pass by her daddy says, "See Samantha's sign? I had that sign put up."

"Why didn't he tell me? I thought it was Carlos," her voice broke, "I even said as much to Lan."

"Honey," Alice eyes were somber as she placed a hand on Samantha's shoulders. "Lan's wife dying in a compromised manner, being with the doctor, Lan was like a man going into a deep sleep. He was angry, he ignored his child. I will say he concentrated on the farm, it saved him by all the hard work, but now, he's coming out of that sleep. If you want him, you're going to have to give up some of your idealistic ways, reach out to him, Samantha on his level. My advice is only if you want him. If you don't, do what you please and ignore what I've said, but take my word for this, he won't be around for long and God is not going to drop him in your lap. The two of you need counseling, to figure out why you fight so quickly, because a fool could see there's a passion between the two of you, you're drawn to each other like magnets." She saw Samantha's expression changing. "Okay, so it's time to take Amy home. I get it."

Amy and Samantha sat in the back. Cuddled close, Samantha read the Night Before Christmas to Amy.

"What do you want for Christmas?" Amy whispered. "I want my daddy to come to Nana's and spend all day with us."

"You don't want a doll or a new bicycle or anything like that?"

"No, I just want Daddy and popcorn and hot chocolate and read the Christmas story. Could you come read the story to us, Samantha, just like now?"

"I don't think I should intrude, sweetheart. That's a day for family."

Amy snuggled closer, pulling Samantha's hands against her chest. "I think you would be the best family, ever." Yawning, Amy's eyes closed and she was drifting into sleep. "I love you, Samantha."

"Love you, too," Samantha whispered.

"You two can't whisper worth a darn," Alice complained from the front. "We heard all that."

"Why weren't you two talking, can't you think of anything to say and not listen to others?" Samantha's voice was cranky. "It's been a day of rude awakenings. On the one hand Alice Jessup Collier, you tell me one thing…but I think I experienced quite another. Did you ever see a man run a way so fast?"

Alice and Pearl laughed so hard, Samantha shuddered. "I thought you were my friends."

❀ ❀ ❀ ❀ ❀

"Nana, Nana, I saw daddy." Amy bounced happily into her grandmother's arms. "I had fun, Nana."

"Take your suitcase into your room, and put things away," Olivia instructed, all the while her own face glowing that Amy was home. To the three, she said, "I miss the little scamp, but you see the time with you all has been a real enjoyment and with me…well, it's just us."

"What would you do without her?" Alice sat across from Olivia. She had motioned them into her living room. Pearl and Samantha sat on the sofa; they were in a cozy circle for easy conversation.

"I would miss her terribly but sometimes love has to let go, doesn't it? I do love that child but she needs young parents and what if I got sick. Landon hardly comes around to check on us, I doubt he would suddenly be of the nature to help me through an illness and I'm at that age." She smiled. "The Lord has been good to me. At this age, knock on wood; I'm in pretty good health. But I still worry about Amy's future." For a moment her face shone concern. "Amy said she saw her daddy. Was my son there?"

Waiting for Samantha to answer, the two were silent, eyes on her. "Well, yes, he dropped in but he didn't stay long. Alice and Pearl were walking with Amy to see the lights they had put up."

"Is he well?"

"Yes," they said in unison and then chuckled together. "He was in his usual form, Olivia," Alice offered.

"That would be angry about something." Olivia shook her head. "No need to ask why, I know my boy."

"Yes, you do," Alice laughed, rising. "We need to be going. We just wanted to ride home with Amy."

Amy came back into the room in time to give them all a hug, but it was Samantha received the best and a big whisper in the ear. "Can I come again, soon? Will you come Christmas to Nana's for dinner?"

Samantha pursed her lips, a bit embarrassed as she met Olivia's eyes. "We…" She began as Olivia interrupted.

"I think that's a marvelous suggestion. Why don't the three of you join us for Christmas dinner?"

CHAPTER 15

THEY WOULD NEVER know. The more he thought about it, the more he planned to do something about it. He had been watching Jess Lassity. He knew when the man left his house, where he went and when he returned. He thought about calling in some of the others that had due cause to avoid Jess Lassity when he was drunk, but the fewer people knew the better it all would be.

It was midnight. He couldn't sleep. A man kept his own demons to himself. Maybe it was her backing him to the door. Little spit fire. He found the bottle tucked in the back of the cabinet and wondered why? No one would look through a man's cabinet. No one darkened his door anyway. It was cold outside, but still he needed to take a drive and he'd check on old Jess. See if he was home.

He sit in the drove of bramble and bush, lights off in the truck, watching Lassity's house. Come out; come out, wherever you are. He wondered, was it true? Did the man kill his own kid? She'd disappeared mighty quick. Pearl was battered and bruised, that night, was it four years, holding an infant in her arms, when he heard footsteps on the porch and a whimper he'd looked out the window as head lights passed by the lane. He listened. There it was again. A

173

whimper and what? What was that, it sounded like a baby's cry? He knew the sound. His own sound like that, except he hadn't kept her either had he? His mother rescued her before he had a thought of what to do with her.

Another secret. He'd never have done anything about that either, except for Pearl. He'd opened the door. There she stood in little more than a thin nightgown, against the cold holding an infant in her arms, Anne Marie she later told him. What's wrong? He'd pulled her into the room, off the bare planks of a porch Lila thought she wanted. He beat me, she said and I can't find Rose Elaine. She's fifteen now, had this baby; her daddy said he'd kill her and drown the baby like a pup. Can we stay here tonight? But you got a momma, he'd said, I'll take you to her. No, no, then Jess will blame her. She started to leave. Come back. You can stay. He'd given her and the baby his room, the only bed there was in a house that wasn't a home. But before she left they'd put a bed for her in the room she called Amy's room.

She'd found milk in the refrigerator for the baby. The baby cried all night. It was the wrong kind of milk. Next day he'd driven to Grandview, with a list, bought the things she told him the baby needed. Went to the Nest because he didn't know where else they had baby clothes and they'd fixed him up with a gift anyone would be proud to receive. Pearl stayed two months and then Jess found her. They'd never thought of sleeping together. She was a woman needing a place to take care of a baby. He was a man whose wife ran away with a doctor and they both died. He and Pearl were both recuperating from evil.

The sound of Jess's old truck woke him from his reverie, he hadn't slept but he'd gotten lost in the memories. Now he followed Jess. Where was he going? All the way through town, toward Samantha's barn; it was Karma, he decided, the man's fate from just cause, whether past or present. He cut the engine. The most ridiculous thought occurred to him, he was a target, dressed as he was, from behind the seat of the truck he pulled out a pair of old coveralls, a dull green in color, and slipped into them, and to further protect himself from the floorboard he found a round metal container of black salve for injuries the men used until they could get to a doctor. It took only minutes to cover his face, and arms and the back of his neck. Then he started a soft padding run toward where he thought Jess would hide the truck. As he thought; in the moonlight he saw the glint of something metal, a gun no doubt. He better be prepared for the worst, mangy and angular, Jess Lassity had the strength of a devil, his reputation as a mad man kept the locals from tackling him. He must be mad to think he could overcome the man. There he was, to the right of the old oak where old man Jessup strung up deer in the fall, and straight in line with Samantha's barn, his gun sight focused on the upper level. Why? Did he think he could take them out, one at a time and he was starting there? Then he saw the ammunition. Jess had it lined up, and that was no ordinary gun. Karma, their fate, Pearl's and Samantha's as surely as his own was being decided. Best he could tell in the darkness, it was more of a Gatling gun, capable of firing a continuous round of ammo. It would splinter the boards of the barn on the way to target. The moon came out from behind the clouds as he stepped on a twig and it broke beneath his foot, the sound could have been a canon to Jess Lassity's ears. He turned quickly to see a rabbit hop from behind the bush.

If he was to overtake Lassity, he'd have to move fast and be swift in punishment. Lassity would have no qualms about gutting him if he could get to the knife he wore proudly on his left leg. Yeah, he was left handed, even in school he'd used either, ambidextrous, near perfection, when he threw a ball or someone he didn't like. He'd been at Jess's mercy a few times, himself. Just as Jess concentrated on and finalized his target, he lunged, caught the man off-guard. Retaliation was as quickly done as he'd imagined. It was taking everything he possessed to beat the man to a pulp; it didn't come quick nor without pain. "Who are you?" Lassity's voice was filled with gravel as he fought back, "Get the hell off me, you can't win."

Win, he had, and he'd driven him to the place they called Hells Gate, a place few knew about, owned by some wealthy family from another country. For a price he worked them until he broke their spirit. It was worth the fee, to see Lassity confined receiving the treatment he'd lashed out on his family. "Did you kill your daughter?" No, he screamed. "Where is she?" I shipped her off to…" He couldn't remember. They lashed his back and it was hard to watch even if he was getting what he deserved. "Did you kill your son?" Lassity began to cry. I didn't mean to. Maybe, all I did was turn the valve. "Valve." The knob. "What if the authorities had looked into it?" Lassity shook until he finally fell in a heap in the floor. "Leave him," the voice said. "Keep the payments coming at the agreed price." You won't kill him? The laughter was something he would never forget. "He will wish we had." Give me your word you won't kill him but you will rehabilitate him for society where he may even fit in as a gentleman. "He will be gentle." The laughter followed him to his truck. They were unseen, but they would know who he was.

He'd had to stay in for a week, until the bruises over his eyes left. He'd taped his rib cage. No one saw him walk with the limp. Lassity had tried to pull his leg out of socket. He'd never spoke a word but Lassity had spewed a continuous line of threat. "I'll kill you. Someone will know I'm gone. You can't win." Six months, they'd said and he will be a different man. "We'll train him to your society's customs. He may become your best friend." He doubted that, two of the six months were almost over. He went in the dark of night to Hell's Gate, spoke into the wired gates intercom. I'm out of money, he said. Release him. Let's see if your method is any good. You promise a lot. If you are as good as you say, two months should do. Next he went to Jess's house, threw the rot out of the refrigerator, got rid of the beer cans and whiskey bottles. When the house was clean of Jess Lassity's old habits, he locked the door and drove away. In a couple of days he heard the buzz, Jess Lassity was back in the area.

"Life is just one hurdle after another." Pearl examined the plaque. "For a man, no doubt."

"What did you say?" Samantha glanced up from jotting an order in the book.

"I was reading the new plaques, and that's what it says. Life is just one hurdle after another." Pearl grinned, "I think it's for someone who plays sports since it shows a guy jumping over...."

"Yeah," Samantha went back to the books, "If it was for a woman, she'd be wearing a hooped skirt." She hadn't had time to go through the mail the last couple of days, now an envelope caught her eye. "When did this mail come in?" She sniffled, "It is one more hurdle, I think I'm taking cold or already have one."

"Let's see, today's Wednesday, I'd say Monday. Why, is something wrong?"

"I hope not." She recognized her mother's casual sling of handwriting. "I think it's from my mother." Hesitant, she opened it and scanned the first page. *"Hello, darling, after all these years I have an urgent need to correspond. Samantha, I want to come back to the area. You are there and Tessia. She tells me you have your own shop. Perhaps I could sell my jewelry line there. I do hope you would allow it. I grew up there, Samantha and I long to see you. I know we've had difficulties in the past, but surely we've grown beyond them. Walt is retiring and I want to be near you and Tessia."* Samantha lay the letter down, and headed toward the door as Alice arrived.

"What's wrong? One look at you and I know something has happened. You aren't well, are you?"

"I have to get some air." She was trying to find her coat, when Alice slipped out of hers and wrapped it around her shoulders. "There's a letter on top of the bills, you and Pearl read it and you'll understand."

"Sam," Alice expression was full of worry. "Surely it can't be that bad. But if you must go outside, button up we can't have you sick on top of whatever the problem is...."

"No, I guess not." Samantha slipped out the door. She walked, tears sliding down her cheeks, and it was cold, but she felt suffocated and struggling for air, so she walked to the end of the pasture, past Jade's poor excuse of failure, mounds covered with the straggles of dirt she'd managed to rake over with the little tractor that was not much more than a lawn mower. Had the neighborhood laughed at her, saying she thought she was playing big game, when all the while everywhere she turned something had needed fixing. And today, why was she feeling so under the weather. She'd tried not to say anything.

She felt defeated. Clarissa always took the wind out of her. How could she allow her mother to steal everything from her? She sat on the old wooden fence, her back to the shop. Alice had volunteered for the day. Shoppers from the neighboring towns would be in to pick up orders and browse. They seemed to like the atmosphere of the barn, and Pearl's brand of hot chocolate. Though her heart ached and she didn't know what to do about Clarissa, away from the busyness she could muse, and as she did her breathing became better, her heart beat settled and she began to feel calm. No one could do anything about Clarissa. Taking a deep breath, she felt of her forehead. It felt hot. She must have walked too fast.

"A penny for your thoughts." She knew his voice and felt the warmth of his body as Lan stepped up behind her. "You're liable to stick to this old fence, girl. That's what we call sitting on a rail." His chin came down on her shoulder, the wide brimmed cowboy hat sitting on both their heads for a moment. "What's going on?" His arms were around her. In spite of circumstance she felt a moment of protectiveness.

"Did they call you?"

"Nobody called me, I was checking a well in the far field, I got a call the cover was off it, and I saw you walking. So what's troubling you?"

"My mother, the one you insulted me about, once when we were fighting. I think you told me to leave your mother alone and make amends with my own."

Although he tightened in a reflex of sorts, his voice was still warm when he replied. "I'm sorry for that. Now what's wrong with your mother?"

"She wants to come back to Riverdale, not to visit, but to live."

"Didn't you tell me a child needs its mother?"

She tried to shrug away. "I'm no child. Isn't my being twenty four a bit late?"

He was at a loss for words. "I'm a pretty sad fellow to ask any question." His lips were on her neck just below the ear. "It's cold as blue blazes, why are you out in this, you could get sick. But then again," there was a smile in his voice if that was possible, "I like this." He kissed her there, a butterfly kiss. She released a sigh that must have signaled her thought to him that this was nice, comforting. For some miscalculated reason his own primal instincts checked in. "I could think of a better way to ease both our pain."

Frustrated Samantha shrugged away. "I thought you were through with hitting on me." She slid off the fence, to find his hands on her shoulders turning her to face him. He shrugged his hands in the air.

"I'm not hitting on you. I apologize for being a man." His eyes were studying her almost lazy, almost amused. "You are a thorn in my side. Everywhere I turn I think of you and I never understand why we irritate each other so quickly. I seem to have such a need for you, you interrupt my sleep. I dream of you."

This was new to her. They hadn't fought. He almost comforted her. Every time she thought she could trust him, something had destroyed that confidence. "I don't know what to say? This thing with my mother weighs heavily on me." She swallowed, before she broke into tears. "And you, why won't you let Amy live with you if that's what she wants? I don't know anything, anymore. Olivia would be alone, so maybe God knows what's best in all of it."

"Think on it. I'm trying. Alice gave me a talk, if I don't shape up I'll lose you completely. Did you really mention leaving Riverdale after working so hard on the barn and it looks like your business is prospering?"

She studied him. Was this the same Land King that burst through doors, tore off door handles and ignored her for weeks on end? She was tired. Vulnerable. God only knew she wondered if she'd have to leave, had she said as much to Alice. "I've got to get back," she said. "Thank you for stopping."

"That sounds lame," he replied. "Like I'm your mail man or something. I stopped because I saw you and I cared you were out in thirty degree weather wearing a light coat, nothing on your head and your shoes look wet. Come on. I'm driving you home. Someone needs to take care of you, might as well be me."

"I need to see my grandmother." She spoke without thought, the words popping out of her mouth.

"We can do that, too." Lan led her to his truck, wondering she hadn't heard the sound as he drove up. "I'll direct the heat down to your feet. That will dry your shoes. Aren't you cold?" He peered down on her subdued form. "This is not like you to let our words go by. Are you all right?"

"I think I've got a cold. I didn't feel so well this morning, but not bad enough to worry over. Please, don't." A fleeting memory caught her. "Didn't you tell me you didn't want Tessia to know we are acquainted?"

"I ask you to let me have the time to rent your grandmother's land on my own, without her associating us as friends. I wanted to do it on my own merit."

"When will that happen? Maybe you shouldn't take me there."

"It's all right. She contacted me and I have the contract there on the dash, ready to deliver. She chose me."

"Then it's all right if you take me to see her. I didn't pick up my cell, would you call Alice and tell her and Pearl I'm with you and they are welcome to run the shop as they see fit." Exhausted, she closed her eyes and let the warmth of the heat go through her body. A few miles down the road she was asleep.

✻ ✻ ✻ ✻ ✻

"John Granger recommends you, Mr. King." Tessia smiled. "It's always good to have an old friend to call up and ask his opinion." She stretched out a hand to seal the deal. "I like your handshake, young man. It's firm. Too many just give you a limp touch as though they're afraid to exert much energy."

"Thank you, Mrs. Cleveland."

"Now, Samantha, come over here." Tessia studied her granddaughter. "You seem a little off your feed, girl. Are you getting enough rest or is that shop running you ragged?" She patted the seat beside her and motioned for Lan to sit opposite. Almost clucking like a hen she was peering with a worried expression into Samantha's face. "Tell me, what's going on. You rode over here with Mr. King, I'm sure you can spit out whatever is bothering you. You just don't seem yourself."

Putting both hands to her face, Samantha thread her fingers through her hair. "I may be tired, Grandmother and maybe I'm taking a cold, I don't know, but its Clarissa. I know she has been in touch with you."

"Yes, she has. Clarissa wants to come home." Pausing, Tessia glanced across at Lan.

"I can leave, Mrs. Cleveland, so you two can talk privately."

"Oh, no, that's not necessary," Tessia flipped her hand in the air. "It's how to phrase what I intend to say to this one, when she and her mother haven't gotten along in a dozen years or so." Her attention was drawn back to Samantha. "Granddaughter," she had addressed Samantha in those terms possibly twice before in their lives. Samantha sat up straighter. "Samantha, I believe Clarissa has become wiser and I know her heart aches to see you and be with you."

Feeling betrayed, tears filled Samantha's eyes. "If you haven't seen her, how could you arrive at that understanding? I just don't get it. My Mother leaves my Dad, your son, and you are so willing to forgive her, when she left us behind and moved on?" Samantha's head went up in a defiant gesture. "I can't be so generous, Tessia." Anger flashed in her eyes. "She will come in all Miss Lady caring, she will ask for forgiveness which you will grant and then she will sashay right back to wherever she comes from. I know because I've seen it before." She stood to pace across the room, returning to look her grandmother in the eye and then moved away, again. "Why can't she stay where she is and not open old wounds?"

"Because," Tessia replied in a soft voice, "with age, comes reckoning and that reckoning showed her, she did wrong by her child and she wants to make right."

"Well, I don't want it."

"Come here." Tessia waited. Samantha was like a hurt child, indeed she was one. "Come here." Samantha came close, finally to kneel by her grandmother's knee. Tessia stroked her hair, "You have to turn loose the anger towards your mother. You are entering a new season of life; no one knows what lies ahead. But you are going to need your mother, if for nothing but the encouragement a mother brings."

Samantha laughed a bitter laugh. "My mother was never around to encourage me."

"But it's never too late." She held Samantha's hand, rubbing her own over the top, again and again. "If we could turn back time, dear, we would. Your parent's would never have divorced to put you through this." She stared across the room until the thought in her mind formed. "Mr. King," she said, "If you have children…I don't believe I ask that question of you, but if you do, it is always best parents stay together, unless something happens that causes a crack, so to speak, in the foundation that is irreparable."

"I have a four year old," Mrs. Cleveland, "that lives with my mother but I'll consider your advice."

Samantha settled more comfortable in front of her grandmother. "Your hands are cold, Tessia. Are you all right?" She peered up into her grandmother's face. "You have to take care of yourself. I need you." She saw her grandmother's expression, "No, don't tell me Clarissa will help me, I won't allow it." They left shortly thereafter and though she didn't know why, Samantha felt concern, usually Tessia had a beautiful ivory glow to her skin but tonight it was gray, especially around her cheeks and mouth.

The phone rang around ten the next morning. "Mrs. McKinsey, this is Doctor Kinder, your grandmother is my patient. I'm not aware if she told you, she needs a pacemaker." Samantha was too shocked to ask questions, immediately. "If you are in agreement we will set up a day and time to do this."

"Shouldn't she have a second opinion? I mean, it may be a simple procedure to you, but I'm thinking of her age." Some little personal thought niggled through her mind of her own problem.

"I am the second opinion, Mrs. McKinsey."

"I'm not married," she managed to squeeze into the conversation but I should be she thought, hanging up the shop phone. It was later, she realized she had not waited for the doctor to conclude his call, something wasn't just right, but she couldn't put a finger on it, instead she had slumped to the floor and when her eyes reopened she was on her bed staring up at Lan King. "What are you doing here?"

"Pearl couldn't get you out of the floor by herself and just by chance she had seen me in the North field. She called me, and here I am. Hi." He grinned. "You slept all the way home, last night. It's kind of hard talking to a sleeping gal."

"Gal?" She rolled her eyes, "and just by chance you were in the neighborhood? I doubt it." She pushed back the light throw they had laid over her. "Really, I don't have time for this. Did the customers see me in the floor?" Embarrassment caused her cheeks to turn rosey.

"Thankfully, the customer had just walked out to her car. Together we carried you in here. Well," he grinned, "I lied, I carried you in. By then, Pearl had a customer."

"Well, I'm ready to go back to work, if you don't mind."

"Hmmm." He pointed to the clock. "I hate to tell you this, but its closing time. You have slept all day."

Now her cheeks really flushed. "Why did you two let me sleep?" She was pushing herself into a sitting position, one foot on the floor and then the other, rising up, anger smattering little darts through her head. "I can't stay in bed just because I thought of Tessia having surgery and evidently I panic..."

"She's down, again," Lan called to Pearl. "Pearl can you come in here." Pearl came running. "I'm not bringing her around, Pearl." His voice was anxious and his expression beyond troubled. "Open the door, Pearl; I'm headed to the hospital." He gathered her up, tucked the throw around her and was on his way to the truck. "Sam, don't do this to me." He crossed the floor, down the steps and had her in the passenger side of the truck in a flash. Pearl was right behind him. She pushed Samantha's cell to him as he passed going around the truck. "Her info is all listed, in notes, if you need it. There's no password."

"Let me try this, it's an old fashioned way," She stuck a damp cloth below Samantha's nose, Samantha gasp and came around but fainting twice in one day seemed to have addled her usual independence.

"What is that?" He was revving the motor. "I'm taking her on. Can't you come later, after you close the shop?" Pearl stepped away from the truck, tucked the cloth with ammonia into her pocket and watched the truck speeding down the lane. She had not remembered to tell him there were trucks making late delivery. She tried to call Alice but there was no answer. When the rush of everything having to be seen after settled, it came to her that Alice had met Kimberly for a football game and to meet Kimberly's new boyfriend. She called Samantha's phone and Lan answered, "No need to come, Pearl, everything's okay," he said, except it wasn't. *Please God, he whispered, I'm sorry I left you, be with her now.*

After an examination in the emergency room, they had taken Samantha to another area of the hospital, thrusting on him a clipboard with a paper full of questions to answer. First he looked at it with complete surprise that they would ask that of him, and then he remembered Pearl saying the information was in her cell under notes. He decided to give it a try, clicking the phone several times and there it was. She had listed a medication for allergies to bee stings, it gave her age, date of birth, next of kin, Clarissa McKinsey something, she had erased the last name, with a line typed beneath, do not call unless I'm dead, followed by Contessia Cleveland, do not call unless you are putting me on a respirator. There was no personal physician listed. Her Insurance company and her own identification number were entered plus her Social Security number. He found he was able to fill out the form and hand to the nurse when she returned. She read the information, smiled, patted his hand and was gone.

It was when the doctor came, patted him on the shoulder and said, "Mr. McKinsey, were you aware your wife was pregnant?" He had sputtered and scrambled around in his chair if that were possible, realizing it was possible he had fallen asleep and needed time to grasp the doctor's words, finally to say, "How long?" The doctor gave him a strange look and said, "First trimester," he saw Land's puzzled expression, thinking he didn't understand, "within the first three months."

"I know what that means." A cold sweat broke out on Lan's brow, that would be around the time her ex-boyfriend came and she said she sent him packin'. Something cold rushed through his veins. He should leave. He wasn't the one to be with her at the hospital. Then who? Her grandmother wouldn't think much of him if he called her and it could be Samantha wouldn't want her to know. Alice was with Kimberly and Pearl couldn't be out in open places, due to Jess's hunting her down.

"We have sedated her but you can go on back." The doctor was mistaking his hesitance for sadness. "These things happen. Something wasn't right, maybe there's been stress or her stamina wasn't ready to carry a baby full term. Do you want to tell her," He waited for Land to speak, "or shall I?"

"This is all confidential, isn't it?" Land struggled a bit wondering how to explain without explaining anything, "I mean, she won't want people to know. She's reserved like that, wanting no sympathy..."

"I see." But the doctor didn't see at all and Land and he both knew that. "Only on her record, sir." The doctor left, going to confer with the nurse until she motioned for him to follow her.

She was sleeping, dark hair fanned out on the pillow, she looked small beneath the sheets, long eyelashes shadowing her cheeks, fragile, he thought, this fiery little angel who kept secrets while evidently her nerves were raw, why else did she hold everything so close to her chest and why did they fight every time they were together? It didn't matter now. She was soiled goods, not because he hadn't made mistakes but because she lied, everything about her was a lie, just like Lila. How could he have had a moment's hope? They were all alike. For the second time he had learned a lesson. With his jaw clamped so tight his teeth felt they might chip, he promised himself there would never be a third.

"I can bring a cot in for you," the nurse said. "Or," she seemed to be deciding whether to confide something, "Or, a lot of our husbands when this happens lie down by their wife and hold her.

It seems to be a comfort and get them both through the first hours. We just look the other way."

He took the chair by the window. "I'll be fine here and if she needs me…" He let the words dangle in air. He hadn't realized how much he cared. No, that was a lie. He pulled himself straight into the fact that he had fallen for her, rejected, neglected and hungered for her. He had made contact with an old friend and he and Kristin had laughed over the fact they were more like brother and sister, or at most cousins and neither marriage nor tryst would ever happen between them. Kristin had enjoyed Amy but declared she was never having a child and have to give up her freedom to wipe noses and change diapers. In the end she had returned to Mississippi, her job teaching at the University, and they hadn't touched base since. Now, facing his own demons it seemed he should call on Samantha's God to watch over her.

"You can turn on the television, if you like," the nurse commented on one of her trips to check on Samantha. He had nodded, settling more into his angry stupor, proud of his ability to sit rather than pace like a raging bull which was how he felt inside. The shock and numbness had left him hours earlier. The drone of the machines should have made him sleepy, but he was as awake as if he'd slept all day. Around midnight, she whimpered. The nurse came immediately. "We have her on monitor," she whispered. "We are concerned because she was running a temp and now it is coming back up."

"We never really know, she thought she was taking cold and had used over the counter meds. By chance she developed a urinary infection, which explains the fainting, but I doubt she had enough of the cold medicines in her to cause the UTI, that often happens with a pregnancy, so she really can't blame herself." She was adjusting something about the IV as she spoke, "but we do have to keep the temp down." She glanced his way. "Does she always sleep this sound? I mean she doesn't hear a thing."

"Yeah, she does."

"Then let me ask, has she been doing any unusual type of work, maybe lifting heavy objects or out in the sun through the summer months? She could have had this UTI awhile and not known it was this serious." Finished, she prepared to leave the room. "Is she an active person or more sedentary?"

For the first time, he forgot his own anger toward Samantha. "Let's just say she leaps tall buildings."

The next hour, Samantha's skin was hot to the touch and she was freezing. The nurse gave Land a questioning glance. Reluctant, he slipped off his boots, lay down behind Samantha and put his arms around her. Evidently the fix was for both of them; he awakened feeling the buzz of Samantha's phone in his pant pocket. Leaving the bed, he draped the extra sheet over her, and hurried down the hall to talk with Pearl. "Yeah," he said. "She has a UTI, whatever that is. I suspect they'll release her come morning." He listened. "I'll tell her you are opening the shop and taking care of business. Thanks, Pearl."

It was six o'clock. The nurses were preparing for the new shift. He found Samantha's nurse. "I've got men working," he explained. "Call me if you think she'll be dismissed and I'll come quickly." The nurse nodded, saying she would relay the message to the new shift and give them his phone number.

She awoke alone, to lay there listening to the pad of feet up and down the hall. The clock on the wall said eleven. An IV hung over the head of the bed, a potty chair by one side and she could tell by the attachments she was being monitored. Fresh pain washed through her mind. She had spent days trying to decide what she must do, stay and face the public, leave the business to someone Carlos would send and take leave of absence, or continue hoping the one thing that would make it all right would happen. Now nothing mattered. She knew her temperature had risen in the night, but had she imagined someone held her or was that a figment of her imagination? No one was there, she guessed the latter.

Trying to remember, from her befuddled state of mind upon being admitted she kept thinking they said her electro lights were messed up, she had an ITU, but nothing confused the admission she was pregnant. She felt of her stomach. She couldn't tell, yet, something inside her said otherwise. A woman would know, wouldn't they? But she had not known a UTI could take one down so quickly and what was it about her electro lights? Was her potassium too low or too high? A tear escaped to run down her cheek. Then another and another, until her body shook quietly beneath the sheet and the sob came broken, almost muted as she put a fist to her lips and the tears stained the sheet as they fell to the side of her face, dripping through her hair, alone, always alone. Daddy. I need you. She wasn't aware where he came from, but someone stepped from behind the head of the bed, where the window looked out onto the parking lot, and strong arms went around her, drawing her up, pulling her into the curve of those wonderful arms as he pressed his hand against her cheek, drawing up, smoothing her hair and letting her cry. In his own way, he asked of the Lord he had turned from to love her and bring comfort.

Lan didn't know why he returned. He hadn't meant to. It was his intention to work with the men, leave the hospital problems behind, and abandon her as she had him for another, except he had no one. The men were doing shop work on the machinery; he could leave and leave he did, barreling down the road, driving eighty plus, not caring if a trooper saw him, he would have to catch him first if he wanted him that bad and he'd returned to the hospital, unshaven in the same clothes, to stand staring out the window. What would he say to her? She loved another and he had no right, anyway. He had brought Kristin in and Amy had told her and he was never going to apologize. But something made him return. For that one time, perhaps, when love had been sweet and they had given to each other, but she had given more because she had set principles and he had scorned them. Either his way or nothing, she had to prove her love and still she had given of herself to comfort him. For that one time, he would return and for a brief second he wondered that he had beaten himself down thinking after all the procrastinating he had done she had not been with another man to find out now she had. Now her sobs told the pain of losing. Without anyone telling her, she knew. Her hurt spilled out in quietness, but he heard her heart ache and felt the loss. It could have been his baby and what would he have done then? His heart was calloused. For this moment, he cared, kissed her brow and smoothed her hair. He had cared enough to ask God to help her through, knowing she would have wanted that.

She was released from the hospital near two o'clock. Her eyes were large with misery. She seemed to crumble to the seat. They had given her a blanket. Now she wrapped it around her body, shivering, whether from cold or private thoughts, he wasn't sure. It didn't seem right to take her back to the busy shop where people would ask question and if they didn't ask they would stare at her and wonder.

"I'm taking you to my house, until night." She didn't reply, just looked at him. "Is there anything you would like to have to eat? The nurse said you didn't touch your dinner." She heard his stomach growl. "Get whatever you feel you want." She turned her head to stare out the window. There were no words, no sobbing, nothing on the way to his house, except he reached to where her hand lay on the seat, between them. "Your hands are cold. Are you?" She shook her head and still he held her hand.

He pulled in, as far as the drive allowed, going around to open the door for her. She stepped onto the truck's step, but her legs buckled and he caught her as she seemed to swarm, trying to set her body down, seeming not to know how. Lifting her up into his arms, he managed to shut the truck door behind them, cover the distance to the porch and get inside. "You've lost weight," he murmured, "you don't feel much heavier than Amy."

By passing the living room with its solitary piece of furniture, he carried her down the hall, past the dining room, his bedroom, and into a room she'd not seen before. A large white rocking chair presided over the empty space. He settled into the chair, drew her close to his body and began to rock. What happened after this day would mean days of not seeing each other and in the end possibly she would be with her ex-boyfriend or maybe someone else in the community. Today, he held her close.

Four o'clock the room grew dim and by six o'clock darkness claimed the windows. "Time to go home," he whispered. "No one will be around to ask questions. Pearl has your room ready and," his eyes held hers, "she seemed to think you needed chicken soup."

There was almost a smile on his face. "I take it you had rather not go into discussion over your night in the hospital."

"No, if possible we will leave it as a UTI and get through this best we can." She saw the flex of his jaw. "Thank you. I'm sorry if this inconvenienced you." She was hesitant and then asked, "Did I imagine it, or did you hold me last night?"

"I did. I don't know why but it seemed appropriate to do so, this afternoon, also." She stood, the long dress she wore for the holiday flare of the shop, falling softly to the floor. "I wonder what they thought of my dress?" Her lips quivered. "I didn't feel like explaining anything."

"The nurse thought I was your husband and I didn't set her straight. Someone laundered your dress."

"Oh?"

"I left it alone, though I wondered if you would have preferred your ex to have been with you making decisions."

"That's a strange thing to say." She hushed. She wasn't up to the usual banter. "Whose blanket is this?"

"You had a blanket. I left with you rather hastily. Then the hospital gave you another."

Pearl tried to keep the dinner time together in a light mood but the undercurrents were nearly bogging them down, each lost in thoughts of their own. Oblivious to the lack of conversation, they ate the chicken soup, she cleared the table and Samantha went immediately to her room. Land at a loss of what was expected of him asked, "Pearl, is it too cold hearted if I head on home?" She shook her head and he left without telling Samantha goodbye.

Peeping in, before retiring for the evening, Pearl found Samantha asleep but there were traces of tears on her cheeks. What hurt, she wondered, were those two piling on each other now but she would never ask. In her room, she counted the money she received for the framed oils. Her heart felt a happy catch. A little more and she could find her own place and bring Anne Marie home. Surely by then, Land and Samantha would have realized they loved each other and make plans for their future, too.

Three days until Christmas Eve. Amy called Samantha, "You are coming, aren't you? Nana's expecting you, Miss Pearl and Miss Alice. She says Daddy can come if he behaves himself." Amy laughed joyously. Samantha bit her lip. Lan hadn't called, nor dropped in. She was at an impasse, whether to go to his mother's for Christmas dinner, or not. Was he that displeased to know about the miscarriage? Then why had he held her so tenderly and took her to his house after leaving the hospital when she felt so vulnerable? Nothing made sense. She finally voiced her misgivings. "Maybe I shouldn't go."

Alice settled it all. "Of course you are going. It was a UTI. That could happen to any one of us. Your gifts are wrapped and we need the frivolity, it's Christmas, for Heaven's Sakes, Samantha, if you hadn't gotten the raw end of the deal, you'd be bustin' with enthusiasm, so come on, let's have a good one."

"What about Jade?" Pearl stopped the threading of a ribbon through the outer edges of a lace doily she was applying in finishing the last gift to be wrapped for Samantha's customer. "If he's released."

"Jade?" Alice grinned. "I already called Olivia and asked if he can come. She was very gracious, said yes to bring him; she had seen Land the day before and she was cheerful over something she gave him and also she had a little task that required two strong men. It was nice to see her and Landon getting along."

"Does that imply her son intends to have Christmas dinner with his mother and child? And a task?" Pearl had worked for Landon King; she knew his mind was an intricate tool." She laughed. "Usually if Land is fighting with one person he fights with everyone. Jess thought I was struck on him but we were merely friends. If he can forget himself, Landon King makes a good friend, but I do wonder what Olivia's task is?"

"All I know she said she had a little task that needed two good strong men, "Alice glanced at Samantha, then to Pearl, "Pearl, our girl here is looking strangely pale."

CHAPTER 16

"SAM, YOU GOTTA stop this fainting stuff, it scares me to death. I'm never sure you're going to come out of it." Alice had picked up a magazine and was on her knees in front of Samantha fanning furiously.

"I just can't help it. I get clammy hot and then the sweating starts and next thing I know I'm waking up."

"Waking up is good. Are you sure there's not more wrong with you than a UTI? It troubles me."

"I can't stand this. Promise you won't let what I tell you go beyond this room." Tears welled in her eyes. "I'm so embarrassed. It isn't something you want to tell anyone and I never intended for it to happen."

Suddenly quiet, Alice and Pearl stared hard at Samantha. "Do you have cancer?"

"No." She shield her face from her friends. "I had a miscarriage."

"Nooo." Pearl was by her side immediately. "Are you all right, really all right. That's serious stuff."

Alice set back on her heels, her hands on Sam's knees. "It didn't feel right, Hon. It was too heavy." She sighed, all the while shaking her head. "I just knew there was more, but I never suspected this. I'm assuming its Lan's but I never knew you two were that close, you were always fighting, and yet I felt the passion and I wanted to shake you both." Pulling herself up, she sat on the other side of Samantha. "What now?"

"That's just it. I never know how he feels. He comes on strong, then he backs off and doesn't speak to me for days. What woman wants someone that does that?" They were looking at her strangely. "You're thinking me." Tears gushed out of her eyes and she swiped a hand across her face. "When your boy's funeral ended, Pearl, for some strange reason Lan stopped by his house when he was driving me back. He was upset, for you, for Jess and over Leon dying young." She took a deep breath. "I don't think he had ever allowed himself to grieve the death of his wife. I think all of a sudden it hit him."

"Lila," Alice said softly, nodding. "He was always too angry and pushing it back, never facing it. Go on."

"He cried. Broken sobs. I had only heard that kind of crying once before, from my dad when my mother left him and I've never forgotten." She tried to pull herself away from that memory. "I was sitting by him on that one piece of furniture he has in the living room."

"The sofa," Pearl offered. "Yes, they never furnished the room, just the sofa came. Lila didn't care."

"Yes, and I laid my hand on his back, sad to see him so upset," She sighed, her whole body trembling. "It's not easy to lay myself bare, like this, I don't know why it happened, other than we were two sad people locked in a moment of time and ...." She sat there tears dripping on her hands, her friends staring at each other. "All I can think, I was tired of the turmoil and at that moment he wasn't angry, just sad."

"Land is aware of this, Samantha?" Alice voice held a note of mystery. "He does know you lost the baby?" Samantha was nodding. "But did the doctor or someone explain to him? They didn't leave him thinking it was a urinary infection?"

"No, I don't think so. No." She had to think back and her mind was in turmoil. "He held me. I was so disappointed. Although it wasn't something I planned, it's still traumatic to think a little life was lost, even if it was two months, and yet the doctor said to me, "I'm sorry, it seems you have had a miscarriage." Now she sobbed, openly distraught again. "I had refused him so many times, I always felt he was trying to get even with women as a whole for what his wife had done and I wasn't responsible for her sins. Just mine," she finished softly. "If we were ever together I wanted it because he loved me."

"He does love you, Samantha," Alice hugged her tight against her body. "He is just so stubborn. He would cut off his nose to spite his face. Ever since Lila, he's like an attack dog, always on guard, never lets down. I wondered if he was hitting on you…and even if he was, that's another of his misguided faults. You are a fever in his brain and he won't admit he has to do his part if there's ever going to be anything between you."

She was wiping her nose on the sleeve of her dress and for a moment the three laughed. "He said something strange, it was strange to me. 'Maybe you would have rather had your ex -boyfriend with you.' Samantha shuddered. "Why would he hold me so loving, and then mention someone I have no use for and haven't seen in months except that time Blake stopped by and I sent him away. He went back to Michigan, as I understand. He didn't spend time alone with me."

Alice rose up and began to pace around the room. "This is crazy, but sometimes men are crazy and drive women crazy. There's no explaining Landon King. He is his own man. I can tell you one thing. If he loves, he loves with all his heart."

"Then he doesn't love me." With that Samantha let out a huge sigh, rose up and wiped her face furiously. "I trust you two to not tell anyone. I couldn't bear it if my grandmother heard about this."

The phone rang and Samantha reached for it. She was able to say, "Hello,' and then the voice at the other end of the line took over. "Samantha, it's Mom. We are in Grandview." She gave Samantha time to reply but when nothing happened, she continued. "I think you should come to the hospital. Tessia was having trouble breathing, so Walt and I brought her in. She's asking for you."

"My mother is in Grandview, at the hospital with Tessia."

"Shall we go with you?"

"No, you have to work tomorrow, I'll be fine. But I do have to change." She started toward her room, stopped and came back to hug them. "Thanks. I didn't mean to burden you with my problems…"

"She doesn't need to be alone, does she?" The two stared at each other. "What should we do?"

"Pearl, will you be all right, by yourself?" Alice drew her shoulders together. "They say trouble comes in threes, first Sam, and then her mother calls and now her grandmother's having problems, but I'm more concerned about you, what if Jess shows up? Some story is going around that he's back."

"It's inevitable, Alice. You and I know he hasn't been drunk enough yet. I'm thinking Christmas eve or day, even, and then he won't have anyone with him to beat on. He's biding his time."

"Just as you are, but you're no match for him. You never have been." Alice was picking up her purse, "There's a bad feeling in all of this. I feel anxious; how about you?" She read Pearl's expression. "Yeah."

Passing by Wilson's Supply, she saw Lan's truck ready to pull onto the highway. He honked and waved her in. "What's going on?" She studied him, wondering what he really knew. "Hey, what's going on?"

"You're asking?" Her conscience waved a red flag. "What do you know about Samantha going to the hospital?"

He shrugged. "Some kind of urinary infection; I was the one took her in."

"Is that all?" She was out of the jeep, standing looking up into his face. "Tell me, now, is that all?" A sudden spurt of anger raced through her thoughts. "Tell me what you know, Landon King, or so help me I'll wipe our friendship off the face of this earth."

Flushed, his eyes narrowed, he spat the words at her. "She told you, didn't she? She had a miscarriage." Fresh anger made him slap the dash. "Yeah, I bet she made you promise not to tell and here you are, is that right? And you're coming after me, but it wasn't mine! Your sweet little fire angel friend got herself knocked up by her old boyfriend; all the while she's playing' cutesy with me. So, what did I do?" He laughed a bitter hollow sound, "I stuck around like a true gentleman, held her hand, filled out her form, let the doctor think I was the daddy, all to save whatever piece of respectability she might have left."

Alice hit the side of his truck with the palm of her hand. "You fool. Did you even think to count how far back the ex-boyfriend came through, and did he spend the night? No she sent him packin'. But you, now you made love to her, what, two months ago, after Leon Lassity's funeral." Alice examined her hand, and then looked at his truck. She'd left a dent all right, but she might have broken a bone, too. "No, we don't tell our deepest secrets unless we're sick to death trying to figure something out, and that's where she is, you big lug. Now she's driving to Grandview, her mother's there for some reason and has taken Tessia Cleveland in with breathing problems. Now let's see what you're really made of Lan King." With that, Alice flounced back to her vehicle, slammed the door, squealed the tires in leaving and never looked back.

He was half a mind to race down the road, tail end her, just to teach her a lesson. Who does she think she is? Without a pause he compared Alice's words to what the doctor said in the first *trimester*, and they'd made love after Leon's funeral. He pulled out his phone, checked something he'd made note of that day concerning the farm and the time fell in place. *It was him.* He knew she didn't look at any other man because he was jealous and he'd watched to see. His heart felt like it fell into his stomach. He felt sick. No wonder she'd looked fragile. She was. She'd been handling the situation all by herself. No doubt she was considering leaving the business to one of her boss's other employees, maybe she would leave for good, knowing no one would take care of it as she was doing. It was her baby. That phrase jolted him back to the now of things. They'd made a baby together but something had gone wrong, maybe hard work, maybe stress, some of it he caused.

Now, what was he to do? He pulled onto the highway, the opposite direction of his home, toward Samantha's barn and he caught her at the end of the lane and blocked her exit. She stopped.

He pulled alongside, rolled down his window and stared at her. "Get in. I'm taking you wherever you're goin."

"No." As weak as she felt she wasn't ready for any person to tell her what she could or could not do.

"Samanatha, just tell me where you are going, get in the truck and let me drive you. Please."

She reconsidered. She really wasn't feeling up to par. "My grandmother is in the hospital."

He nodded. "Okay, I'm taking you." If she hesitated, he didn't notice, his thoughts were so scattered nothing made sense. His imperfect little world had become decidedly more complicated the last few minutes. "How're you feeling?" He asked as she slid into the seat and when she didn't answer, he said, "Uh huh, I figured as much." They didn't have anything to say to each other or else, too much to say to each other, he surmised, but when they arrived at the hospital and he parked the truck, she came alive.

"Just how do I explain you're bringing me? How do I introduce you?" She glared. "My mother is here."

"Tell them I'm your boyfriend, nah," he could see that didn't go over. "Tell them I'm your landlord. Hmm, that's a lie, isn't it? Just tell them I'm a friend. You don't like that either?" He considered their situation, "give me a minute here, I'm thinking." She was walking toward the entrance to the hospital. "I tell you what; tell them I'm the guy you are going to marry if we can get our wits together."

She turned on him. "Do you really think that's funny? I've been through hell the last two months and now I'm upset and disappointed and," frustrated, she wiped angrily at the tears that had slid down her cheeks, "and I'm sad and you dare say that to me when my grandmother is in the hospital." She said grandmother with such agony, she saw him roll his eyes and stop dead still in the middle of the parking lot, his shoulders slumped forward. She wanted to slap him. How dare he be so uncaring, so frivolous with her when she'd suffered such loss? "I don't know what they will think of you, I don't care. I need to face my mother with calm and yet here I stand looking at the one person who could have made things right and you didn't."

She was a pitiful mess. It hit him all of a sudden. He loved this mixed up, stubborn as a bull dog girl that had defied him in every way a woman could, proving him wrong about the barn, the land around it, and that she could build a business from nothing in the middle of nowhere, and people would come. He felt some of her animosity toward himself. So how did he make her see the difference in him? He advanced. Put his arms around her, bent his head, even as she struggled, and he kissed her, bruising her lips and his, too, he supposed, until she went limp in his arms and opening one eye, with their lips still engaged he said, "You aren't fainting are you?" That's when she bit him. "Oww," he yelped, tasting blood.

"I'll introduce myself," he said, wiping the blood off his lip, with his right hand, his left holding tightly to hers. "I'm in the process of trying to make things right. This is all new to me. So just bear with me. I'm bound to get something right before long."

They found Clarissa and her husband in the waiting room. Clarissa came to meet her, placing a kiss on her cheek. "How are you darling?" Her attention turned to Lan. "Who's this?"

Before Samantha could say a word, "Landon King, Ma'am. I'll be farming Mrs. Cleveland's land next year and Samantha and I are more than friends, wouldn't you say, Sam? We may get married one day."

"Really?" Clarissa smiled, patting his arm; it seemed to Samantha, sympathetically. "Welcome to the family." Then she hugged Samantha. "I couldn't be happier for you."

"Mother, he hasn't proposed, so don't start planning my wedding. How is grandmother?"

"They decided to do surgery, tonight. I don't know if it's an emergency procedure or if the surgeon was on hand and they decided not to delay; they told us to wait here and when there's something to tell they will find us." She led Samantha to where Walt was sitting. He stood taking her hands into his own.

"Hello, Samantha." His smile was genuine; evidently he held no hard feelings and eight years had passed. He listened to her introduction of Land, "Just call me Walt; first names are always easier to remember." He and Land sat in chairs facing each other as Clarissa pulled Samantha aside to question her about Tessia's last month of not feeling well and they could hear the discussion.

"Where are you staying, Mother?"

"We are at the Inn, but Tessia has graciously offered use of her home, since she is registered at the Nursing Home, presently. She said she was there to let her get her bearings and not have daily duties, do you think that's what's behind her admitting herself?" There was concern in Clarissa's voice. "And we wouldn't take up space in her home without your approval, Samantha." Clarissa left the question hanging between them. "What do you think?"

"Why would it matter what I think about your staying in Grandmother's home?"

"Because, should she die, dear, it belongs to you; in fact the papers are already in your name. She told me."

"That sounds so final. I don't even want to think about losing her. Not now." Samantha shrugged impatiently. "Stay there if you wish. It doesn't matter to me. I think if the pace maker makes a difference she will return to her home. We could talk to Mary and I'm sure Mary would check on her daily." The question remained. Clarissa was waiting. "If you were there, it would be easier for her, too."

Clarissa hugged her again. "Mother you don't have to hug me. That's not our relationship and you know it." She saw sadness flit across her mother's face. "I don't mean that harshly," and even as she spoke she thought of the baby she would have liked to hold and one day hug and her heart softened. "Give me time, Mother."

"I think there's a promise in those words, darling," Clarissa whispered. "When you are ready; I've missed you. There's never been a day I didn't think of you and say a prayer for your well-being."

"Do you pray, Mother?" Samantha studied her mother's face. "I always wondered if you prayed, or had any thought about me, by the time I was in college I let go, somewhat..."her words died off, "but I still wondered."

"I pray, darling. Walt and I had to make peace with leaving our families behind in order to be together. Had we not found peace through learning more about God and his forgiveness, I think we would both have fallen by the wayside." Her attention was drawn to a young lady crying as she entered the room.

Obviously a family followed; it seemed in overhearing the conversation, a young man injured in an automobile accident was now fighting for his life and they were rerouted from the Emergency Room to be near where the surgery was taking place. "Let us pray," a young man stood, placing his bible under arm, in order to hold hands with the group. "Father, God," he began, "Let us ask your forgiveness as we come boldly before your throne requesting life for our loved one, who is son, husband, young daddy and dear friend and church member to each of us as we join our hearts and prayers, Lord, that whatever the obstacle, whatever his need, Lord that you will bless the surgeon as they work with his body, using the skill you have provided, the knowledge that comes only from you and the healing power you have given through the blood of your son who died on the cross that we might have life and have life more abundantly. Lord, God, our Heavenly Father we ask that even now as we speak the tables are turning, the life that the doctors fear has been snuffed out with only a short time to exist, Lord, take that time table away and grant healing in Your name. Bless the members of this family Lord as we wait, and increase their faith, as we ask for mercy, for it is in your gracious heavenly name that we ask. Amen."

The four had bowed their head, listening to the young man praying, assuming he was a pastor to the church where the young man attended and that the young woman so terribly distraught and softly crying must be wife to the young man in the accident. Lost in his own thoughts, Lan considered the omnipotence that the Lord they all served could be called upon wherever one sat, whatever the situation and he wondered that on the previous day he and Samantha had not called on anyone, and yet in his own feeble attempt he had ask the Lord to watch over Samantha, not knowing at that time how dire the need was or that her life and his was connected.

Samantha had heard the person praying saying the patient was a young daddy. In her mind she could see a baby as a mother was leaning over a crib preparing to pick him up. The baby smiled and then went limp. It was as near a bad dream as the one she had suffered alone in the darkness that first night. Raised since twelve, by a single father, she struggled to remember Clarissa being the mother who cuddled her, whispered calm or taught her something new each day. Being a mother was part of her own dream, but being a wife to a man who loved her was first, in all of her dreams for the future when she was growing from child to a young woman, Samantha had dreamed someday a man would love her and never leave her. In the last twenty four hours she had reconciled herself to waiting and it might take years. Possibly never. Tears smarted, and she blinked quickly, his teasing had hurt her miserably. Why would he do that?

It was Christmas eve, the last sale of the day was made, customers left with gaily wrapped packages and Pearl was preparing to clean up her own decorated corner that housed the hot chocolate stored out of sight in a huge thermos and the crystal punch bowl Samantha had brought from her grandmother's house. "This will be my best memory of working here, Sam. You just gave me full reign to see after your customers with something to drink and something to nibble on. There's nothing but a crumb left on this cookie plate. Hot chocolate's all gone and the punch," she paused, "Lets' just say it no longer resembles punch, what few dribbles are left." She raised the lid on the insulated pitcher she used to pour the hot chocolate into cups. "Might be a cup and a half here, you want to split it?"

Samantha eased down into the director chair no one had bought. "I'm glad we still have a place to sit."

"Did you over-do?" Pearl placed a cup in her hand. "There, you go, it's still hot."

"Oh, it's good. Who told you about slipping chocolate curls into it after its poured into the cup?"

"My daughter." Pearl seemed to look into the past. "She was a wonderful girl, but when she got pregnant, Jess couldn't handle it. It's been five years now I've not seen her." Sadness worked its way across her face, "But come February, Sam, I think I'll have enough money to move out and make a home for me and Anne Marie, God willing. Maybe we will move away. California, maybe."

"I'll miss you." Samantha sighed. "Who will sit with me and Alice at church? Who will sing in that wonderful alto voice?"

"Oh, my goodness, have you been listening to me sing?" Embarrassed, Pearl covered her face. "I declare, can't a girl even praise her Lord?"

"What do you think the Lord thinks about me, Pearl?"

"As Alice would say, Honey I think he loves you." She sighed, sitting across from Samantha on a knee high wooden box full of candles, each hole providing individual space. "You know, this could be used to store bottles, like a wine cellar, couldn't it?"

Samantha laughed, "Do you drink much wine?"

"Well, no, none actually but you know, what about for the bathroom, roll up the towels…"

"Sounds good to me, now answer the question? It bothers me. I've talked to the Lord about it."

"Then it don't matter what anyone else thinks, does it? That's between you, the Lord and Landon King."

"What does he have to do with it?" Samantha flushed. "I mean, I know he did but now that it's over, why would you say that?" She had a flash back of him with Clarissa, Walt and her grandmother.

"I need to mind my own business and let you handle yours. I don't know why I said that, I got all I can handle, there's always something in the back of my mind saying watch over your shoulder, girl, and I do." She had that far away look in her eye again. "Something about Christmas makes a person think a situation is better than it really is, makes us lose focus. I can almost remember the good days with Jess." She shook her head. "The Lord knows I better turn loose that because the last five years there was nothing good. Now I'm asking where is he that he hasn't come back around to kill me or take me home."

"Would you go?" Samantha leaned forward. "I've told myself to turn completely loose of any misconception there's even a remote chance Landon King and I have a future. Time has proven…"

Pearl's smile spread across her face. "I wouldn't discount Landon King's intentions, if I were you. I told you, I know him. He had a lot of baggage to turn loose of and its taken four years for that to happen. If you hadn't come along it might have been another four."

"Riverdale or Grandview, for that matter are not void of young women that would fall for him."

"Don't you get it, Samantha," Pearl's voice was low and mysterious, in the dimming light she reminded Samantha of a mystical being, always wearing those headbands that set off her oval face, dusky eyes and full lips. "If God had wanted Landon King to fall for one of those available women, it would have happened but he didn't, you were supposed to show up here, work your fingers to the bone to make him notice what a fine person you are, and in the meantime he found it hard to keep his hands off of you." She grinned, "Now I'm not sayin' that was part of God's plan, Lan was just bein' a man and he found your independence enticing." She saw a flash of something in Samantha's eyes, "That's what I mean, girl. Lan King can't keep his hands off of you, because he's drawn to you like a magnet and you are him, you just got better control of those emotions that happen between a man and a woman."

"Lord have mercy." Samantha stood up. "You start out telling me about God's plan and end up spewing something else. If that were true, certain people could not go out into public places."

"It's called love, Sam. Land is just starved for your attention and has mistaken it for lust. He'll get hold of the problem and when he does he will make a fine husband."

"If you know him so well, why didn't you marry him? I can tell you for us it would be on a wing and a prayer. You understand that? I can't comprehend thinking something might work when I know it won't."

Pearl's laughter rolled through the room. "To answer your first question, I had Jess, remember?"

"Was he as, let me rephrase that, was your Jess as enticing as you think Land King is?"

"I don't know," Pearl replied. "But I don't think it's over between you and Land and I think God is going to bless you both. As for me, it's hard to leave Jess behind. I'd feel sorry for him, if it wasn't for the fact he nearly beat me to death a couple of times. I always prayed to God, asking him to change that man." The smile was gone, now she looked sad. "But it was as if God tried to tell me, Jess has to do that, himself."

"And you don't think he can or will?"

"Nothing's impossible with the Lord, Sam. Haven't we been hearing that every Sunday? Look at Alice, all of a sudden without even knowing it she is sprucing up the nest, fixing Jade a room and looking forward to him coming home. Of course, Kimberly will be home for Christmas and that will keep them in line."

Samantha reached for the ringing phone. "It's Tessia," she told Pearl. "Hi, how are you feeling?"

"I'll be going home the day after Christmas." Tessia was quiet for a moment. "Do you understand what I'm saying?" Samantha held the phone, staring down as though bad news had been delivered. "Sam?"

"I was registering that. I believe you are going home, to your home, where Clarissa and Walt are staying." Her voice gave away her concern. "You want me to give you a granddaughter's blessing."

"Yes," Tessia's voice sounded troubled. "Is that all right with you?"

"It's good if that is what you want, Grandmother."

They were both quiet. "I don't want to hurt you, Samantha, but I've always loved Clarissa. She's the daughter I never had."

"I know." What about me? Samantha was thinking how the two loved each other and their history was not hers. "If you are up to it, I'll come see you tomorrow evening late."

"Could you come around five, dear?" Tessia gave an embarrassed laugh of sorts. "I know it's foolish, but John Granger and his lady friend are coming around four. I think I know the woman, but I'm not certain. He tells me she is younger than him, he's eighty two you remember, but it seems he wants my blessing."

She hung up the phone. At first she thought she was being passed over by Clarissa and Walt, but John Granger's lady friend? Evidently it wasn't Olivia, how could she host a dinner and be at the Nursing Home by four? That schedule would tire a young woman. That thought led to wondering if Lan would be present at his mother's table. Finding the box of chocolates she had set aside for Olivia, she decided to add one of the fine lace scarves new to the season and intended for spring wear. For Amy, she had ordered a set of paints and brushes and all kinds of pencils. Then it was time to see to her own personal needs, her nails were split from wrapping gifts for others, her hair…she glanced in the mirror in passing. What she saw was a sad young woman who presently didn't know where her place was in the world; and she wondered after all Pearl had been through how it was that she now exuded confidence in herself enough to have laid plans for the future. Merry Christmas, Samantha, she thought, and her hand came to rest on the Bible opened to the Christmas story that lay before the nativity scene that sat under the mirror. Soon, another year would end and she would say it was much like the ones before, but the words burned in her memory, *IT came to pass in those days.* Nothing's impossible with God.

Pearl came out of the bathroom. "Are you okay, Sam?" She had her bath and her hair was wet.

"I think so, considering everything and it being Christmas Eve."

"I know the feeling."

"Would you go back, Pearl?" She knew Pearl understood the question, but she added, "Home?'

Pulling the towel around her shoulders, Pearl closed her eyes to give the question thought. "I don't know, Sam. I did love Jess in the first years of our life together, but lately I've been thinking, to escape the beatings I'll have to take myself and Anna Marie to another part of the country."

"That said and not needing discussion, what are you wearing to Olivia's?"

"I was thinking that maroon set you gave me of your mother's, the big legged pants and the tapered tunic top. It has that abstract scarf with all the good colors in it, to brighten it up for the occasion." She fluffed her hair, "and what about you?"

"It's either the light gray or the red dress with the sweetheart neckline." Samantha sighed heavily. "I've been procrastinating all by myself this afternoon, thinking, maybe I wouldn't go but then that would upset Amy and Olivia might question why?"

"Oh, Sam, I want you to go. I wouldn't even have the invitation if not for you."

Laughing, Samantha reminded her, "You have known this family since you were a kid, don't say that."

"My families poor, Sam. Land's family has always had something more than my folks."

"They don't seem the type to look at your bank statement before they look at you."

"No, they're not. Olivia's been really good to me two different times in life. I respect her."

"Well, right now I think I shall shower and maybe wash some of these cobwebs out of my head."

Grinning, Pearl started toward the bedroom, "Thank you, Sam, you have saved my life."

"Thank you for being such a hard worker and keeping a part of my life sane when I am completely ignoring it. Now, I've got to get a shower before I take an all-night nap right here on this chaise lounge."

✳ ✳ ✳ ✳ ✳

Christmas morning, the two had coffee together and then each went to their own room to dress. "You look ravishing," Samantha complimented Pearl, who was studying her quite openly.

"You look pale. What's going on?" Pearl saw that Samantha was still in her long flannel nightgown. "I can tell something wrong, so you just as well tell me. Where do you hurt?"

"Really? You can tell? I'm off my feed, a little. My stomach is hurting. It's like the kind we got when we were kids." Hurrying back into the bedroom, she looked askiance at the bathroom door. "Honestly, what is it about my having a stomach ache, besides the little darting pains; I think I'm all right." Then a pain hit and she went scurrying back to the bathroom. When she returned to the living area, Alice had joined Pearl. "I don't think I can go. I guess my immune system is down and I'm going to take everything that comes along. I can't explain this overwhelming weariness I feel today. Maybe I could come later."

"Are you sure? We want you along with us. As you can see, Jade hasn't arrived home yet. No Jade."

"It's these pains. I'm not sure what they are trying to tell me. Possibly nothing but stay home." She tried to smile but the effort was too much. "Go, and if this lets up I'll be there, hug Olivia and Amy for me."

※ ※ ※ ※ ※

"Surprise. Surprise." Land was there, helping his mother by setting the table with the white china plates on a red table cloth. "Merry Christmas,' he greeted them, "Where's Samantha?"

Alice explained. "She's a bit under the weather." She saw Amy's shoulders droop.

"How's that?" He kept an eye on his mother, making sure she didn't hear from the kitchen.

"Tummy ache," she said, "Occasional sharp pains. She hasn't let up since she arrived home."

"Something tickled his memory but he couldn't pull it up; it was something the doctor said. "Watch her in the next few days that she doesn't get any pains. Having a miscarriage is one thing, but hemorrhaging or even a possible blood clot is something else." Handing Alice the napkins, he said, "Here, you go, Alice I'll let you finish, for some reason I feel an uneasiness about Samantha, I think I'll go get her."

"Mother....Mother," Olivia met him in the doorway to the kitchen. "Mother, I'm going back for Samantha." She smiled agreement. He stooped to lift up Amy. "I'll bring her back, how's that?"

"He's pretty calm, for Landon King," Pearl quipped, "And setting the table for you, Olivia?"

"He can be wonderful, if he wants," Olivia agreed, "but on the other hand, he can be quite confusing." She opened the oven door, stooping to peer in. "There, my girls, is a twenty some pound bird and it's baking beautifully." Closing the door, she said to them, "I pray Samantha is well and will return with Lan." She didn't miss the glance the two gave each other.

Pretending whatever was happening inside her body was not so bad was almost more than she could manage. It was the pain in her back that worried her, like a heavy menstrual period magnified. Pulling the covers aside, she laid a thick towel doubled and folded again over the sheet; it was coming on stronger now. She lay there too tired to think what was happening and then she felt the sticky flow coming from her body, and if anything her back pain was escalating. Now she tried to think whether to go to the hospital or find the heat pad and lanquish in her own misery. Could she drive herself to the hospital? Anxiety made her legs weak as if they would buckle and not hold her up to walk to the car. But she had to. The decision made, she collected the keys, more towels and a coat, determined to go.

She made it to the car, opened the door and fell across the seat somehow managing to pull the door shut. I'll rest a minute, she thought. Once, she heard the roar of a motor, but dismissed that to her own shakiness. If she could just shut her eyes for a moment, then she could drive.

Good. Her car was still there. Land left the motor running, as he bound across the yard, wondering why she had left the outside door swinging. When he was standing in the middle of the room where Samantha and Pearl lived away from the front section that was the shop, his mind was riddled with questions. Why was the door open and swinging in the wind? Where was she? Walking into the bedroom he saw the bed covers turned back, but no Samantha, instead a horrifying sight of bright red blood more clots than anything stained the white towel folded there. Now his heart beat fast enough to make him panic. She was in trouble, but where was she? He opened the bath room door. No Samantha. Hurriedly he walked through the rooms to the front that housed the shop, calling her name, but of course she didn't answer. She must have tried to get to her car and maybe fallen and he had walked past her. He left the house to walk around the property, going as a last resort to the car and there she lay crumpled across the console, her body more in the driver's seat, legs drawn up, almost in a fetal position. It appeared she was asleep, but he feared the situation was worse. Running back to the house he secured the door, returned to his truck and opened the passenger side, to lay the seat back as far as it would go in order to transfer Samantha from her car to the truck. How could she be asleep?

He had seen the patch of blood on the seat of her car and her coat was ruined, but one could buy a new coat, it was Samantha he was concerned with. Getting her settled, the seat belt around her, he shut the door and going around the truck slid in to begin the trek back to the hospital she'd left several days before with instructions to rest and let others run the shop. Knowing her, she wouldn't tell anyone if something was going wrong, she would handle it herself. She slept all the way to the emergency room.

The nurses in ER, picked up a phone and called the attending doctor. Lan could hear them saying, "she was here last week, a miscarriage, yes. It has evidently crossed over into more than we thought, Yes, I'd say she is hemoragghing," She listened. "Yes, sir, blood clots are possible, but that's not what I'm seeing." The doctor had a lot to say. "Yes, sir," she listened again. "Yes sir, we will do that."

"I don't want to stay in the hospital," Samantha fret. "Please, do the best you can and let me go home."

When the doctor arrived and looked his way, in view of her protest, Lan wondered if she could understand the seriousness of her ordeal "Do you understand, you are not out of the woods, yet. I'm thinking the idea of you going to sleep as easily as you do, your blood count is very low and the labs we've run hold the answer to why you go to sleep so easily." Land guessed he was in his early fifties but old enough to know a thing or two. Now he ask, "Did the problem of falling asleep happen in the last month, or longer?"

"It's been going on a while."

"Has she been under stress or perhaps doing a lot of physical work that would drain her body of...."

Samantha interrupted, "I am right here, you can address me with your questions." She was cranky. "It is Christmas Day. My problem today is not that I'm asleep but that I'm bleeding, now what is the official medical reason for that?" She didn't seem to realize she had truly been out of commission, snoozing away. "I mean," she searched for words, "I would like to go home. Do you have a prescription for me?"

Land chuckled and received a chilling glare from Samantha. "Is it too much to ask what will help?"

The doctor shook his head, staring off into the distance. "Yes, we'll start you on Methergine tablets but if you start bleeding again, get back here. You have lost a lot of blood. I'll call your prescription in to the hospital pharmacy, otherwise on Christmas Day I don't believe you'll get it."

Samantha started to rise, when a bilious feeling hit her and she almost went down. The doctor just shook his head. "I'm assuming you will be with her?" Lan nodded while Samantha looked stormy eyed. "I should admit her to the hospital and I world insist, but for the fact the flu epidemic has reached Grandview. That's where I've been all morning." He glanced at the clock on the wall, "I won't be having Christmas dinner. There are five children from different families in bad shape with the flu, running temperatures all the while they are freezing." He glanced at Samantha, "In your condition, your immune system as it is, if you take the flu now, it will be a battle to overcome." For the first time she didn't seem as hostile. Lan thought perhaps the doctor was finally getting through to her. "Could I see you out in the hall, while the nurse helps Mrs. McKinsey dress?" Lan knew to not even look at Samantha as he followed the doctor.

Once there, he smiled at Lan and said, "I see you are quite concerned with your wife's attitude. You don't need to worry on my part, she has lost a lot of blood and loss of blood brings trauma to the body and our thinking. If it weren't for the flu I'd have her in a room on IV's, but rest is what's most important for her. I have a feeling she went back to work after the miscarriage and that's part of why she's having problems now." He offered his hand and Land shook it and thanked him.

"I apologize, but she can be rough on a person when something wrinkles her ire."

"Tell me about it. I have a wife at home and nine nurses telling me what to do all day long."

Samantha, white faced and weak was coming through the door. "Mrs. McKinsey, if you would be so kind a nurse will be bringing a wheel chair any moment. If you fall and break something, I believe there'd be no alternative but to keep you here in this hospital." Turning to Land, he said, "I leave her in your hands. Remember, this time she has to rest and not be alone a few days."

"I believe you've been dismissed, but you are not to stay alone." He was studying her, a worried expression on his face. "I'm not sure Pearl can handle you. Alice could, but she has Kimberly home."

"I heard." She seemed to be considering her options as the nurse arrived with the wheelchair ready to take her to the outside entrance.

"Wait right here and I'll get the truck." He gave the nurse a sympathetic nod. "Don't let her get up."

Every effort drained more strength from her body. "I can't do this," she whispered. "I feel as though I'm going to faint." She had stalled, one foot on the ground; the other could not reach the interior of the truck. The nurse was alone, wondering what she was supposed to do, and then he was there.

"Let me help you. We've done this before." Picking her up, cradling her just so, Land set her up on the seat. "Now, lie back, I'll put the quilt over you and you can sleep on the way home."

"I'm sorry," her eyes were already closing. He heard the misery in her voice and leaned in to kiss her.

CHAPTER 17

$\mathcal{S}$HE AWAKENED TO find herself in his bed, not the gray walled room she remembered thinking was intended for Amy. She hadn't seen it since she and Land had spent the day shopping for Amy. She saw his feet stretched out beyond the foot board of the bed before she saw him; his toes pointed upward, his head the same and sound asleep.

She lay there thinking. How had they come this far? Two people, stubborn beyond means, hurt by another and not willing to take a chance with each other when their paths had done nothing but cross. She almost chuckled, but the effort affected her breathing and that was another thing. Maybe the doctor had found the reason she slept so easily. Could it be something as simple as he said? Devious, she couldn't help thinking of all the times Land had carried her, dead weight, and put her to bed and she had missed it because she was asleep. But then, they were in fight mode, and by now they were worn out with that process. Sighing, deeply, she closed her eyes and went back to sleep.

"Landon King," his mother's voice stepped through his dreams. "I declare, Son, couldn't you get more comfortable than that chair?"

Olivia had Amy waiting in the kitchen by the door they had found a key to fit. "I didn't think there would be anything clandestine, but one never knows." She continued talking until she reached her son to lay hands on his shoulders. "Wake up, dear. Amy's been so disappointed. I decided if as the saying goes, Mohammed didn't go to the mountain, the mountain would come to Mohammed. So here we are, and it's still Christmas. Wake up." She raised his head which was in an unreal position, "You will have whip lash if you stay in this position much longer." She shook her head, "I must say, you have to be tired to sleep in that straight backed chair." Tsk, tsk, tsk. "Can't believe this."

She called Amy. "Sweetheart, come in here." Amy came running but when she saw her daddy in the chair and Samantha asleep in the bed, her face turned immediately sad. "What's wrong?" Olivia asked.

"Are they dead?"

"No, just tired. Samantha had to go to the doctor. Your daddy found out and went with her. I called the hospital to know this, so don't tell anyone…" Olivia sighed. "The nurse is my next door neighbor. She said Landon was bringing his wife home." Olivia chuckled. "Wonder how Landon received that info."

"I think he should marry Samantha." Olivia smiled and hugged her. "Can we wake them?"

"We can try. I'll start with him, you climb up on the bed and see what you can do with her."

"Merry Christmas, Samantha." Amy snuggled up close, peering down into Samantha's face. "I was afraid I wouldn't get to tell you that. I made a gift for you, but you have to wake up." Amy pulled the covers away. "Look, Nana, Samantha is asleep in funny clothes. Is she a nurse?"

Olivia studied the scrubs Samantha was wearing. "I think, for some reason, the hospital sent her home in those, dear. I tell you what. Why don't you bring the little tree you made for Samantha and the gifts, in here? Two trips, all right?" Olivia's mind was running a mile a minute. Evidently, Samantha's own clothes were out of the question, for that matter she now understood the nurse saying, "That's all I can tell you, Olivia." She had to wake these two, minutes were turning into an hour and Amy's Christmas had been completely different than her very excited expectations. "Landon King, wake up." She patted the front of his chest rather brisk and finally got a response. "Merry Christmas, darling, it's not every day I drive over here to see you in your bedroom sitting in a chair with a woman asleep in your bed."

That truth rolled around in his brain. Was he dreaming? He slid his hand across his face. His neck felt as though it would break and then he jerked upright. His mother stood there, smiling. "Hello, Son."

"Mother?" Then the memory hit; he had brought Samantha to his house. He turned to check the bed. "This is no dream, is it?" Olivia was laughing. "My word, Mother, you could warn a person."

"Who would that be? You were dead to the world, but shape up your daughter's on her way in here."

"Samantha fainted, some kind of female problem, I think." He lied. "Anyway, when I arrived to bring her back to your house she was slumped over in her car. I took her to the hospital and sit with her, and then the doctor said she was better off not staying in the hospital because of the flu epidemic there."

Patting his shoulder, Olivia said, "Son, it's all right. You don't have to explain. I can see everything is honorable...but I did notice something hasn't transpired yet, has it?"

"No. Is it still Christmas?"

They studied the clock on the wall. "It appears there's five more hours until it is officially over." Olivia pointed to Samantha. "Has she slept long enough to wake and spend the remainder of Christmas day with Amy? That has been Amy's one thing she wanted for Christmas, to spend it with the two of you."

He stood, shrugging his shoulders. "I think this problem is going to get better," his mother was staring at him, when he realized she knew nothing about the sleeping disorder," Sorry, Mother, I'm still trying to get my bearings."

"Are you sure you aren't having second thoughts about the whole proposition," she laughed. "I guess we can call it that."

"I have second thoughts about everything." He was aware his mother left the room shaking her head. The minute he was certain she was out of hearing, he leaned down to whisper in Samantha's ear. "Can you wake up? We have someone here who wants to spend what's left of Christmas with us." He shook her gently. Her head rolled on the pillow. "Sam, please, please wake up. We have to do this for Amy."

"Amy?" She rolled over, frowning, her hand patting the pillow beside her. "Am I dreaming?" She opened her eyes, but it was Lan in her line of view and then Amy was coming through the door with Olivia close behind. Startled and embarrassed, she sat up, wiping her arm across her mouth. "I look terrible," she said, zeroing in on Lan as though it were his fault, he shrugged as she met Olivia's amused expression. "Olivia?" She pulled the sheet up over her arms, shaking her head, "I don't know what to say."

"Merry Christmas, Samantha," Olivia stooped to hug her. "We were so worried when the two of you didn't appear for dinner that I called the hospital and they told me you were admitted, but they wouldn't say why, so when Landon didn't call we began to think it was very serious, a bump on the head and either a concussion or maybe amnesia." Olivia began to laugh. "Don't be embarrassed. My son was sitting in that straight backed chair sound asleep. I could tell everything was honorable and I said so."

Amy hopped up on the bed. "Did you eat, today? Because if you didn't my Nana brought food."

Samantha found herself smiling through tears. "You, Amy King, are the most wonderful little girl I've ever known and you ask me if I'm hungry? I don't think I've eaten a thing today and I'm starving. Now ask your daddy." Amy went to her daddy. He picked her up and hugged her tight, nodding yes. And then Land was right there, his hand out helping her up from the bed. His expression one she didn't remember as he held Amy in one arm, the other waiting for her and she found that expression very interesting.

"Oh, my, Olivia, you are an excellent cook." Samantha felt stronger and her head was clearing of the closed off feeling she'd experienced earlier when all she wanted to do was sleep. "I think your food and the meds the doctor prescribed have both kicked in together and today will be the best Christmas I've had in many many years." She watched as Land cleared the table and stored the excess food.

"Why, Samantha?" Amy's eyes were large and curious as Samantha pulled her up onto her lap.

"I spent so many Christmas alone, because my mother and Daddy separated and I felt I had no one."

"Me, too," Amy's voice lifted in sharing. "But this is the bestest ever, with Nana and Daddy and you."

"We should all say Merry Christmas on three, so we will never forget we were together. Ready?"

Amy counted. "One, two, three;" Laughing and on the count they all said, "Merry Christmas."

"And we have to go home, Amy." When Amy's countenance fell, Olivia's eyes were on Land.

He stooped, drawing her into the hollow of his body. "How about if Samantha's up to it, tomorrow night we drive over and pick you up to spend a few days with me, unless Nana has plans for you." Amy's face glowed seeing Olivia nodding agreement. "And when you and Nana leave, tonight, we have to decide whether Samantha should go home or stay over, which means if she stays, I'll have to sleep in your bed." Amy's laughter and goodnight kisses saved the three adults an embarrassing moment.

The car left the drive. Land turned out the lights and led her back to the bedroom, motioning she was to lie down. She patted the space beside her. "Are you sure?" He asked. She nodded and he kicked off his boots.

"You're not going to hit on me, are you?"

"No, but I want to kiss you." His eyes had turned mysteriously darker as he lay down beside her and pulled her close. He was raised on one elbow, staring down into her face. "I've wanted to kiss you and hold you all day." He kissed her three little butterfly kisses.

"I thought you had left me at the hospital. I was surprised when you stepped away from the window."

"I did leave you," he admitted, his fingers creasing the hem of the top, until his hand came to rest, flat, on top of her stomach. "But I couldn't stay away. I was so miserable; I drove like a maniac getting back to the hospital scared to death something might have happened to you while I was gone and there you were sleeping and I was never so glad about anything as finding you asleep and then you moaned and the nurse gave me that look and I did the same thing as before, laid down and held you and we both slept." He closed his eyes. "I'm sorry you lost the baby and I'm sorry I took advantage of you the night of Leon's funeral." He laid his head on her shoulder, not letting his weight press down. "You were right, I wasn't thinking of your need, only mine." He gripped her hand. "You gave yourself to me in my need and all the times we differed on things, I remembered. Every time I saw you I wanted to pull you close and make things right but we usually fought over something and I'd leave thinking you didn't deserve it." She laid a finger on his lips as if to stop him. "No, let me say it," he shook his head, his eyes troubled, "My fantasy was that I would open my arms and you would come willingly, I needed you so much."

"My fantasy was that you would open your arms and pull me in so close I would know you wanted me." She sighed, "But your absence kept me emotionally unsettled and then when I didn't have a period," she put her hands on his cheeks, "The first month I was hopeful, but when I missed the second I was worried." He started to protest. "If you are going to say you would have done the right thing, that wasn't good enough for me. I have to know it's more than the right thing. I was always trying to tell you when I fall in love it's for keeps. I found out I didn't love Blake. I wanted to love him, to build a life, but what I felt with you was so much different, I can't explain it," She laughed. "Once I met you and we had this ungodly magnetism of needing to touch each other." His hands were wrapping her tight, "we do have it don't we?" His smile relayed he was amused she ask. "If someone would have mentioned his name, I think I would have said *who's that?*"

217

"You are a fire in my blood," he replied, his voice husky. "And I've vowed I won't go against your wishes but I've been pushed nearly beyond a man's control and I'm thinking I'll be taking a lot of cold showers." He kissed her again and when she responded he groaned. "You truly are a fire angel. You look like an angel, you speak like one…until you're mad…but you stir up this heat in me without doing anything really, you just look at me…" He groaned. "What are we going to do about this? I know you feel the same way, don't you?" He waited and then finished, "You want to be obedient to God's plan?"

She grinned. "Yes, but I feel your pain." The grin turned into a dusky lowering of her eyes, the top buttons to his shirt had come open. "I doubt I'm any different than you. I want to wrap my arms around you and never let go." But she set the expectations and she knew it was up to her to keep them on the right path. "We've messed up, once and we lost a part of ourselves," sadness crept into her voice and dimmed her eyes. "I've kept pushing it to the back of my thoughts, but we formed a baby in my womb, you and I and if there's a chance that could happen again, we have to make it right. Otherwise, let me go, now while I can walk away, not without loss and heartache but still walk away knowing I've tried to do what's right in God's sight, honorable and true. Do you understand?"

He kissed her, a chaste kiss that lingered, almost reverent, pulling her back into the warmth of his arm. "I understand but that doesn't mean I'm not suffering…" He gave an embarrassed laugh. "The old me would cajole, threaten, promise about anything and even make you feel it was the right thing to do, but I actually feared losing you, one way or the other, so I'm going to listen to you but I'm telling you we've got to do something quick, I mean tomorrow, the next day…" He grinned. "You get my message?"

She gave him a tolerant look. "Maybe our sin is like David's in the Bible when he and Bathsheba lost their child."

"If there's sin, then it would be on my shoulders, but I prefer to think our God is a forgiving God." He pulled himself free, found the sheet at the end of the bed and tucked it around her shoulders, and stood. "Now don't go to sleep. There's something I have to do. All right?" She frowned at his seriousness.

"Would you like to take me home?" Evidently he'd allowed himself a quick assessment of their situation and decided against commitment. A pained expression crossed his face. "I understand, Lan, I would never want you to make a fast choice about something so important. If I'm staying, I'll just turn over and go to sleep, if I'm going, tell me now." Inside her body was shaking, it would not be easy after their talk.

He lay a finger across her lips. "I have to do something," he said. "Don't go to sleep." He left the room. She heard the water running and believed he was taking a shower. Rising, she found her purse, took out the small make up bag she carried, and using the mirror to comb her hair, saw the dark circles under her eyes and dabbed make up there, correcting her face best she could and slipped the bag back into her purse and found her shoes. She would be ready when he said he was driving her home. In the small suitcase he carried in, she found the set of clothes she had packed, thinking she might need something if the reason she was going to the hospital proved serious. She slipped on the black slacks, the white laced camisole and the drop necked white sweater that allowed the camisoles lace to show; grimacing that it gave a nice feminine touch that meant nothing, now, to a woman being set free and driven home. And still she sprayed the small bottle of cologne on her wrist, behind her ear and there in the hollow of her throat. Her small diamond earrings were in the little black velvet box and she slipped them into each ear, screwing the backs on carefully knowing these were the only diamonds she owned and she treasured them.

With her bag packed, her shoes on, the scrubs folded in the clothes bag the hospital had supplied, she carried her belongings into the living room and set the suitcase by the door and sit down on the sofa to wait for the man to whom she had just bared her soul. She had been honest; she would try not to regret admitting her love for him and on that thought realized he had not said he loved her only that she was a fire in his blood. As usual words that seemed to ring with sincerity and draw her in had once more ended with his pulling back. She must remember this in the future. How vulnerable she was in his presence.

He found her, half lying on the one piece of furniture in the living room. Had it not been for the black slacks she would have blended with the white material. Though she was pale, she was beautiful. She had changed clothes and he noticed the lace peeping from the wide v in the sweater. Her lips were pink and full and soft and he bent to kiss her lightly as he wondered, should he wake her or let her sleep. The kiss answered his question; she opened sleepy eyes, her hand straightening her hair, her feet touching the floor where her shoes had landed by some degree of remembrance, freeing her to lie comfortably on the sofa, sometimes half on and half off. "Why are you dressed in your suit?" Or, am I dreaming, she wondered as he leaned close, the clean brisk cologne he had applied making her inhale and make an appreciative sound. Yes, she was dreaming, Land King did not dress in a nice suit, smell wonderful and kiss her in real life. She snuggled back to the sofa wondering if she should delight in its comfort.

"Samantha," he was kissing her again. Her arms went around his neck. He kissed her again, brushing her hair onto her shoulders, liking the feel of it against his skin. "Babe, why did you change clothes? You could have slept in the scrubs, couldn't you?"

She liked the sound of his voice. "Lan?" She heard him laugh. That irritated her. She sit up, awake, maybe not completely but enough to see he was on one knee, looking down at her. "Did you kiss me?"

He grinned. "I did." Now he stood. "Are you awake enough to see I have dressed for you? You are such a stickler for perfection. And I see you dressed, was that for me?"

She was cross. "No, I didn't want to go home in scrubs and answer questions if Alice or Pearl ask."

"Hmm. You were going home?" He saw the tear slip from the corner of her eye and run down her cheek, another and another. He sit beside her and pulled her into his arms. "Why are you crying?"

"Why would a man take a shower and dress in his suit if he was taking a woman home?"

His laughter was joyous. "I can think of only one reason." He wiped away her tears with a handkerchief.

"What is it?" She was waking up. "I waited and then I fell asleep." She reminded him of Amy.

"I know," he said. "Now," he took a little black velvet box, a bit worn around the edges, from his pocket.. "I wanted to give you your Christmas present, if you will accept it."

Remorse shone in her face and her voice, "but I don't have a gift for you." He was back down on his knees, one on the floor, one bent, staring into her face, opening the box. She was stunned, speechless. "I love you Samantha. Will you marry me?"

"Did you ask me to marry you and did you say you love me?" Her voice was filled with amazement and joy as her eyes filled with tears, again. "Yes. Yes. Yes." She was breathless. "I thought you were taking me home. My heart was breaking." She moaned, "Oh, it's beautiful. Oh….."

He was slipping the ring on her finger. "This was my mother's ring that my dad gave to her. I ask her to go with me to find a ring for you." He smiled. "This is what she asked, "What would Samantha say if you gave her my ring?"

"Oh," Samantha's arms went around his neck. "What mother in law loved her son's wife that much?"

He saw the question in her eyes. "She didn't love Lila that much; I think she hand-picked you."

CHAPTER 18

EXT MORNING HE drove her home. She had slept like a rock after tiring herself out dressing and then putting the scrubs back on. "We have a slight problem," he said, as he was unlocking the door, helping her inside and carrying her belongings to the bedroom. "Just how many days do you need before we can be married?"

She sank onto the bed. The effort of coming home had used up all of her energy. She huffed, trying to draw air into her lungs. "Tell me your thoughts but take into consideration I really do need to get over this issue and if the doctor knows what he's talking about he said the shot he gave me should get me up and going."

He sit beside her, taking her hand in his, kissing her fingers, and shaking his head at the same time. "It's my fault, the miscarriage caused the blood loss and evidently your blood count was already low. I'm sorry."

They heard the door open and hushed laughter as Pearl came from her room to find Alice. They sat there expecting them any minute and they were right. Pearl and Alice peeped around the corner, grinning when they saw the two, but the grin faded when they realized Samantha was very pale. "What's up?" Alice sidled up to the bed, arms folded to her chest, waiting for Samantha's explanation.

When Samantha didn't answer but lay back on the pillows and stared at them, Land replied. "We got a problem here, ladies. I'd get married today if my lady, here, felt up to it, but she needs time and she tells me there's things to do….which I can't imagine what."

"What is the problem, Sam?" Alice scooted her over and lay down beside her.

Wearily, Samantha replied, "it may not sound important to anyone else but it would be easier to get Land's home in shape if we could do it before we moved in and I know Amy would like that, too."

"Is there one room that is in sleeping condition?"

"Yeah, the one started for Amy," Land looked to Samantha for agreement. "Isn't it? What about it?"

"I could stay there and you two get married and live here while work's going on there."

Land lay back on the other pillow, turning to face Samantha, "Now isn't this cozy?" He grinned. "Board meeting among friends, in the bedroom." He put an arm around Samantha, "I like that solution. Do you?"

Pearl moved to the other side, pulling a small bench from beneath the dresser to sit on. "I'll still be here early enough to open the shop, say the word and tonight I'll have my bag ready and leave you two alone."

"No. No. No," Land grinned. "I like that plan too, but we've turned over a new leaf, actually I have. She had no problem, except to constantly keep me in line." He gave an embarrassed laugh. "We stay as chaste as Saint Mary's Nun, until we're officially Mr. and Mrs., then I get to move in. Right Babe?"

She was immersed studying the ring on her finger; it was throwing fire in the rays of sunlight coming through the slats of the window blinds. She turned her hand toward Pearl, then Alice. "It was Olivia's. I'm overwhelmed and happy." She yawned. "I can't imagine anyone loving me that much."

Taking time to admire the ring, Pearl finally said, "Sam, we can do things you need if you give us a clue what you're talking about." Pearl leaned closer. "Is it the wedding or the house you need help with."

Struggling, she remembered their conversation." You all plan it and I'll be there. I'm so sorry," she yawned again, "I'm simply out of it but I do want to marry this man." She snuggled closer to Land's body ready for sleep. "You have the list we made out last night for your house?" Land nodded.

"This is not our Sam talking," Alice said. "But plan things we will. We will think as she does. Watch out." She patted Samantha's shoulder. "Sam, do you hear me? Where do you want to be married?"

The words were muffled and left the three chuckling. "Did she say barn?" Alice and Pearl's eyes met. Pearl nodded. "Then a barn it is. Land, could you bring a couple of your men over for us to finish out that big old empty space downstairs? She's been thinkin' it would be perfect for parties and special events. Let's go for it. This girl," she glanced down at Samantha, "She's a perfectionist but I've been taking lessons."

Reluctantly, Land drew himself up and off the bed, pulling a comforter over Samantha's shoulders. "I slept in Amy's bed last night, since she was in mine, and I think that bed of Amy's is a foot short." He stretched. "So I'm headed home to bring back a couple guys and we'll work out here today, then tonight I promised Amy I'd pick her up and she can stay with me. You girls got the shop, right?" They nodded and listened as he stomped down the stairs, whistling.

"There goes a happy man," Alice quipped. "Did you notice they didn't quibble one time? No fighting?"

"I noticed," Pearl was hesitant to continue, "But, for some reason, I don't think our Sam is out of the woods." She shook herself mentally, "I've never been in charge of anything, before, but I saw her list and she had Winter Sale begins the twenty eight. So, I guess we put up the sale signs she ordered."

"Please," Alice looked heavenward, "Please don't let anything happen to her when things are going right." She leaned closer to her friend, laying a hand on Samantha's forehead. "It's cool."

Word traveled fast, the shop was busy with Alice and Pearl constantly on their feet, the delivery truck brought more of the late supplies and Alice asked, "Can I stop this Doctor's order from being sent,"

"What doctor and what did he order?" Pearl held up a hand full of licorice sticks in holiday wrap.

Laughing, Alice said, "Her doctor and that's what he ordered, so let's keep them safely put away until he stops in, supposedly this week." She heaved a big sigh; "It may be he will need to check our Sam."

Land came in near five, saying he had sent the boys home, and the barn was looking good. "How's my girl? I know she can't ride over to get Amy with me but I wondered if you'd seen any improvement."

Pearl saw Alice had a customer, "Come on," she needed his advice on something, anyway. From her pocket she withdrew the letter she'd received in the mail that day. "What do you make of this?" She asked. He stopped by the lamp and leaned down to read it.

"You didn't say who it's from?" Land was scanning the handwriting. "It isn't anyone I know."

"I think it is." Pearl was leaning over Samantha's sleeping form, her hand on Samantha's brow. "Land, I think she's burning up with fever." Pearl was looking ahead to Amy's visit, knowing she shouldn't come.

"I'll call the doctor." He was already dialing. "Yeah, I'm calling about Samantha McKinsey. Yes, she was there. The problem is she's burning up with fever right now. I don't know what to do." He paused. "Yes, I'll wait." Then he was giving directions before he hung up the phone. "The doctor is coming this way."

"Shouldn't you call Amy or maybe Olivia?" She saw the meaning was heavy and it hit home with Land. "I mean, Samantha may have the flu, or it could be something…" Her words dropped off. "I've had an uneasy feeling, Lan; it could be the letter, but it has seemed to center around Sam, all day."

He glanced at the letter again and read, *I want you to come home, it's not the same and I think we can work this out, if you'll just come home. I'm not threatening, Pearl, I'm asking.'* Now his eyes met hers. "Are you thinking this is Jess?"

"Who else? He used my name." Without realizing she was, Pearl began to tremble, the tremble progressing to a shaking and she wrapped her arms protectively around her mid-section. "I've not been beaten all these months. I've learned to laugh again, all because Samantha took me in and I'm so close to getting Anna Marie back," tears filled her eyes and ran down her cheeks. "I can't go back to that."

"What do you need me to do, Pearl?" He glanced at Samantha, his own face dissolving into misery. "I thought she was on the road to recovery and she did too. For the first time we weren't fighting and it felt good."

"There's your priority. I don't know what mine is, to alert the sheriff, or to see if he has changed but I'm afraid, Lan, afraid I'm vulnerable and I'll be taken in and then he'll kill me." She seemed to try to pull her emotions together. "Right now, let's see what the doctor thinks. The shop is past closing hours and I can't do anything about my problems, so let's concentrate on Samantha." She heaved a breath, unfolding her arms, "I'm sorry."

"Hey, we're all in this together, because we're friends. Don't give up, let's just say we're all thinking on the matter while we take care of another and God willing, the answer will show up."

Alice came to the door. Keys were dangling from her finger, "I just got a call. Jade's on his way here. You all right with that, Lan? If not, I'll go pick him up." A nervous laugh lay between them. "He's walking here." She realized Pearl was mouthing, *Sam's not well.* "Trouble does come in three's, doesn't it?"

CHAPTER 19

CLARISSA AND WALT took the chairs along the wall. Tessia and Olivia sat close to Land. The doctor had stayed. His words circled silently in side Land's memory. "This year the flu is killing people." Three hours earlier he had arrived, asking for a place to wash his hands. He had then adorned himself with a sterile gown and mask, explaining he had visited Mr. Colter who lived down the road. "He has the flu and if that isn't what Mrs. McKinsey's has, I don't want to bring any germs to her." They led him into the bedroom. "Temperature is good," he said, as if talking to himself, "of the room, I mean, don't want a hot room when someone's got a fever. Now let's see if she has a temp. One hundred three and you've given her the medicine from the hospital stay? And you think it was more when she was talking in her sleep?"

Pearl nodded, "The medicine seemed to work until late evening and then her temp began to rise." She glanced at the family she had called, knowing it would have been against Sam's wishes, but she had an uneasy feeling that Sam was worse than they imagined. Now, they were all concerned because the doctor continued to monitor her. "Like I said, she seemed almost delirious at one time."

"I know you are wondering why not call an ambulance and admit her to hospital." The doctor shook his head, staring at the floor. "We've lost three, already, to the flu. The medicines aren't working, or the strain has mutated and we don't have anything that works, yet." He glanced to Land, "I say that to say this, if we can get her temperature down and keep it down, I don't think she has the flu, but her own infection that her body is trying to burn out. Who knows? It could be the flu. If you are praying people then pray and help get this woman well."

Tessia lay a hand on her granddaughter, glancing across the room to take in Samantha's mother. "Clarissa," she called. "Come over here. God knows there's nothing stronger than a mother's prayer for her child. Now Olivia, let's hold hands and let Clarissa pray, shall we?" Everyone stood, Clarissa took Olivia's hand on one side and Tessia's on the other, and Land was holding to his mother with the doctor, Pearl, Alice, Jade and Walt completing the line around Samantha's bed.

"Before we pray, are we all in agreement? If there's one who does not agree there is power of prayer over the sick, that person must step out of the group." No one moved. "Let us bow our head," tears were running down her cheeks and her voice was husky as she began. "Father, God, we come to you with thanksgiving for Samantha and what she means to each of us; we ask forgiveness and favor now as we come to you in her behalf. Lord, remove the illness that is claiming her at this moment, strengthen her body that she shrugs off the poison that is attacking her system and rendering her listless and unable to respond. Lord, we claim your scripture *'if any is sick among us the prayer of faith will save them,'* and we thank you for giving that scripture to us in the book of James.' Lord, we ask you to grant our prayer that Samantha advances beyond this fever, this illness, to be healthy and able to do all things in your name. We love you and we praise you and thank you... and everyone said, Amen."

Something held him in a stronghold; he couldn't say what was going on. Leaving the group Lan went outside to sit in his truck. His heart was heavy. They had come so far from the unrest they had known. He couldn't understand, with peace and calm they could be happy and make a home for Amy; was that going to be ripped away? His hands gripped the steering wheel, now he laid his head there. It had been a long time since he wanted anything. "Lord, if this is all my fault, I ask your forgiveness. Please, make Samantha well." The words circled in his mind, round and round. He must have sit there an hour or more, reliving the times he'd done something to disillusion her and she'd shone nothing but stamina and a will to persevere in spite of him. "Let her have that now, Lord."

Inside, Alice left her seat by Jade; Pearl was in the kitchen, which was where she chose to be. "Pearl, it's as though the devil has moved in. Isn't this heaviness we feel, his work? I mean, we were talking this morning, expecting good things and now Samantha is lying in there near unconscious. Are we under the throes of man's doings, like the preacher said one Sunday? Or, is it just the flu and we can do nothing?"

"Young lady," the doctor spoke from behind the kitchen wall. "I'm aware you spoke not knowing I'd overhear but I want to tell you, it's never just the flu, it's whether a body has been under attack, all things considered; a struggle whether the body and the person are strong enough to survive. We have strong healthy men come in, we're impressed with their strength and then they are gone and we can't explain why."

"Are you saying there's no hope?" Worry stressed each word. "This is too quick. We were making plans."

"But she is very still, isn't she? Her pulse is rapid but her blood count dropped dangerously low at one point." He sighed, the weight of his profession on his shoulders. "I wouldn't be here if I wasn't concerned. This very thing happened to my daughter, no explanation. Then there's my wife's uncle, Mr. Colter, I came out to see. Did God bring me near Mrs. McKinsey's home for a reason?"

"It is all unexpected and unbelievable that something changes so quickly."

"Yes, it is," he agreed, "but there's always hope one can overcome, God willing. So it's in God's hands?" The doctor's head dropped for a moment, and then he said, "Yes, it is."

The door opened, they heard someone coming up the steps. Land King's face shone with determination. He headed for the bedroom, wishing they would all get out of the room, but he wouldn't ask. Going to the bed, he reached down, now his actions turned gentle as he slid an arm under Samantha, straightening he lift her up and to his body, his eyes searching for the strange chaise chair they'd rocked in before. For some unknown reason it was empty. He settled into it, holding Samantha close, as Alice brought a light blanket and draped it across her body. Finished, she motioned everyone out. Olivia offered Tessia an arm to steady her. Now the two were alone and Land began to rock.

"You have to wake up, babe. I can't do this without you and Amy's at her little friend's house waiting to hear." A tear drooped on her arm. "I've asked God to make you completely well. I've made a few promises too. I may not be the best husband in the world, but I'm going to try. You remember all those fights we had? They're nothing compared to you fighting to wake up, to let your mind feel all our prayers and your body let go whatever the problem is that's trying to take you from us. You hear me, babe? I figure I love you more than I've ever loved anybody or anything. I'm going to sit here and hold you until you realize God is willing, I know He is because He gave me a little shove to do this." His tears dripped continuously. "You know why I'm crying? Because God put peace in me, and he wouldn't have done that if you weren't going to be all right. So if you hear me, it's time to wake up."

He rocked and thought and whispered his thoughts to her. "You told me, once, our getting together was like wishing something was done or would happen, you said it was like being on a wing and a prayer. Well, babe, so be it. I prayed and I'm waiting for you. I'll take a wing and a prayer, any day. That's a lot more promising than nothing at all." He could hear the ticking of the clock and found himself nodding.

Alice came in, "I'm taking Jade home. Call me if I can do anything. There's no one here, now, but Pearl."

"Tell Jade, I didn't have the presence of mind to even speak. I apologize for that. What did the doctor say?"

"In the beginning he said, time will tell." She didn't tell him, upon leaving he admitted his daughter died.

"You are going to have a crick in your neck." Her hands were on each side of his neck, trying to center his head. "Boy, are you a glutton for punishment." He slept on but he tightened his hold on her. "I kind of wonder if you still want to go through with marrying me?" Her voice was wistful. "It's a wonder your Mother wouldn't come take back her ring if she heard about this little episode." She sighed, wiggled her toes and shifted in his arms. "I would like to tell you I love you and maybe kiss you. Once, you said, "the next time we kiss it will be because you want to." A slight laugh ended in her coughing. "Well, I want to now."

"Would you now?" Land's hold on her made her gasp. "Too much, huh?" He was staring down at her. "Do you know how long I've sit here holding you?" He kissed her on the forehead, tip of her nose and claimed her lips. "How's that? Mrs. McKinsey?" He laughed. "I didn't have the heart to tell the doc."

"That I'm not a Mrs. Anything, yet?"

"Oh, you're something, all right. You scared the daylights out of all of us." He saw the puzzled look. "Your grandmother, your Mother and Walt and my Mom were all here." Her eyes flashed but the spurt of energy was more than she needed. He laid a finger across her lips. "Before you jump to conclusions, it may well be your mother's prayer held with God, because here you are, fire darting out of your eyes." Tilting his head, he studied her face. "Your color is not as pale." He was feeling of her brow. "I don't think you have fever, either. Now, if I just knew your heart rate and that you're not going to faint."

"I'm fine." She placed his thumb and forefinger around her wrist, "count, and you'll know that, too."

A knock sounded at the door and Pearl stuck her head in. "I thought I heard voices." She began to laugh. "Sam, is that you?"

She danced a little jig before entering. "You had us worried, but you know what?" She was grinning, "Before he left the doctor checked you over and he said you were going to be just fine but," she laughed harder, "he wasn't sure about that man asleep with his head about to fall off."

❊ ❊ ❊ ❊ ❊

If ever there was a silent celebration, Pearl was thinking, it's happening here. She wished for a place to go, to leave them to their selves without thinking she would hear them. Alice had Jade. She still feared going to her family, in case Jess went on rampage. She paced the floor, worrying, half praying, not knowing what to pray for until it came to her muddled senses, pray a prayer of thanksgiving for Samantha coming out of the fever and pray she continued to be well. Pray Samantha and her mother reached an understanding and pray for Landon King. As she prayed, Jess face appeared in her thoughts.

Maybe there was one way she could answer the letter she received that day that someone hand delivered. She left a note and slipped into her coat and quietly out the back door. She made one detour before driving Sam's car out to Hell's Acre. As if expecting her, Jess was standing at the window when she arrived. He opened the door and met her, reaching out a hand when she came up the steps.

"I was afraid you wouldn't come." He led the way inside.

"I'm here. Your letter sounded insistent." She was keeping a safe distance from him, her eye on the door. "What's important, that we discuss?"

"Rose Elaine."

"Is she alive?" She had never dared ask before; he had threatened to kill her if she did.

"She's alive." He seemed to be studying the toes of his shoes. "The California branch for missing persons found her." He shook his head, as if he wasn't the reason their daughter was missing. "I have the letter." He pulled it from his pocket, folded down to nearly nothing. "There's a picture. She'd be twenty now."

"Come June." Pearl's fingers trembled as she worked with the paper. "You've had this awhile."

"Yes. It's been in the mail box but I've been away."

"Where?"

He stroked his chin. "You don't know? I thought you had a hand in it."

"I have no idea what you're talking about. It took months for me to heal, properly. I stayed in."

"Come home, Pearl. Let's start over." He saw her back toward the door. "I was made to think what I did to you." She didn't believe him. "Do you know about the real Hell's Gate?" She shivered, thinking he was lying. "Someone jumped me, bound me, put a bag over my head and dumped me there." He looked sad. "Your life is not your own. I didn't know in this country there was such a place. I never want to be there again." She was looking around the room. "You feel this way about our home? Did you come clean it up?"

"I never came back." She gave him a withering look. "My arm was broke, my hip out of place, I had double vision, but I didn't tell anyone the worst parts, all they knew was my arm was broke."

"They broke my fingers," he held up his hand to reveal crooked fingers. "I tried setting them on sticks." He kept his eyes on her. "Every time they broke a finger they said your name, this one's for Pearl. So someone knew I was there. Someone knew your name, and Anna Marie's, then on the last Rose Elaines." He was beginning to fidget. "You had no money, but someone you know paid for me to be there."

Pearl was backing out the door. She'd seen him tremble with agitation and start beating her before. "I'm different," he called out as she ran to the car. "God as my witness, I'm different."

"I haven't seen you in church," she said, wondering that he heard. "Don't get your gun, Jess, I'm not alone." Her feet were full of lead. The hundred feet to the car seemed a mile and she fumbled getting in.

"I don't have any guns. Someone took them." He saw lights come on in the bracken of trees beyond the road. "Who is that, Pearl? You got a boyfriend?" She didn't look back. The Police car followed her into town. She drove the rest of the way watching over her shoulder, every car setting off tremors in her body.

Lan came into the kitchen as she tried to think how to walk past Samantha's room without disturbing them. "Pearl, I'm going to leave the door open. I'm staying over to be sure she is all right. I'll sleep on my side of the bed and keep things normal. You got anything to say?"

"I'm the last person, Lan, I just faced Jess Lassity and I can't tell you if he's lying or telling the truth. He said someone ambushed him and carried him off to a place called Hell's Gate. I've never heard of it. He said it changed him." She sighed, her hands trembling with nervousness. "It will take time to know if he's lying. I lost confidence in him every time he beat me until I was nearly dead." She held up a hand before Lan spoke. "Don't say it's my fault. A woman becomes cowered after a while and if there are children...."

Within two weeks, Samantha was up, making wedding plans, smiling and happy.

Pearl laughed, watching Samantha. "You hold that ring up one more time to let the sunlight make those prisms on the window it's going to explode." Samantha danced over to where she stood and hugged her. "You hugging me makes me think you are just practicing up, say what is it, five more days. Right?"

"Yeah, one night and five days. I am so happy, and to think Land's mother would part with this beauty. Did you know this ring was in a vault since her husband died and she didn't know the combination? Christmas day, Lan and someone else took the door off that was why she needed two men."

"What?" Pearl squared off, standing hands on hips. "Wait 'til I tell Alice. We helped take that door off. Girl, it was heavy, but we never knew why we were doing it."

The big day arrived. Balloon lamps were strung around the barn, inside and out. For all the gray wood grained boards of the barn walls, everything was polish clean; the ivory bows with sprigs of holly dangling from the center added a quaint charm. Mahogany folding chairs with padded seats had been set up; a baby grand piano with silver candlesticks graced one side of the built up floor where the minister would stand with the wedding party and a string ensemble balanced the other, two violins, a bass, a cello and a harp. "Ah," Alice was overwhelmed with Samantha's touch. "It is going to be wonderful and I heard the ensemble practice." She sighed. "It was Heaven on earth, so why the piano?"

Pearl snickered. "Do you not know, Samantha's grandmother is the great Contessa Cleveland that taught piano to nearly every person in this community and surrounding area. She will play the wedding march, the ensemble will accompany." She sobered as quickly as she had laughed. "Lan tells me Jade is going to stand with you and Jimmy with me."

"Yeah, he thinks something might rub off on Jade." Alice grinned. "I hope so. And you know Jimmy?"

Pearl nodded. "You know, I never saw Jess in a tuxedo, why would I think of that?" Alice hugged her. Glancing at the tablet in her hand one last time, Pearl said, "Everything's go. There will be a large vase of red roses by the piano and one to the left of the ensemble, on a pedestal to bring them up chin high and not block anyone's view and the caterers are going to set up at the front where everyone enters. It's all white mock china plates, crystal goblets and a five tiered cake. Can you believe it? And there's one last thing, it's a secret, right after they're pronounced man and wife and before cutting the cake. The photographer will have the pictures during the ceremony its self. Oh, Alice, it's all beautiful."

It was a fairy tale wedding, all the church people came, dressed in their best, happiness written on their faces as their own Pastor prepared to perform the ceremony. Land and Samantha had agreed not to see each other the last two days and when Contessa Cleveland was seated at the baby grand, they held their breath in great expectation. If the string ensemble blessed their soul, now listening to the matriarch of the McKinsey family in action was something, without knowing, they had waited for all their life, a journey at times reaching great heights moving to calm as the sparkling summer brook, drawing them in to settle in their mind and then the first chords of the Wedding March began.

Jade came first, then Jimmy and at last Landon King, in tuxedo; his handsome face wearing a serious expression. Now, Contessa's music softened as Pearl and Alice came down the aisle, wearing off-shoulder, tea length, ruby red gowns with all eyes on the ladies as the men smiled appreciation; and then there was Amy dressed in a cloud of pink and carrying a small white basket filled with red rose petals. The ivory sash mid waist was tied in a perfect bow as Amy's hair fell gently down her back.

The ensemble joined Contessa, the violins wafting a lonely calling to the one waiting on the steps. Samantha moved forward, the ivory gown glowing beneath the lantern's glow, her dark hair swept up, the tiny diamonds sparkling in her ears, and Landon King smiled, his eyes on Samantha as the smile widened, his lashes closing over the dusky look he gave to Samantha only. Samantha, walked forward, facing the minister, Land stepped by her side, leaning to place a kiss on her forehead as the people took a deep breath. Amy stepped center of the two, slightly in front, and the minister cleared his throat.

"Dearly Beloved, we are gathered her to witness Landon King and Samantha McKinsey in holy matrimony." Landon reached for Samantha's hand. Amy glanced up and smiled. Samantha was radiant. "It is time for the giving of the roses," the minister reminded and Samantha handed three red roses to Amy. Clarissa, Tessia and Olivia were the recipients. "Now the vows and the giving of the rings;" The minister smiled, "if you will repeat after me."

When those who had become their friends thought it could not get any better, the minister pronounced them man and wife. Land pulled Samantha into his arms, staring down into her eyes. "You are beautiful," he whispered, "I will love you forever. Thank you for being patient." Except, the minister's microphone picked up Lan's voice and the people clapped. "Now," if you will all rise and move forward, the ushers are going to relocate your chairs," he smiled, "but you won't be discomforted as you listen to Landon and Samantha, finishing their marriage ceremony by singing to each other. As the chairs are relocated you may take your seat once more if you wish."

Land held out his hand and Samantha taking it followed him to the piano. The magnificent chords rang out, Land's own professional astuteness lead into the first chords of A Bridge over Trouble Water; his was the first verse, Samantha, the second and as the marriage of a man and a woman combined with music that built, crescendoing, until the string ensemble's bass joined first and then the strings, the people could have been in Carnegie Hall. Last, came the settling notes of an old, old, hymn, Morning Has Broken... blackbird has spoken.... With tears in their eyes, the people clapped and no one realized in a short span of time, the room was cleared, the caterers prepared, as Land's own men as ushers worked magic; tables with white cloths circled the perimeter and the floor had been cleared for the cutting of the cake and Samantha's special touch to a tasty repose followed by the first dance of the evening.

The ensemble folded at nine, the people beginning to leave. "It was a beautiful evening," many said. "I've never experienced such a beautiful wedding." Mother's complimented Samantha, saying, "my daughter's engaged, I'll be by to see you." It went on and on.

Land pulled her aside, kissing Samantha in the dark of her old bedroom. "Can we slip away?" His hold tightened on her. "I want our time to be special, too. Mother's ready to take Amy home with her, and your mom...." She smiled against his lips. This man had become all she ever dreamed. He had seen her through heartache, recovery of her health and now their time ahead would be blessed with Amy.

"I'll tell Mother and Tessia good night and we can leave. Alice and Pearl will oversee the clean up."

"I guess you noticed the new man with the ushers, and of course Jade helped."

She stopped, "I wondered, who is he?" Land was smiling. "They all looked handsome in their tuxedos but I have never met that one; only your men and Jade." She was waiting.

"It was Jess Lassity."

She was shocked. "Did Pearl recognize him?"

"Mrs. King, do you think you will recognize me after ten years of marriage?" He pulled her back into his arms. "Jess wanted to come. He has a job on our farm now and I'm to watch over him, according to some new order Pearl has on him. The Sheriff's department delivered it during the two days you and I were apart. He asked if he could wear a tux, too, like the others. It was a small thing, and I figured he wanted Pearl to see he was trying." He shrugged. "Alice had her Jade, Pearl got Jess." He was wrapping his arms around her again, "are we staying here? If we are, I'm sending these people home."

Samantha started to unfold from his body. "I'll need to change," she said.

"I'll help you," he whispered in her ear. "I love you, Mrs. King, my little fire angel."

"I love you back, Mr. King," she said. "Let's tell our parents good bye."

"Why don't we just wave and walk out?"

She rolled her eyes. "When dreams come true." He groaned and then smiled.

The END

Betty invites you to join her on her blog

Forgiven by Betty Lowrey

on Facebook

www.ingramcontent.com/pod-product-compliance
Lightning Source LLC
Chambersburg PA
CBHW050350190726
48284CB00007BB/2225